The Keeala Series

The Road Home

Kumari Gorman

By the same author

The Keeala Resort Series

Book 1 - The Last Resort

Book 2 - Village Secrets

Book 4 - Crystal Clear

The Keeala Resort Series

The Road Home

© Kumari Gorman 2014

This book is a work of fiction. The names, characters, places and incidents are products of the writer's imagination or have been used fictitiously and are not to be construed as real. Any resemblance to persons, living or dead, actual events, locales or organizations is entirely coincidental.

National Library of Australia Cataloguing-in-Publication entry (pbk)

Author: Gorman, Kumari, author.

Title: The Road Home/ Kumari Gorman.

ISBN: 9780992388041 (paperback)

Series: Gorman, Kumari. Keeala Resort Series

Subjects: Resorts—Queensland--Fiction

Dewey Number: A823.4

Published with the assistance by www.inhousepublishing.com.au

The Keeala Series

The Road Home

Acknowledgements.

I would like to thank Ocean Reeve for his wonderful words of wisdom and his freely given support. He arrived at a time when I was about to give up. He guided me back on to the right track and I am very grateful that he inspired me to keep going. Thank you Ocean.

To my husband, John. Thank you so much. Thank you for your time, patience, advice and support.

Well, for some of your time and patience.

Well, perhaps tolerance is a better word.

Maybe I mean a bit of your time and occasional patience.

Definitely some tolerance and some occasional advice.

Whatever. You know what I mean.

Kumari Gorman

October 2014.

Chapter One

Terror sucked away Margaret Dougherty's breath as she tried to come to terms with her predicament. Fear froze her muscles. Dread deprived her of her voice and her heartbeat thumped an incessant, deafening rhythm in her ears. Sweat oozed from every pore of her almost paralysed body as she sat rigidly and gasped ineffectually for air. Her chest felt like it was in a vice. *Could death be this bad ?* repeated in her head, like a broken record.

The only sound her husband could hear was her laboured struggle for breath. Ethan shuffled hesitantly in the impenetrable darkness, arms outstretched and waving at the wall of black.

"Margaret? ... Margaret?"

No answer.

Ethan strained to pinpoint his wife's shuddering respirations, but they were masked by the scuffing of his bare feet along the cold, crumbly, earthen floor. He stopped –

cocked his head to the right – concentrated – slid his foot to the left.

An involuntary shudder shook Margaret as something touched her leg. Her heart raced and a strangled, high-pitched scream choked in her throat.

"Oh, Margaret!"

Ethan felt the thin strip of leather cut into his tightly bound wrists as he edged up next to his wife. The back of his shirt snagged and threads pulled, as he slid down the rough surface of a wall and sat beside his wife.

Margaret realised it was Ethan she had felt. The warmth of her husband's body should have reassured her, but it was the unexpected contact which had terrified her even more. Her breaths continued in uncontrollable, sobbing gasps.

"Margy, I want you to breathe in and hold, and then breathe out. Now, breathe in slowly, slowly ... hold ... breathe out, slowly ... and again, in ... hold ... out again ...now keep going, slowly. Close your eyes and concentrate solely on your breath." Ethan's voice was soft, consoling.

Margaret began to respond after a couple of minutes. Her breathing gradually slowed and the pounding of her heart started to ease. She became more aware of her body. The panic attack gradually loosened its hold.

The recall of recent events returned to her in a series of flashing images. It was all too vivid and her mind would not let it rest.

She remembered the touch of rough hands that had shaken her from the depths of sleep in the early hours of the morning. She had been pulled to her feet, and dragged up to the motel door. She recalled the strength was of a well-muscled arm steadying her as she staggered out of the room and threatened to fall. Someone had stuffed a wad of cloth into her mouth and pulled a bag over her head.

The same hands had pushed her in the small of her back, as a man's voice, muted but menacing, commanded, 'Walk'.

Margaret tried to stay calm, as she relived the panic she had felt when her knees had collapsed and her body folded, as she crumpled to the ground outside the motel room. Unseen hands had immediately flipped her roughly onto her back. She remembered how the same hands then slipped under her armpits and yanked her, so effortlessly, back to a standing position. Her unseeable assailant had dragged her limp body a few metres along the rough concrete path outside the motel room. Margaret relived the pain as her head had hit the side of a vehicle. She remembered how she had screamed a muffled, ineffectual protest. She thought how she had raised a hand and gingerly touched her forehead. The hessian bag over her head was thick with what Margaret thought was chaff dust. She could not tell if she was bleeding.

'Get in!'

The short, sharp command resonated in Margaret's memory. She could recall her vulnerability as she heard the door of the vehicle click open; the quick shove in her back. As she had pitched forward, she had thrown her hands out in front of her. Her torso sprawled across the upper step of the vehicle; her head bounced over the edge of the seat and her forehead struck a seatbelt buckle. Margaret winced at the thought of the pain. Her breath expelled with a grunt as she landed. She remembered thinking how strong her attacker must have been as he then lifted and turned her in one motion, then slid her across the bench seat so that she was jammed upright against the far door. In her mind, she could still hear the muted, breathless noises trapped in her throat, as she tried desperately to scream. She had struggled as she felt her hands pulled together and tied behind her back. She remembered the relief she felt as her captor backed out of the rear seat and moved away.

Margaret had heard voices; a quick exchange, spoken softly. She could hear another sound; speech, but it was an unintelligible jumble. The sounds came nearer, and Margaret could hear a scraping, shuffling noise approaching.

A heavy thump startled her. She felt a body dumped on the seat, next to her. She could feel the struggles and hear the stifled protestations and knew it must have been her husband, as he too resisted the same rough treatment.

Margaret realised now, as she sat with Ethan in the silence of their captivity, that she had not known at the time whether to feel relieved or alarmed by Ethan's presence beside her in the vehicle.

She recalled that she had tried to call out. She could still feel the scrape of the hessian bag across her cheek as she was whacked with an open palm.

'Shut up!' a voice had said softly, but with menace. Margaret could remember the intimidation she had felt at the time. She had heard the doors of the vehicle shut quietly, and a moment later, they were moving off slowly out of the motel car park.

As Margaret sat now and tossed the scene around in her mind, she recalled just how efficiently the whole abduction had been.

After they had left the motel, it was a couple of minutes before she had heard a new voice from the front seat. 'Everything all right?' it said.

'Perfect,' said the other. 'Just drive and keep your eyes on the road; we don't want to get picked up.'

It was clear to Margaret that she and her husband were being abducted. She was in the middle of her worst nightmare. Thoughts of torture, rape, and being dumped and left to die, assailed her. She tried to move, tested her bonds, and shook her head. They were tight and there was no way for her to loosen them. The blackness inside the hood disoriented her; for a moment, panic took hold, and she sensed she was close to hysteria. A sound from the rear seat jolted her back to her senses. Margaret made a muffled response as Ethan tried to communicate with her. It was pointless. They both hunched quietly on their seats as the vehicle bumped along, throwing them left and right, the security of seat belts a luxury missing from this journey.

They turned onto a rough, unmade road and continued for what seemed like hours. When they stopped, the driver and his mate got out and slammed their doors. Their voices trailed off as they walked away from the vehicle, a disquieting, shrill laugh the last evidence of their presence. The captives heard the sounds of night; small birds and animals in the distance, as quiet descended.

Ethan grunted. He struggled against his bonds and thrust his body against the car door; he stamped his feet and bit down on his gag. He became frustrated and desperate, but eventually gave in and relaxed enough to rest against the door of the van.

"Wakey, wakey – all out."

The door was flung open. The driver and his mate reached in and dragged Ethan out first, then Margaret. They shoved the pair ahead of them. Unable to see, Ethan and Margaret stumbled around, almost falling with every step.

"Take off the bags," the driver said to the other man. "I'm not carrying these buggers down there."

Margaret and Ethan felt the soft night air against their faces as they looked around. It was dark, but it was obvious to the couple that they were in some very desolate location. There were no buildings, no trees, just piles of rocks and mounds of dirt where the pale light illuminated what could be a moonscape. They were in mining country, Coober Pedy, the opal capital of Australia.

Their captors turned on their headlamps and one of them snapped, "Come on, we haven't got all day, step it up."

"Move, ya buggers!" said the other man.

The taller of the two men pushed them forward, directing them with a torch.

Hesitantly, they picked their way across the rocky surface to a dark circular hole in the ground.

My God, thought Ethan, *It's a mineshaft.*

One of the men untied their hands.

Together, Margaret and Ethan peered in. They watched one of the men descend a rope ladder. It swung loosely downward into blackness. Margaret shuddered as she recoiled from the threat ahead of her. Ethan took a step backwards.

"Right, you first missus."

The man spun the pair around so that their backs faced the edge of the shaft. The headlamp made it difficult to see the man's features but Margaret had a strange feeling about him; he was familiar in some way, perhaps it was his voice. The feeling persisted but the answer eluded her. She baulked once again when she turned her head, and saw the first man's headlamp swinging from side to side, as he disappeared into the dark hole.

Ethan moved close to his wife, trying to transfer some kind of reassurance and comfort that he did not feel himself.

Margaret teetered on the edge of the hole and almost fell. She recovered her balance, turned her head, and could barely make out the top two rungs of the ladder behind her. Two star pickets stuck out of the ground either side of the top of the ladder. The iron posts secured the top rung. Margaret grabbed onto them, and gingerly placed her right foot on the first rung inside the shaft.

"Come on, you stupid bitch!" The man grabbed Margaret roughly and held her in an iron grip. "Come on, foot – hand – foot – hand – it's not bloody rocket science!"

Margaret was terrified but slowly began the descent, one shaking rung after another.

The man made Ethan wait for a minute or so. When Margaret had descended the first few rungs, he told Ethan to follow his wife.

As he began his descent, Ethan could feel Margaret's fear below him, as the flimsy ladder shook and swayed. After several minutes, Ethan reached the bottom. He turned around and saw Margaret, her face lit by the lamp on the head of the shorter of the two men, who had been first to go down.

The man removed the gag in Margaret's mouth, then Ethan's.

"Margaret? Are you okay?" Ethan asked his wife.

A muffled sobbing was the only reply.

"It's okay, darling, the worst is over. I'm here," he said.

"Shut it," said the man, standing between them.

The erratic, swinging beam from his headlamp broke the darkness into random slabs of light. The second man descended with ease, and seconds later, he stood at the base of the ladder. Their headlamps picked out the details of a cave-like room and revealed a passageway leading away from one side. One of the men walked around and kicked at a spot on a wall.

"Get over there." The rougher of the two men pushed Margaret to the wall.

The other shoved Ethan to the opposite wall, several metres away from his wife.

"Get down on the floor, both of you," he said.

Ethan and Margaret stood their ground, but the men grabbed them roughly and threw them to the dirt floor, punishing them for their defiance.

"Are you just plain stupid?" asked the shorter man, not really expecting an answer. "We don't 'ave time for 'eroics. Put your bloody 'ands behind yer back."

After restraining their hands again, the captors started to walk away.

Margaret, panic stricken, tried to scream but choked and coughed uncontrollably. The two men turned around to see her convulsing on the ground and having some kind of seizure; her body appeared to stiffen, then lie still.

"Margaret, Margaret," Ethan yelled.

He began to edge toward his wife on his knees, but the shorter man walked over to Ethan, grabbed the collar of his pyjama shirt, and dragged him back to the wall. He placed Ethan's torso flat against the wall, and pulled his legs out straight in front of him. He repeated the action with Margaret.

"Gag 'em again, mate?" he asked his accomplice.

"No, won't hear a thing from up there," said the man who had done the driving. "Anyway, wouldn't want them dying on us, would we?"

The kidnappers turned and walked away, taking the relative comfort of the light with them. They clambered up the ladder and disappeared from sight.

Chapter Two

Three weeks previously, Di Watersen had rummaged through the bottom desk drawer in the manager's office at Keeala Resort, an Over 50's Resort on the outskirts of Brisbane in South East Queensland.

"Have you seen that pile of travel brochures I left in this drawer here, love?" she asked.

"Yes, I put them over there on that shelf." Jim, her husband, pointed to the shelves behind the door, stacked with anything not current or too hard to deal with.

The heat of a Queensland summer and autumn over for another year, Jim and Di Watersen were beginning to enjoy the mild winter and the peace and quiet that had reigned since their first challenging summer in the job as joint managers. Over the past year, they had been involved in helping to uncover a drug syndicate and catch the murderer of one of the residents.

The summer had provided a little more excitement than they had bargained for and they had considered resigning on more than one occasion, but they were still there when winter descended and were looking forward to a very peaceful season. They were close to retiring age themselves and the events of the past year had put a great strain on their marriage and their health.

Having made many new friends in the resort now, Di had begun to toy with the idea of joining forces with some of them on a touring holiday. She noted the signs of stress in her husband and started to research all possibilities for getting away from the stress for a while. What had captured her interest was a bus tour around Australia for a coach of around twenty or thirty people.

While Di considered the possibilities of this, Jim continued with his head in his accounts and a world of worries on his shoulders. He usually thought the best of people, although he said occasionally that 'being old did not automatically make you nice.' After a long, stressful career in financial management, he enjoyed the interaction with the residents and the regularity of the day-to-day life at Keeala Resort.

Jim was tall and well built. He had a lined face that said he did lots of smiling and a thick head of grey hair that said he did lots of worrying. He would probably say it was worrying about his wife, Diane, but she would probably say it was thirty years of his concern for other people's money in the finance industry.

Jim now considered himself in partial retirement because, theoretically, he got up at 7 am and knocked off at 4 pm. Of course, this was not accounting for being on-call 24/7, and dealing with problems or disputes 'after hours', but mostly he had time to enjoy the less hectic pace of this appointment. Jim also found a nip of vodka, taken at times of stress, helped him sustain his equilibrium, a practice that had continued to increase in recent times.

"I'm going, meet you on the balcony in ten minutes," said Di, as she swept out of the office with her arms full of travel brochures. She made for the manager's residence along the pretty path bordered by petunias, impatiens and delicate ferns.

"Sure." Jim watched her go, always amazed at his wife's ability to move so quickly from one task to another. Di did manage very well; she set a punishing pace for both of them and Jim often struggled to keep up.

He locked his office, walked to his house and went directly to the fridge. Jim carried a cold bottle of wine to the balcony where Di had set out glasses and nibbles on a tray.

"Whew, that's good," he said, as he dropped into his favourite chair and looked at the distant hills on the horizon. No matter how many times he took up this position, he never tired of it.

"Another day over," he said, as he smiled at his wife and reached for the glasses and the chilled, sparkling white wine. Jim tilted a glass and poured some of the wine, waited for the bubbles to subside, then filled to three-quarters and handed it to Di. He did the same with the second flute and raised his glass. "To us," he said, "because we deserve it."

She responded with a similar salute, took a sip, and put her glass on the tray as she reached for a pile of travel brochures and spread them on the cane table in front of her. Using both hands, she shuffled them round like cards waiting for the one she was searching for to come to the surface. She stopped and stared, a picture of a Balinese hut looked back at her. This image immediately brought up thoughts of how drug runners used this little island to traffic drugs to Australia and New Zealand. For several moments, she was lost in thought.

Jim watched her surreptitiously from behind his glass.

His wife was small boned and delicately shaped. Her movements were graceful, yet quick. She carried herself with confidence and determination. Years of working as a registered nurse had given her the self-assurance to be decisive and follow decision with action. Her brown hair was long and softly drawn back into a loose knot. She usually twisted it when deep in thought or watching the television. Di looked younger than her 55 years, her skin showing creases around the mouth and eyes that added to a look of character and maturity. Di shook her head and realised she had been daydreaming, or perhaps reminiscing, but whatever it was, she was wasting time. She put down the Bali leaflet and quickly found the pamphlet she was searching for.

"Bus tours around Australia, yes!"

"Find it?" Jim laughed.

Di waved it in the air. "What do you think? This could be us. No driving, no looking for accommodation; going directly to the best tourist spots without getting lost for days on end;

no listening to everybody's complaints morning, noon, and night. Could this be us?"

Jim sighed. "Hold on, I don't really see myself in a bus full of seniors, singing songs from the last world war."

'Oh really, Jim! In case you hadn't noticed, you are older than some of the residents here anyway."

"Well, well, I really don't know." He was shaking his head negatively, desperately trying to think of why he did not want to sit on a bus full of oldies watching the country fly by.

"So, exactly what is your major objection? I'm sure I can arrange a relief manager. The weather will be perfect. It'll be a change of scenery, good company, total relaxation, no stress. And the best part – get ready for this – it's free."

"What do you mean, it's free?"

"I spoke to Joan, the travel agent, yesterday and there are several special offers going, including a free trip for two if you can get fifteen other people to go along. This would be a small charter coach."

"Well, how can we do that? We don't know anyone wanting to go on holidays right now. We'd have to drag along half the resort to take up that offer. Oh no! No, you don't mean take along our own rent-a-crowd?" Jim looked suddenly afraid.

"Why not?" Di raised the palms of her hands in question.

"You just finished saying, 'good company', that's why."

"I didn't mean take everyone along. I thought I'd just quietly pass the word around to some special people, like maybe Harold and Robert, and the newlyweds, Margaret and

Ethan. Maybe Hank Fletcher, he's good for a laugh, and Martin Judd could do with a change of scenery after the stress of the trial and everything. Hey, Joy Rayne would be a good match for him."

"So what is this, Blind Date? You can't be serious."

"Well, I guess I was just joking. There are many nice people here, who would enjoy a trip, and they could afford it. We could all have a good time." Di had obviously already passed the point of no return. She was ready for action.

"Let me think about this, please. Don't push me into a situation where I feel trapped, with everybody waiting for me to make a decision." Jim stood and refilled his glass.

Di looked sheepish, "I'm sorry, I had no intention of being pushy, but the time to decide is limited and the weather waits for no one."

"So, what you're saying is that you're waiting for me to decide, maybe tonight." Jim laughed at his own joke, and then looked up at his wife to see she was serious. "You *do* want me to decide tonight?" He sounded incredulous.

"Well, you've got until I spread the word to the usual suspects, maybe a day or two."

"You realise it may not be a strictly ethical thing to do, to take along a select few of our friends, leaving the rest to feel like they are rejects." Jim could see problems arising already.

"Yes, I've thought of that. I'll be quick and discreet. We'll be on the bus and away before the general population even knows, we've organised a trip. Most people wouldn't want to go anyhow. They'll have their own plans, or tripping around in a bus won't be to their liking."

"I can relate to that," Jim mumbled, as he threw back the second half of his glass.

"So, what else is new?" she said, changing the subject. "Did I hear you on the phone to Frank Pekalski today?"

"You mean, your friend, the newly promoted Detective Inspector Frank Pekalski?" Jim let the sarcasm drip off the comment.

"Yes, as a matter of fact, he was telling me that Allen Sinclaire has been transferred to a separate, secure lockup. There's been an attempt on his life since he went to gaol. I think he'll be lucky to survive his term; you can't sell out your buddies and not expect them to be pissed off. Drug dealers have very long arms and I suspect there're plenty of them already on the inside - just waiting for Allen. Thank God he's no longer our area manager, though. I can't imagine what we might have ended up being drawn into."

"Yeah, well let's hope young Matthew Weatherlee settles things down. It'll be a big responsibility for him, looking after all the Sleighmen Group's Queensland resorts. I hope he's up to it."

******

Di and Jim were still considering retirement. After the events of the previous year, they were wondering if perhaps they would be happier in a less demanding job after an extended holiday. Finances, however, would probably not stretch to an early retirement so they were staying put until they decided on a better alternative. A free holiday would not go amiss right now. Di's practical idea was not really a bad one and Jim knew he should give it serious consideration.

"Who could we get as a relief manager?" Jim asked, as he followed Di back downstairs to the kitchen.

"I've rung head office and they'll call me back in a couple of days. We could have asked Matt Weatherlee to do it, but they want him to stay in Adelaide to complete his training. It's too good an opportunity for him to miss and, if he does become our permanent area manager, we'll then have to have a new salesperson. That won't be a hard position to fill, most likely a woman this time, more suited to the position."

Chapter Three

The manager's office filled with the insistent buzzing of the emergency alarm, and "Pool – Pool – Pool" flashing on the indicator board. Jim could hear shouting in the distance. He ran out of his office and sprinted toward the noise. There was no doubt it was coming from the swimming pool. A crowd gathered around the gate. Jim pushed his way forward and stopped at the pool's edge.

He saw the sisters, Penny and Lottie, both treading water and holding up a little dog. It was Ben, from Unit 27. Two men reached down to the women, giving them a hand to wade to the side. They handed Ben up first, and he immediately shook all over his rescuers. Everyone pushed back; it was not really swimming weather. One after the other, the two women climbed the ladder out of the pool, dripping and smiling. The crowd clapped and cheered. Everyone spoke at once as several big towels arrived to wrap around the heroes.

"What on earth happened here?" Jim finally got a word in. About five people answered at once. Jim put his hand up and pointed to Lottie who sat on the seat and wiped her face. Her sister was shivering by her side, her hair dripping in pools on the cement under the seat.

"A man threw Ben into the pool. I saw him. We were going down to the community centre for our Yoga class and I heard barking and then a splash. When Penny and I looked over, we saw a man turn and run through the gate, leaving poor little Ben struggling to keep afloat. We ran over and the creep nearly knocked us down trying to get away. He took off down the path toward the gate. We tried to get Ben out and eventually we jumped in. He was definitely drowning, poor little bugger." Someone was rubbing Ben vigorously and talking soothingly to him.

Just then, his owner arrived. "Oh, Ben what happened?" She rushed to crouch down next to her little pet and hug him. Once again, everyone wanted to answer and she finally gleaned the story from three or four different versions.

"Did anyone see who the man was?" Jim asked.

"Yes." Penny looked up. "It was our old gardener, Kevin," she continued. "We recognised him because he has a very distinctive limp and we got a close look at him."

"Oh yes, it definitely was that gardener," said Lottie.

"Could make sense," Jim said. "Last year, Ben bit him and his wound got infected. I also remember he threatened to kill Ben several times after that." Jim looked at the sisters again. "Well, it's probably best you go home and get dry, now. I'll talk to you later today."

Rachael went over and thanked the women again for saving her little dog. She held Ben close as she headed back to her unit.

Lottie and Penny were escorted to their home with lots of chattering and back patting. They had missed their Yoga class but got some exercise anyway.

For the next few minutes, Jim checked around the area. As he did so, he wondered why Kevin would want to do such an awful thing. It seemed to him that sacking the man had not been enough to get rid of him. He had been an irresponsible employee and now he was back, but why? Kevin had been a suspect when Detective Frank Pekalski, as he then was, had an accident in the grounds only a few months ago. It all seemed very strange to Jim, especially with the closure of the previous matter. Jim shook his head and wondered why this resort seemed to attract so many odd people.

He made his decision. *I need a holiday.*

******

When Jim arrived back at the office, Di was waiting at the front door "What happened? What did I miss?"

"It seems our old gardener, Kevin, has paid us a visit again and he threw Ben into the pool for an unscheduled swim."

Jim moved past his wife into the office, flicked open his notebook and picked up the phone. "Hello Frank," said Jim, when the Detective Inspector answered at the other end. "Sorry to interrupt your busy day but I thought you may be interested to know that your old friend Kevin is back. He dropped around to throw little Ben into our pool. You remember Jessie's poodle? Whether he was here for some other reason I don't know, but he went to the trouble to pick up the poor little bugger and carry him over to the pool and dump him in."

"Did anyone see this happen?"

"Yes, I have a couple of witnesses. I believe they're reliable. The women who saved Ben recognised Kevin. He is well known around here."

Kevin was suspected of tripping the detective up on a path in the resort some months ago. Pekalski ended up in hospital with a broken leg and other minor injuries. He had only recently recovered sufficiently and returned to full duties.

Although thought by the police to be only small fry, Kevin was also suspected of involvement with certain drug runners who were now in gaol. He obviously did not know when to quit; if he had disappeared, he would probably have been forgotten. However, here he was, back again. *But what for?* Jim asked himself.

Jim finished his conversation with the detective and hung up. He turned to Di who was standing and staring wide eyed at him.

"What next?" he said to her. "Can you believe that sod? He can't stay away from the place. I thought Frank may be interested – he was." Jim walked around the desk and took Di's hands in his; he looked into her eyes and said, "Can we please go on that holiday before anything else starts? I don't want to be here if we're about to break out in our next major crime. I want to be sitting at Uluru, in the shade of a wattle

21

tree, with a very long, cold drink in my hand when the police or the relief manager rings to say that the village has just been sacked and then burnt to the ground, the women raped and the children sold into slavery." Jim sat down heavily, drawing Di down to sit on his lap. They grinned at one another.

"So let's get this show on the road then, shall we?" Di patted Jim's cheeks and kissed him on the forehead. "We'd better get you out of here quick before you run away." She stood and scooped up her workbook and pen. Let's have lunch first though and I can tell you all about the plans so far."

Di and Jim walked over to the manager's residence. It was a well-appointed, medium sized house, surrounded by delightful gardens. There was a giant, spreading Poinciana tree that dipped its branches onto the front upstairs deck. This was the managers' favourite place to sit at day's end. They could see the mountains in the west and watch the sunset in all its glory. They looked over the beautiful gardens, so lovingly tended by old Tom and the new young gardener, Lachlan.

Di spread her book open on the kitchen table and started to explain the plans she had made for the bus trip so far. Jim did the honours and made sandwiches for their lunch.

"What I thought would be nice is a six week trip around Australia."

Jim dropped his knife on the kitchen bench, "That long?"

"Why not? We have it coming and you really can't do justice to this beautiful country in less time. As it is, we'll only skim the surface. We'll be very selective about what we see. We're certainly not just going off on a jaunt all over the place. We'll plan our journey carefully."

"Okay." Jim had not really expected such a grand plan but continued to listen.

"This is a list of who's coming so far." Di pushed a foolscap sheet toward Jim at the table. As you can see, we have the new woman from number 27, Rachael Ross, and she's friends with Freya Holman. There's also, well, you can see who's there. So far, I only have thirteen and that includes Harold and Robert, even though they haven't said a definite yes, yet. I think they'd be great company on a long trip, they're always happy and into everything. Underneath their carefree facades, I find both of them to be deep thinkers and always have a responsible attitude. Whatever my opinions of gay men were before, those views have been radically changed since I met Harold and Robert. I don't think we would have survived the previous eighteen months of problems if it weren't for those two. Moreover, they gave us so much insight into the residents to start with. Yes, I really hope they decide to come."

Jim cleared the table and sat back next to his wife to study the maps she had spread out.

Di said, "I have in mind to travel south from here to Sydney and Melbourne, before it gets too cold, then on to Adelaide via the Great Ocean Road – from there to Alice Springs where we can see Uluru and Kata Juta, also Kings Canyon. It depends on the bus company, but I'm assured we can submit what we want and see what they come up with. I thought Katherine Gorge and Kakadu National Park and on to Darwin. From there to Broome, the Kimberley and in Western

Australia to Perth, then across the Nullarbor and finally home via western New South Wales and western Queensland. I haven't included much of the Queensland coast but my research tells me that most of our travellers have seen it. The one place most of them have seen is the area from Brisbane to Cairns."

Di sat back and looked at Jim for his response.

"That certainly is some trip. I really think forty days would be ample though. Can you imagine how fed up some people will get with certain others after many weeks of such close proximity?"

"I hadn't really thought about that. But it takes time for everyone to settle in and after a while most petty problems are resolved."

Jim looked at his wife askance. "Do you really believe that?"

"Sure. Wait and see, I think you might be surprised at how people can get along when they have to. I remember a bus trip when I was at school; we all came back great friends. It was a time of bonding, and in adversity, people have to stick together."

"In adversity?"

"Well, you know what I mean, when the going gets tough the tough get going – that sort of thing."

"What sort of thing? You're beginning to worry me now, Di."

"Oh, how did we get on to this? Yes, I agree there may be some personality differences that will surface, but that's why I'm being selective about who comes. I'm making sure everyone has a partner or mate so that no one feels lonely. These people already know one another and have an established social bond. If there are real differences of opinion or any incompatibility, then they just won't come." Di seemed satisfied.

"And you believe this too?"

"Sure."

The phone rang and Jim reached to pick it up. He nodded and said, "Okay."

"I've got to go, Di, someone waiting to see me at the office. Talk later." Jim was gone.

Di sat there with the pile of paper in front of her. She had heard her husband's reservations. She had had the same reservations herself, but did not want to voice them. She wanted to feel confident that all would be well, whether it would or not. "Oh, damn," she mumbled.

Chapter Four

Judy Robilliard wiped her brow with a tissue and then stuffed it into her jeans pocket. Despite the cool weather, packing up was hot work and sometimes she wondered if it was necessary for her and her brother to move around so much.

Judy spoke loudly to her brother as he stacked the back seat of the vehicle. "I'm feeling a bit over all this constant moving, you know, Pat. The thought of hitting the road again just doesn't turn me on anymore."

"Yeah," he grunted in response and went on with his pushing and shoving.

The brother and sister had been orphaned at a young age and they had grown up, together, in a series of foster homes. They had both been abused, and for reasons neither could understand, they had always found it difficult to fit in anywhere, so they had been shunted from home to home. On one occasion, they were sent to separate homes. They had both run away and were re-united when they were picked up by the Department of Child Affairs. Margaret and John Robilliard had become their next foster parents, and the children had stayed there until they were in their early teens. Despite the fact they were both well treated and loved there, they left their home and made their own way. Their life experiences had taught them that it was the two of them against the world. They had no idea when they were finally well off. Trust and respect for others was not something they understood.

Judy was two years younger than Patrick, and relied on him for everything. She had often thought about how desperate they had been at times, sometimes not knowing from where their next meal would come. She marvelled at how Patrick somehow always came up with the goods, even if he had to steal it.

As the years passed, the brother and sister established a nomadic lifestyle of casual work and travelling, never staying long enough anywhere to make lasting friendships or develop loyalties.

Judy slammed the back door of their new, four wheel drive wagon. She jumped into the front seat and sorted through the glove box while she waited for her brother to join her. For the past three months, up until that day, they had worked for a poultry farmer in North Queensland; it was time to move on.

Judy looked around at all their possessions, stacked in the vehicle that was now their whole world. The excitement of a new adventure was wearing thin; sometimes she longed to live with Patrick in a house of their own again, and go to work at a normal job.

"Ready to go, mate?" Patrick swung up into his seat and pushed the keys into the ignition. He looked at his sister questioningly; she stared back at him.

"I was just wondering if we could settle down some day. You know, buy another house like that one we had at Surfers - and I would like to study."

"Study what, for shit's sake?" Patrick put the car into gear and swung out on to the track.

"Maybe horticulture, landscape gardening." Judy's voice was barely audible.

Patrick burst out laughing, "Bloody hell, you can't be serious!"

"Oh, shut up." Judy turned her head, and stared out the window. She knew he would make fun of her, he always did. She should just keep her mouth shut.

"Anyway, we could never get that much dough together again. Since one of us managed to lose most of what Margaret left, the only way to get back into a cashed-up state would be to hijack a bank. You volunteering?"

A sudden vision of herself pushing money into the poker machines at the Casino in Broadbeach, reminded her of how irresponsible she had been on the only occasion they had had any decent amount of money.

Following the death of John Robilliard, their last foster father, Margaret, his wife, had sold up and followed Patrick and Judy to Queensland, where she lived with them for a time and had paid off their mortgage with her life savings.

Margaret had told them she hoped it would give them the start in life they so badly needed. With so little concern for her, and no appreciation for the sacrifice she had made on their behalf, they decided to cash in. They sold the property and moved on. They left Margaret with just enough cash to buy a small unit in Keeala Resort.

Thoughts of Margaret brought a cloud of depression over Judy's mind and she dropped her head in regret and sadness – a depression that waited for these unguarded moments of silence. Driving gave her long periods of introspection, until Patrick or the radio interrupted her.

Patrick was grateful to be able to drive on in silence.

******

Di knocked on Margaret's front door. "Are you there, Marg? It's Di." She smiled as the older woman approached the door. "I wanted to discuss the bus trip with you, if you have a minute."

Margaret stepped aside to allow the manager to enter the lounge and Ethan joined them from the kitchen at the same time. "I've just put the kettle on for a cup of tea. Will you join us, Diane?"

"Love one, thank you." Di sat down and looked around. She took in the expensive new furniture and curtains and the paintings on the walls. Obviously, one or both of these people had very good taste.

She had first met Margaret not long after she and Jim arrived at the resort. Margaret had a problem with the sun coming into her bed-sitter and she was very concerned about her security, as the window was exposed to the street, albeit within the resort's perimeter fence. Di had heard of Margaret's concerns from her friend, Ethan, who at that time lived in a neighbouring unit. The two women had hit it off straight away and Di had gone to great lengths to organise a solution to Margaret's concerns. She had managed to get a special awning that not only gave shade and kept the room much cooler, but also provided security for the exposed window. Di had been able organise the work at no cost to Margaret. Nice people deserved a break sometimes, she reasoned.

"Tell me Ethan, how did you and Margaret meet?" asked Di.

"Marg and I were friends at school. My God, that's a long time ago. We competed for the first place in class for three years running. I won once and Marg won twice. I'm sure you can tell she's still the smartest," Ethan laughed. "Anyway, Marg and I drifted apart when I went to Vietnam and by the time I came home she had married someone else. They had a long and happy marriage and lived in a beautiful home in Sydney. After the death of Margy's husband, she moved to Queensland to be near her foster children. I must say this is the part I really don't understand. She had to have been very low at the time because she'd had many problems with both of them and yet she packed up her home, bag and baggage, and came to Queensland to live with them. She paid their not inconsiderable mortgage, settled several other debts, and purchased a new vehicle for them. She did this believing they would provide her with a secure home for as long as she wished. I have the feeling she tried to buy their love. And, of course, that never works, does it?"

Ethan looked at Di. "Sometime after that, they sold their house, bought her a tiny bed sitter unit here in the resort and moved away. They left Marg high and dry with virtually no money in the bank and, of course, no family support."

Di was appalled when she heard the story from Ethan but it was not the first one like that she had heard and, as Di shook her head, she thought it probably wouldn't be the last.

Ethan went on to say that their story had a happy conclusion.

"Or, as Margaret says, a happy beginning," he said. He explained how he and Margaret had been reunited after so many years and began a relationship that had brought immense comfort for them both.

"As you know, Di, we were married at the community centre only a few months ago. What you probably are not aware of is that one special guest Margaret invited to the wedding was a beloved uncle, almost 93 years old. Unbeknown to us, he had discovered the skulduggery Margaret's foster children had engaged in and he decided to give us a fabulous wedding gift. He presented us with the ownership documents of this beautiful, three-bedroom unit we now live in, plus a cheque for $500,000. Needless to say, we were overwhelmed by his generosity."

"Wow, that's an amazing story." Di wondered whether she had ever heard a happier story. She knew they could now afford to go on the bus trip and money was no object. She was glad to know the newlyweds would be coming along; they would be good company.

"Well, let's keep on happy subjects. I've a stack of information here, all about the bus tour." Di plonked herself down on a dining chair and spread out her portfolio. "Now, all this is subject to minor alteration and I'm completely open to your suggestions and requests at this stage. Once I've talked to the others, we'll come up with what I'll take back to the travel agent. This is the list of who's coming, it's almost complete." She pushed the list across the table to Ethan and he and his wife huddled together to see who their travelling companions would be.

"Oh, yes, these are most of our friends in our little social circle," said Margaret.

"Yes, I've tried to keep it as comfortable a group as possible. Oh, and this is the rough itinerary, so far," said Di. "Please feel free to make a note of anything in particular you want to see or do and, if it can be slotted in, it will be, okay?"

The pair chatted quietly as they read the plan. "I'd like to fly over Uluru in a helicopter," said Ethan.

"Write it down. I'm sure that'll be possible and we can book ahead. There are some who won't want to go and some who can't afford it. Whatever, we'll endeavour to accommodate as much of that type of thing as possible. This will be the adventure of a lifetime." Di was grinning from ear to ear.

"I'm really looking forward to buying some original art. I know that Alice Springs is the place for that but I was wondering if we will get to go to any Aboriginal communities," said Margaret. She was obviously the one who had chosen the artwork now hanging on the walls around them.

"I don't think so Marg," said Di. "I believe special authority is required, and we can't just pop in and intrude on people's lives uninvited. We can arrange for you to get to see some artwork, though, I'm sure of that. I'll talk to the travel agent about it."

They pored over the maps and lists. Di checked her watch and realised there were still lots of people to talk to.

"Have a think about it and let me know if there's anything else you want to add before next Monday. That's the deadline." Di got up and made her way to the door where she turned to the couple who were standing, holding hands, and said, "And by the way, did you finally hear from your kids. Do they know you're married now?"

Margaret looked down and Ethan answered, "Yes, Margy's daughter, Judy, wrote a note telling her she should watch out for some old bugger wanting to take her for a ride. Can you believe that? After them ripping her off, suggesting I would do the same. I can't imagine what they would say if they found out about all the money we've come into. We certainly won't be telling them."

Di said, "It's hard to understand what would have motivated them to treat you the way they did, Margaret, apart from sheer greed. Surely they must have considered the distress they would cause you?"

"Oh," said Ethan, "originally they were foster children who could not go back to either of their biological parents. They'd been in several different foster homes when Marg and her husband adopted them both when they were about nine and eleven. Perhaps it was too late to undo the damage that had already been done to them."

"They were both very sad children." Margaret looked up and added, "They'd come from a violent, dysfunctional family and had really stuck together through events no child should ever have to suffer. Anyway, it seems we never really bonded and they left home as soon as they got jobs. They really didn't know how much we loved them both and they couldn't recognise love when they were surrounded by it. I was a romantic, gullible woman for ever trusting them, especially with all I had in the world. I see now how simple it was to set me up the way they did. But, that's all in the past – and look at me now." She turned her head and smiled at Ethan, "Look at us now."

Di walked over and kissed them both on the cheek. "Yes, just look at you now!" She turned and left with a smile on her face.

******

Di's next stop was unit number 39, Robert Wieland and Harold Smith. These two mature aged men had been together for many years and were at ease with each other. They were a happy couple, and never failed to make any potentially awkward situation lighter with good natured banter. Jim and Di had become staunch friends with Harold and Robert since they had taken over the management, and often attended the music appreciation evenings that the men had on a monthly basis.

"Knock, knock," Di called from the open doorway. "It's Di, may I come in?"

Robert, appearing from the inner coolness, waved her in. "We were hoping to see you today, Mrs. Manager, do come in." He directed her to a seat on the lounge, and called to his partner, "Diane is here, Harold."

The other man walked into the room with the vacuum cleaner trailing behind him. "Hello, I'll be with you in one minute," and he disappeared again.

Di looked around the room; she had seen it many times but was always able to find some new objet d'art to attract her attention and admire. Both men had previously been collectors and antique dealers. They had a shop for many years and had kept their most precious pieces, some of which were quite ugly but must have been rare or valuable.

Harold was thickset, but only compared to Robert who was extremely health conscious and very slim. They both had thinning hair and were quick to smile. Di often thought of Robert as the more aesthetic and Harold more practical. One of their loves was their little dog Gypsy. She was a King Charles spaniel and very pretty; very naughty according to Robert. She jumped straight up onto Di's lap when she sat down.

"Get off there, you bad girl." Robert leaned over to wave the animal away.

"No, no, she's fine. I actually miss having a dog around. Since Ben went back to unit 27, there's been no one for me to make a fuss of." Di looked down at Gypsy and began to stroke her soft fur. "What will happen to Gypsy when you go away? I presume you are going to come on the trip?"

"Yes, yes we are and that's always a problem. However, we can leave her with my sister; she lives in Brisbane. She's a widow and really loves Gypsy. She has a Shitzu of her own. The dogs don't get on that well but Meredith enjoys being in the middle. Unfortunately, she gives them crap to eat, as well as their normal food, you know – sweet treats and so on and our little darling here always puts on weight when we go away. When we get home, she won't eat healthy food and holds out for rubbish which is simply not forthcoming from us. It always takes me months to retrain her and get her slim again. But it's worth it, because we know that she'll be treasured and want for nothing."

"Well, I guess that's the main thing," Di said.

She looked up as Harold came in with a tray of coffee in delicate porcelain cups.

"Sorry, no nibbles today. We're on our preparation diet for the trip. Rob here has decided we have to slim down before we spend the next few weeks sitting on our arses in a bus. He also tells me we'll be walking every afternoon when we stop, before we eat, and we'll be eating cautiously – whatever that is."

"You know perfectly well what I mean – no rubbish – just good healthy food, and small servings. When one uses no energy, which we'll be doing, sitting looking out of a window, one doesn't need much fuel, does one?"

Robert looked from one to the other and raised an eyebrow at Harold, waiting for a response.

Harold obliged. "Are you sure you really want to go, old son? You're sounding a bit doubtful; perhaps you should stay here near the gym and the walking paths and the veggie garden."

Harold knew his friend so well he could never resist pulling his strings.

"I'm dying to go, you stupid man. I simply want to be sure our health doesn't suffer and maybe one of us end up in an outback hospital or being transported by the Flying Doctor Service."

"Oh, that does sound like fun."

Harold had the last word.

"So, you've told me what I came to find out. You're coming and here's the list of other contenders and the possible route, yet to be finalised." Di handed them more notes. "Please go over it all at your leisure and add you special requests or suggestions. The final draft has to be ready for the travel agent next Monday, so don't muck around."

"Yes, Sir" they both said together and saluted.

Di laughed and stood up. "I have heaps more people to see so I must away. I wanted to see you two, to make sure you weren't going to deprive us of your company."

"Wouldn't dream of it," said Harold and walked her to the door. "We're both quite excited now and Robert already has reminder notes hanging off every surface."

******

Di laughed again as she walked down the path and shook her head. She looked at her list. *Who's next? Ah, Rachael in*

27 and Freya in 41. I should ring them and get them together. I should get them all together. No, of course I can't do that. The others will say we're having a secret meeting which is what we would be doing. Then a mutiny will break out. No, I have to continue and see the bus people in ones and twos.

The next two days were taken up with dozens of cups of tea and coffee and descriptions of the proposed trip to all those on the list, which now reached 16. *Well, if I've missed anything, too bad,* thought Di. *Enough is enough.* She was pleased with the response to the trip and went to see the travel agent on Monday morning with sheets of hand-written notes and a head full of questions.

Chapter Five

It was midnight when Lottie finally turned out her bedside lamp. She and her sister, Penny, had been talking for hours. It had started with a discussion about what they hoped to see on their trip and that led to a discussion about what each had already seen. They were both widows and had very many different experiences. No one was more surprised than they were when they moved in together to live out their senior years.

Penny was the oldest and, in all the ways that mattered, very typical of a first born – the most responsible, the decision maker, the academic achiever and, of course, the boss. She had had a successful marriage with a good man, a boyfriend she had met while still at school. Penny had her own business as well, her own fashion label. She had designed clothes for women and at one time had owned two very up-market shops in the city of Melbourne. Penny sold out when her husband died in his fifties. They had planned to retire in Queensland when they were much older, but once Des died the heart went out of Penny and she had no desire to continue their business.

"I'm moving to Queensland" Penny had informed her sister after her husband's funeral. In 1990, she moved to Noosa and hoped it would be a fresh start and her loneliness would be over. Unfortunately, the move only exacerbated her isolation and she found herself with severe depression.

"You should come and spend some time with the sister who loves you," Lottie had said when she saw how down Penny had become, living on her own. Penny agreed and went off to Brisbane for a holiday. Within weeks, they were playing golf, attending gym and fitness classes and going to art lessons every week.

Lottie turned out to be the companion Penny really needed. She was heard to say, 'there is so much that does not need to be said between siblings'. Lottie discovered her older sister had mellowed. She was no longer the authoritarian, pushy, demanding pace setter. Her sister had become wise, thoughtful, and very kind.

Penny had always thought of Lottie as a rebel and one without a cause as well. Unable to compete with the high achievements of her sister, Lottie simply opted out. Leaving home at seventeen, Lottie earned enough in a chorus line to pay for her airfare to London. Once there she made her way in musicals and stage plays. Lottie saw herself as a dancer, but in fact, her talent lay in acting. Eventually, she toured Europe and lived many years in Britain where she married an older man who died when he was seventy and she only fifty.

Finally, Lottie came home to Australia and settled in Brisbane. Neither of the sisters had children, so, when they found fate had thrust them back together, they were both surprised. They both finally acknowledged they had more in common than they had ever been prepared to admit. They pooled their resources and bought a home together at Keeala Resort. In the three years they had been together, they had not only learned a lot about one another but also learned a lot from one another. The bus tour was to be an adventure they could share and tighten the bonds that had formed so long ago.

Chapter Six

"Shit!" Di fell the last three steps of the stairs into the entrance hall of their home. For a moment, there was complete silence, not a sound. Di lifted her head and moaned. Her hand reached down to her ankle and she screamed aloud, "Bloody hell!"

She lay back down and tears ran down her cheeks. *Oh no, not now, please not now.* The pain was excruciating, and for a few minutes, Di lay on the floor panting and wondering what to do next.

The front door opened and Jim almost walked on her head. She screamed and he jumped so far he almost fell over as well.

"Shit. What are you doing?" Jim looked at his wife in astonishment.

"Not much – just thought I'd try out ..." but she could not finish the sarcastic comment on the tip of her tongue. "I fell down the stairs," she screamed and started a new flood of tears.

"So I see, and have you broken anything?" Jim approached her hesitantly, as if he may catch whatever had thrown his wife down the stairs.

"I think so, my ankle. Can you take a look at it?"

"Well, I don't know how I could tell if it was broken. Does it hurt?"

Diane looked at Jim disbelievingly. "Of course it bloody hurts. Do you think I'm just lying here for fun?"

Jim bent down, frowned, and peered at her foot. "Will I ring the ambulance? I don't want to touch it and hurt you."

Di attempted to sit up but winced with pain. She sprawled back down again. "Yes, I can't stand and I don't feel like conducting the rest of my life from the floor. Wait – no, you can drive me. It's only five minutes away. It'll be in range of your beeper. Grab the wheelchair from the office."

Within a few minutes, Di was lying on a trolley in Accident and Emergency, answering questions, the same questions, for the third time.

"What's the point of writing anything down if nobody looks at your answers?" Di was getting cranky and, as she was approached by another nurse, she was ready to tell her to look at the file and she was not about to answer the same questions again.

The nurse, however, held a kidney tray containing an injection for pain. "What is your name, please?"

"Diane Watersen," Di answered, gritting her teeth as she exposed her upper arm for an injection.

"We'll be taking you for an x-ray in a few minutes." The nurse looked harried. Di nodded in understanding. She had been there and done that.

Jim stood nearby. "This could present a problem, in relation to going on holidays, that is," he said. He had a vague look of satisfaction lurking around his mouth.

Di stiffened, but looked away from her husband. She decided not to acknowledge his comment.

Minutes later, she was having an x-ray and a half hour later a handsome looking Indian doctor pushed back the curtain and walked to her bedside.

"You will be happy I'm sure to know that your ankle is not broken. A bad looking sprain but something you will recover from, there is no doubt of that."

"Oh, thank God. I'm so relieved." Di reached for Jim's hand and squeezed it. He looked down and smiled indulgently.

"You will need some medication for the pain, to take home with you, I am thinking," Dr. Gupta explained, "So you will be taking it easy for a few weeks also." He nodded and smiled. "We are giving you some support to that painful area and you can then be on your way home again. Rest, and foot up on the bed, ah yes, that is my recommendation to you. Goodbye, Madam."

Di gratefully accepted the medication. An assistant wheeled Di to the car, which Jim had brought to the entrance.

"Be careful," shouted Jim, as he watched wide eyed as his wife lunged for the seat of the car, after hopping and jumping from the wheelchair. Distracted, Di almost missed the seat as she grabbed the car door for support. She landed with a thump, and Jim slammed the door behind her. They drove home, both very subdued.

With borrowed crutches and Jim's assistance, Di made her way to the lounge and declared she would go no further.

"This will do me for tonight. Please, darling, a cup of tea, oh, and a pillow here, oh, and before you go, could you hand me those pills please. Oh, and I'm going to need a blanket."

"Hang on, one thing at a time. I'm..."

"Can you hand me the phone please, before you go? And turn the light on, darling. I'll also need a pillow under my foot to elevate it, you know."

Jim left the room, turning on the light as he did so. He returned and handed his wife the phone.

"And where is my pillow?"

"Why is it that I have the idea you're feeling a little better than you were when you left here a few hours ago," he muttered.

She sat thinking, *Reiki therapy should help speed up recovery. Now I need my phone directory. I wonder what's taking Jim so long. I can't believe how slow men can be; give them more than one chore to do and they fly into complete confusion. I'd better be on top of things tomorrow.* Di drummed her fingers on the coffee table, and waited for her wayward husband to return.

The next day was Sunday. Di woke and looked at her foot; it was very swollen, and painful. She began to talk to herself as she swallowed her analgesics, looked around the room, and wondered why she had never noticed how many cobwebs were forming in the corners of the ceiling. *The room needs a good clean – a spring clean – maybe even a coat of paint. Carpets are looking shabby as well. I wonder if Jim knows what time it is. He could be getting so much work done this morning. I wonder if he remembers I can't get up and start breakfast. Actually, I'll have to call him anyway. I need assistance to the toilet.*

"Jim, Jim," Di shouted several times. No answer. She called again, a little louder.

"You don't have to shout the house down," Jim answered, as he came thumping down the stairs.

"Sorry, darling, but I need a hand to the toilet."

He handed her crutches to her and together they made their way to the downstairs toilet between the laundry and the kitchen.

"Could you put the jug on for a cup of tea while you're waiting, please dear?"

"It's on." Jim had a faint sound of exasperation in his voice. Di detected both impatience and frustration just below the surface.

She thought, *Well, that's tough. I certainly didn't plan to fall down the stairs. We can't always have everything our own way.*

They danced together to the kitchen table. Di sat heavily and almost missed the chair. She put her hand up. "I'm fine,

I'm fine," she said, as Jim lurched toward her to break her fall.

"Now. What do we have to do today?"

Jim rolled his eyes, "It's Sunday."

"Yes, that's good."

"Darling, do you seriously think you'll be fit to go on this bus trip in a week's time?"

Di sighed, "I really want to be, Jim, after all the trouble I've gone to organising it. I can't let everyone down now."

"Well, *they* could all still go."

"No, most of them are only going because we're going along."

"I see. It puts a lot of pressure on us to be responsible for everyone, and it's not as if we'll have any authority, away from home."

"I hope not. It is unofficial, and we all just happen to be going on the same bus."

Jim added "At the same time, to the same place."

"Yes." Di was feeling pretty down.

Jim began to feel sorry for his wife, who had been known to bite off more than she could chew, occasionally. "We can do it. What do you want me to do today?" he said.

"Thank you, love." Di reached for Jim's hand and squeezed it. "I'll need all my info about the trip. It's on the desk in the guest room."

By lunchtime, Jim and Di had contacted all the travellers and informed them that the deal would be finalised tomorrow morning. They would be on the road in a week.

Mid afternoon, the buzzer went in the manager's residence. Jim followed his usual protocol, rang the unit first, in this case Unit 70, and when it didn't answer he grabbed his keys and took off to that unit in the one-bedroom section.

Jim arrived at the front door and knocked. Helga den Ronden answered with a smile on her face. "Hello, Mr. Watersen, come in."

Jim stepped inside "What's the problem, Helga?"

"Sit down, sit down."

"No, thanks." Jim looked around "You rang the buzzer?"

Suddenly Helga looked a little flustered, "Well, as a matter of fact, Mr. Watersen, it was just my little experiment, you see. My daughter told me I could not rely on anyone to assist me when I go on the bus trip. I said she was wrong and that both you and your wife were very reliable people. You could be trusted to help me, if I needed it, I said. Therefore, I have just proved my point. It is Sunday, your day off – and here you are."

Jim felt like a stunned mullet. He opened his mouth several times to speak and closed it again. He clenched his fist in anger and frustration. He sat down.

Helga sat next to him and smiled. Suddenly she noted his silence and looked up startled. "You're not upset, are you?"

"That, Mrs den Ronden, is an understatement. If you can't see anything wrong with demanding my attention via the emergency call bell, for no good reason and, on a Sunday as well, then there is really not much I can say. For your information, we certainly cannot be relied upon to look after you on the bus trip since it is not an official village excursion.

If you have chosen to go along on the same bus as us, then that is entirely your concern. We are on holiday ourselves and bear no responsibility for anyone at all. I suggest you take your daughter's advice and stay home where you'll have the support of the facilities here in the resort and there'll be a relief manager to respond to any emergency you may have."

Helga was in tears before Jim finished speaking. "I'm so sorry. I can see it was not wise to call you on your day off. Please forgive me. I don't want to miss the bus trip; I've been so looking forward to it. Please don't make me stay home."

"Madam, can't you see it is not my decision who comes or stays. If you go along you must be prepared to look after yourself entirely. We are on holiday ourselves. We will not be looking after anyone but ourselves. Please understand that."

"Yes, I do. I am afraid I'm just a very silly old woman and I've always had someone to take care of me." Helga sniffed and blew her nose. "I was Mummy and Daddy's only little girl and then my dear husband was such an attentive man, he never let me do anything for myself. Now my daughter looks out for me and she is always saying I'm helpless and I'm sure she is right. I think it's time I showed everyone I can take care of myself." Helga stood and sniffed again. "You are absolutely right Mr. Watersen, I'm sorry for calling you out for no reason, it was most inconsiderate of me. Moreover, heavens, I could become like the boy who cried wolf, you know. No one comes when I do need help."

Jim stood and walked to the door. "Please consider it carefully, Helga. I'll ring you this evening and see how you feel about going on the bus trip after you've had time to think about it thoroughly." Jim strode off and did not look back, his only thought, *I can't believe that happened.*

Chapter Seven

Jim and Di visited the travel agent's office the next day. It took more than two hours for them to go through the details and when they left, Jim carried out a bag containing pamphlets and a suggested itinerary for each of the other residents.

"I suppose I can't complain. It's a free country and really James and Julie were only doing what anyone else could have done," Di commented to Jim as soon as they got into the car to drive home. The travel agent had told the managers that a couple from the village, James and Julie O'Brien, had come in and booked onto the bus trip independently of the circle of friends. She mentioned that others from the resort had also enquired and shown interest. Despite the best efforts of the original participants, news of the tour had spread around the resort soon after Di had proposed it. Jim and Di agreed the O'Briens may not have been their first choice as travelling companions, nor would some of the others mentioned by the agent, but the fact was it would have been very difficult to exclude anyone. That meant seventeen from the group of friends, plus Di and Jim made nineteen. It seemed possible that another half dozen or so from the resort may also tag along.

Mid-morning next day, Di took a call from the travel agent. "Hi, Joan, hope there's not a problem?"

"No, on the contrary, Di. I've got good news – well, I hope you'll think it's good news. I've had some interest in your tour from the friends of some of your people and even from some residents of another resort in the area, who have somehow heard about your little jaunt. I know it was meant to be a tour for your resort residents but with the amount of additional enquiry from outside, it would be quite advantageous cost wise, to fill the next sized coach. You would still only require the same drivers but, with the cost spread over a greater number of people, even allowing for the running costs of the bigger coach, there would be a worthwhile saving on your fares."

"Oh, what the hell, Joan, it's already escalated from the original idea, I'm sure you're right, and the more the merrier, eh?"

******

The following week was a series of dramas and events that had Jim running around all day and up half the night, since Di was still not on two feet. The relief manager, Sonja, arrived and moved into their house with bags, boxes and two dogs. She seemed to Jim to be a little naive, despite her recommendation from head office. Consequently, he spent much more time with her than he had anticipated. The guest room was overflowing with Sonya's personal stuff and the dogs made themselves very comfortable on the lounge, either sleeping or scratching.

Di shuddered every time she saw them there and almost went head over heels in the kitchen where there were two bowls of dog food and a large water bowl right in the main walkway.

Di and Jim tried to leave things in order as well as pack for the trip and make contact with family members. There were insurance and personal papers to deal with. Going away for six weeks meant checking their wills were in order and paying bills that might arise in their absence. There were so many details to finalise and residents were constantly ringing up to check on one thing or another.

Two days before their departure, Jim circulated a flyer for the residents of the resort, bringing them up to date with their dates of absence and introducing Sonja, the relief manager, assuring everyone things would continue as normal. The night before the trip was due to commence, Jim sank into bed and pulled the covers over his head. "Don't wake me, ever!"

Hearing his muffled cry, Di said. "Aren't you even a bit excited about tomorrow, darling?"

"No!"

******

The much-anticipated day dawned, not a cloud in the sky, a perfect day for sight-seeing. The bus arrived at 10.00 am, already carrying six other travellers. They peered out of the windows to see hugging, kissing, and waving, luggage stowing and going back for last minute forgotten items. The six already on the coach were fully entertained watching the dramas unfold as everyone from the resort finally got on the bus and settled down. After they had changed seats, moved pillows, set up snack containers in the seat pockets, and then, some still not satisfied, changed again, the bus driver finally stood at the front and introduced himself.

"Morning ladies and gentlemen, my name is Roger and I will be one of your host--drivers for the next six weeks. I'll get to know you at our first lunch-stop, but now, let's get this show on the road, shall we?" He slid into his seat, started the engine and let off the brake. The shouting and whistling could have rivalled the departure of the Queen Mary.

The bus had not gone more than ten metres when a voice shrieked, "Wait, wait, I don't have my handbag." The whole bus froze. "Oh, yes I have. Sorry, it's right here on my lap."

Everyone breathed out again, accompanied by some not so subtle grumbling and, for about five minutes, there was silence as the bus picked up momentum down the road.

Once out of the congestion of the suburban streets and onto the motorway, the bus driver adjusted the fit of his headset microphone and spoke to the passengers about the trip; what to expect from the extended sight-seeing, what to do in an emergency, and the general housekeeping and safety issues of long-distance coach travel. He asked his passengers not to speak to him while the coach was in motion and reaffirmed he would introduce himself to each traveller on a first name basis at the first stop. They all sat back and began to watch the world go by outside their window. Their great adventure had begun.

******

"Knock again, they must be there."

Judy knocked again, louder, "Anyone home?"

"No one lives there now," a voice from behind called to the couple standing on Margaret's doorstep.

They turned to see an elderly lady with a round, smiling face standing at the end of the path to what was Margaret's old bed-sitter unit.

"I'm looking for Margaret Robilliard."

"She doesn't live here anymore."

"What do you mean, she doesn't live here now?"

The elderly woman walked up the path toward them.

"She married Ethan Dougherty and now they've gone on a bus tour around Australia." The woman looked smug and self-satisfied to be the bearer of such news.

Patrick and Judy stared back with mouths agape and finally Judy asked, "But where do they live now?"

The woman started to answer, but stopped, "And who, may I ask, wants to know?"

Patrick stepped forward, hand extended. "Patrick Robilliard. My sister Judy and I have been overseas and came to see Mum and meet her new husband."

"Oh, well, nice to meet you Patrick and you too, Judy. I'm sorry to say you only missed them by one day. Why don't you come next door to my home and have a cup of tea and I can tell you all about them. My name is Lillian Gossett, but you can call me Lil."

They all walked back down the path and into number 111, where Lil offered the couple tea and biscuits and which they accepted happily.

"What a fairy tale story it's been. I'm sure it couldn't happen to a nicer pair than Margaret and Ethan. By the way, your mum's name is now Dougherty.

Brother and sister nodded. "Well, unfortunately we've been out of touch, overseas and all, but we were looking forward to meeting our new dad."

"Oh, what a shame. You could probably ring them. The relief manager would have a mobile number you could contact them on, I'm sure."

The pair nodded again. Patrick thought fast, "And so where do they live now, Lil, if you don't mind me asking?"

"Not at all, son, they have a lovely new home right here in the resort. I don't think they even considered moving anywhere else. This is their home and all their friends are here."

"Well, this new dad of ours must have a bit of money, buying a new house and all." Judy was digging for information.

"I wouldn't know about that, dear, but they got a lovely surprise at the wedding. A fabulous gift from an old uncle, a very wealthy one I would say."

"Oh, really, which uncle was that?" Patrick and Judy glanced quickly at one another.

Lil thought, "I'm not sure, maybe Roddie something. No, I can't remember his name, but I remember he not only gave them a new home, but $500,000 in a bank account as well."

Patrick almost choked on his drink. Judy stared, mouth open.

"How much did you say?" Patrick asked.

Lil laughed, "Quite a sum of money to get from someone you haven't seen for years, $500,000, and with no strings attached, apparently."

Patrick recovered first. "Wow, and you say they've gone on a trip somewhere?"

"Not just a trip, a trip around Australia. We don't expect to see them again for about six weeks. I would have gone myself if I hadn't already seen most of the country. I've done a lot of travelling in my youth you know. Actually, I wonder how some of them will stand up to such a long drive and being in such close quarters with the likes of Helga den Ronden and Joy Rayne. I really couldn't do it myself."

Judy and Patrick stood up before Lil finished talking. They seemed to have heard enough and made their way to the front door.

"You say the manager will know their phone number and what bus they're on?" Patrick asked.

"Yes, dear, if manager is what you can call her. Personally, I would just call her useless. I, for one, will be glad to see our rightful managers return to where they belong – if we are all still here when they return." Lil found herself talking to the backs of the couple who were already walking briskly along the driveway. "Didn't even say thank you for the afternoon tea. Not very well mannered, if you ask me," Lil said, to no one in particular.

******

"So, Jude, we have a whole new ball game, looks like we may soon come into some money."

"Might not be that easy, Pat."

"Well, I can hardly wait to meet our new Daddy. Maybe we'll have a better idea of what our prospects are, after that. I hope he doesn't have any kids already. Mind you, I doubt they'll be making any more at their age."

"They could live for years yet."

"Maybe and maybe not – so many things can happen on a trip as long as theirs. Accidents ... , you know what I mean." Patrick smiled at his sister as they walked over to the manager's office.

Chapter Eight

Despite the never-ending speed restrictions and delays caused by road-works on the Pacific Highway, the tourist's spirits were buoyant as they left their home state and travelled south through the far-north coast of New South Wales. After a lunch stop at Ballina, at which Roger, their coach driver, introduced himself to each passenger, the group continued to their first overnight destination, Coffs Harbour. Most of the passengers belonged to the same loose alliance of friends in the resort and were at ease in each other's company. They laughed, joked and sang their way south and made a special effort to include the strangers amongst them, especially a couple of those whose reserved manner was probably no more than shyness. After having spent the whole day talking and singing, many vocal chords would need at least one full night's rest before they could perform again.

In the motel restaurant that evening, Jim sat next to Harold and they exchanged their day's experiences.

"I really can't understand this great need to tell another person one's whole life story, no matter how irrelevant it may be," stated Harold. "I always manage to sit next to some motor-mouth who simply will not shut up, even though they are given absolutely no encouragement whatsoever."

Jim agreed and said he made a practice of always carrying a book to read in such cases, but noted that even that did not deter some people. Harold and Jim went on to discuss the recent court case that had stimulated so much interest at the resort.

At this point, Helga den Ronden walked up behind Jim and leaned over his chair. "Please excuse the interruption, Mr. Watersen," she turned her back to Harold and pushed between the chairs. "I wonder if you could check my mobile phone for messages." She poked her phone in front of Jim.

Jim lifted his hand to take the phone but Harold reached in front of him and took it. "I'm afraid, Helga, our manager is on holidays; I'd be happy to take a look if you like." He looked up at her and she scowled at him in return. She snatched her phone and blustered away to her table with nothing further to say.

The men exchanged knowing glances. Harold shrugged his shoulders and said, "Rude? Ignorant? Bigoted? Take your pick. Oh, I'm sorry Jim, I shouldn't speak like that about a fellow resident, especially to you, but sometimes, even after all these years, such narrow-mindedness still gets my goat."

"As they say in the classics, Harold, you may very well say it, but I couldn't possibly do so." Jim gave a conspiratorial smile and, with a twinkle in his eye to set Harold at ease, added, "Not that I wouldn't like to."

"It seems there is no end to the prejudice levelled at Robert and myself. It just continues, no matter how we respond, or don't respond, they never change." Harold scratched his head and took a deep breath, hating to expose his feelings in Jim's company.

Jim turned to look directly at his friend. "I'm very impressed with how you handle these narrow-minded idiots. I can't begin to understand how it makes you feel and considering you have to deal with it on a daily basis; I really take my hat off to you."

"Thanks Jim, I appreciate you saying that. Robert is the sensitive one though, and it is hard to stand by and watch how much he has been hurt in the past. The likes of the den Ronden woman is typical of what we constantly have to deal with."

"So how do you deal with it?" Jim spoke softly.

Harold took a deep breath, "We've tried all sorts of tactics; ignoring the criticism, meeting it head on and defending our relationship, striking back. I can't understand what our sex life has to do with other people. We're not interested in theirs. You wouldn't credit the lengths some individuals will go to. We've had poison pen letters shoved in our mailbox; we've been threatened that our house will be burnt down if we don't move out; oh you wouldn't believe how foul some people are. Sometimes it's the ones you least suspect as well. They never fail to surprise me, Jim."

"This is awful. I find it hard to believe. Unfortunately I do, and it makes me ashamed."

"Let's not dwell on this subject though. We're here to enjoy ourselves and that's what we're going to do, hey?"

"Absolutely!"

They both chuckled and started to talk about the A-League football, or soccer, as Jim still called it. The arrival of the beautifully presented main courses slowed the conversation. The food was delicious and their enjoyment of it ensured Helga den Ronden's rude interruption was soon forgotten.

******

The bus offloaded the group in North Sydney the following afternoon at a comfortable and charming guesthouse. Everyone was looking forward to the next day when they could either join a local tour or spend the day wandering freely. Freya Holman had pared up with Rachel Ross and they were waiting on the front steps of the old building the next morning when Di waved to them from the breakfast balcony.

"Excuse me," said Freya, and she went up to speak to Di. "I'm not sure if you know, and I realise it's not my business, but I'm a bit worried about Lorna McDonald."

"Really, why?" Di sat with Margaret Dougherty, who had her mouth full of toast.

"She's very sick."

"What do you mean? When I saw her yesterday, she looked fine. Mind you, she's never been a good colour and she's always fairly quiet. What do you think's wrong with her?"

"She's dying. She has cancer. Sorry, I assumed you knew. I'm afraid I may be talking out of place here but I heard her last night vomiting in the unit next to me. I already knew she had cancer, because her daughter and mine both attend aqua aerobics together. I found out by chance. I have the feeling she may not have told anyone, but I thought you may have known."

"No, I did not." Di was shaking her head and looking quite stunned. She locked eyes with Margaret and thought for a minute. "Well, thank you for telling me, Freya. Perhaps you should not mention this to anyone else as Lorna is such a private person. I'll take it from here and thank you again." Di reached for Freya's hand and squeezed it. Freya left to catch up with Rachael.

This is certainly a surprise. Perhaps one of many? Di thought as she lifted her cup to her mouth.

"That sounds bad," said Margaret. "What can you do?"

"I don't know, maybe nothing until Lorna confides in me. I'll just keep an eye on her from a distance for the time being I think."

"So will I," Margaret nodded.

******

Day three went along happily with everyone going off in couples or small groups. There was a city tour and sightseeing at the botanical gardens and the opera house, the museum and the harbour. Shopping and eating were high priorities. That night, many of the group were exhausted, and went off to bed very quietly.

In the lounge of the guesthouse, Di found Lorna sitting, reading, and she thought it a good opportunity to approach her.

"How was your day, Lorna?" she said, as she sat opposite her on a big leather lounge. Lorna looked up and smiled.

"Very interesting, and quite fun actually. I went with the sisters, Penny and Lottie, and they really kept me laughing at the silliest of things. They both have quite different tastes and they make fun of one another. It must be nice to be so relaxed in someone else's company."

"Well, you must be good company too or they wouldn't have invited you along."

"Oh I suspect they took pity on me and decided there was room for one more. But still, I did appreciate the gesture; however I won't make a nuisance of myself."

"Is that something that worries you? I mean making a nuisance of yourself?"

Lorna looked a question at Di.

"Lorna, I think you may have something to share with me about your health."

"Did my daughter tell you?" Lorna looked worried.

"No, in fact, one of the residents told me because she was worried. She had been told, indirectly by your daughter, that you had cancer. Now, only two people beside me know, and of course, we will respect your privacy. But I would feel much better if you discussed the extent of you illness with me now and then. If needed, I may be able to help."

"But this is your holiday. I know you're a nurse but I had no intention of burdening you with my problems."

Di reached for Lorna's hand. It was cold and moist. "I think I like being useful. You know, since I hurt my ankle it has been the worst experience I could have imagined. Having to wait for my husband or someone else to attend to my needs or to just fetch and carry has been dreadful. I assure you I'm impatient and demanding and would make the worst kind of sick person. Jim will attest to that. However, give me a challenge and I'm happy – it makes me feel important."

Lorna smiled at that. "I think you need a rest like anyone, but I am very grateful for your offer to talk. Since my husband died eighteen months ago, I've been alone and I wouldn't wish that on my worst enemy. I mean, after we had been so close and he died of cancer over a three-year period. He died at home and I cared for him with the help of a nursing service and a very good G.P."

Di nodded. "And when did you get your diagnosis?"

"Eight months ago. I must have had it for some time before Jay died, but was just too busy to realise it. So now, I have a prognosis of about three to four months as the cancer has gone to my liver and other parts of my body. I had surgery and that relieved some of the pain but now that is coming back again."

"Oh dear, I'm so sorry. Are you content that everything that can be done has been done?" Di asked quietly

"Yes. I feel I'm a bit knowledgeable now after going through all the alternatives with Jay. And I have little desire to prolong my life now he's gone." Lorna sighed sadly and looked up at Di. "It means a lot to be heard in a sympathetic way. Thank you."

"What sort of pain relief do you have, Lorna?"

"I have this cannula in my arm and can give myself injections or use the syringe driver. Of course, I plan to check in with doctors in several different towns on the way. I have oral medication as well – something for every symptom just about. I understand the procedure to alter my medication and the effects of the drugs I'm using. Please don't worry too much; I really am pretty experienced with all this stuff."

"I accept that. I'm not sure I understand why you decided to come on this trip though." Di looked at Lorna.

"Well, my daughter isn't aware of how little time I have left and I didn't want to just sit at home and deteriorate, waiting with everyone watching me and hoping for it to be over. I considered that if I got a lot worse I would go to a hospital, any hospital; it doesn't matter – and only contact Janie at the end. That way it will be almost over before the family have to go through the end-stage again. Jay's death was very hard on everyone. They've had enough, I think." A tear slipped from Lorna's eye and splashed on to her hand. She wiped it away quickly.

"Have you considered that Janie might be very upset after you die that she was not allowed to share your pain. She'll want to grieve and she may even think you couldn't trust her to be there for you."

"I hadn't really thought of it that way, you may be right. Perhaps I'll stay with the group for a while and then go home by plane in a couple of weeks. What do you think about that?"

"A better idea, yes. Don't take away your family's chance to say good-bye properly. They certainly may not thank you for leaving them out – even though you are trying to spare them. That's what families were invented for, you know, to help with the burdens of life as well as share the joys."

For a few moments, the women sat together and cried almost silently. They shared tissues from Lorna's handbag and then a hug.

"Thank you," said Lorna

"Thank you for sharing and trusting me. Come on, its bedtime. From now on, you keep me abreast of you current condition and I won't pester you. We are definitely going to have a little fun before you go home." Di and Lorna smiled.

Chapter Nine

When Patrick and Judy left Keeala Resort, they were both deep in thought.

Pat asked, "Do you have any idea what a difference that much money could make to us? I mean invested in a profitable business, several of which I already have in mind."

"But how on earth are you going to get them to part with it? You know they won't just leave it to you in their Will and they won't just write you out a cheque. For shit's sake, Pat, this new hubby may not even let us talk to Margaret. He has no reason to let us into their lives."

"Calm down, kid." Patrick had heaps of character, some of it bad. He had been looking after his sister all his life. They had been through very rough times together and no one ever came between them. Not that either looked for a partner since they had always been all things to each other – including lovers.

"I'm having lots of ideas already. But we're going to need help and I know just the person to provide it." Patrick punched a number into his mobile phone as they drove off down the street. Their car was their latest indulgence and represented almost the bottom of their bank account. It was a four-wheel drive Toyota, brand new and fully equipped. They had about ten thousand left after the purchase of their car and thought a loan from Margaret would be very timely. Patrick began to think he would need to invest some of their savings to insure against hard times.

"You can't have too much well-invested money – that's what I always say," Patrick said.

******

An early start on day four saw the bus on its way to the sights and sounds of the tour's next major stop over, the garden city of Melbourne, the capital of Victoria. As the coach left the built-up areas of Sydney's outer suburbs, Di commented to Jim that the atmosphere on the bus had changed. There was a definite feeling that the travellers were dropping their guard, their stress, and their inhibitions. Most of them had sung at the top of their voices and there was nothing like loud group singing to release tension and increase laughter. Everyone had taken a turn at commencing a song and then the others had to join in. Of course, what had started out as good, clean fun ended with the songs getting smutty and finally downright dirty. By popular demand though, a DVD of Billy Connolly was played over the coach's multimedia system. Passengers could watch the performance on a screen set into the back of the seat ahead of them. Some, who had never seen the comedian's stand-up routine, were so shocked at the language that they turned their screens off and sat stony-faced, waiting for the tears of laughter to stop rolling down the cheeks of the other passengers. It was a hard act to follow and, when the DVD finished, a relative calm pervaded the cabin, but was broken every few minutes by sudden guffaws and giggles as Connolly's jokes were recycled.

Di wiped her eyes and realised how long it had been since she had felt so relaxed. Spirits were high when they broke the journey at a motel in a small country town, about six hours after having left Sydney. When the bus drew into the motel parking lot, the atmosphere sparkled with bonhomie and there was friendly pushing and shoving to get out and stretch legs.

"Anyone wishing to join Lottie and I on a brisk walk is most welcome," announced Penny, as she descended the bus steps a little shakily.

A straggly line of crumpled oldies made their way down the main street of the town that later no one could remember the name of. They came back starving and made their way to their rooms to wash and repair for dinner.

When Di joined Jim and Harold at the bar, she commented on the amount of friends already there drinking merrily. "I didn't think either Joy or Martin drank alcohol." Di was referring to Martin Judd and Joy Rayne, who came separately, but who were obviously enjoying a traveller's romance while on the road. Neither could stop laughing as they sat together at the bar, telling funny stories.

"Oh, it's so nice to see them let their hair down," said Robert, when he came up behind Harold and put his hands on Jim's and his partner's shoulders. "What are we drinking, boys? Because I want some of what they are having!"

"We're having very dry martinis if you must know, and I've already ordered one for you, sir. Please be seated." Harold waved to the bar tender and moved along to let Robert sit next to him.

Lorna was again with Penny and Lottie and the three made a happy scene. They were looking at the photos on their digital cameras, jostling each other and laughing. Di was pleased to see the three women together; they were about the same age, all well educated and refined widows and they had a lot in common. Di noted that Lorna was participating and not just hanging on in the background. She was genuinely enjoying herself. Di smiled.

******

"Good to see you, mate," said Patrick, as he shook hands at a planned meeting with a new friend. New, because their paths had crossed fortuitously at a recent buck's night, but it was an old friendship, rekindled from their days in the Army Reserve. Patrick had immediately recognised Russell as a kindred spirit, not an equal in some respects, but complementary nevertheless. Patrick, despite his turbulent life as a foster child, had the intellect to exploit his years of learning and emerged as a well educated young man. Russell, on the other hand, had not made it past primary school. He had come from a broken home and never seemed able to concentrate in class. His manner of speaking would never win him a prize in the elocution section of an eisteddfod, but rough as it was, it belied a rat-cunning intelligence and practical nature that was an integral element in his survival. Unlikely as it would appear possible, Russell had somehow taken to computers as if he had been hatched from a hard drive. His reputation in the world of hacking was legend, though he was only ever identified by his hacker nickname. It was easy to see why he was Patrick's first choice as an accomplice in his scheme to separate his foster mother from her fortune.

As Patrick outlined his plan to his new, old friend, he noted that Russell had, like himself, stayed fit. Russell was shorter than Patrick, but strong, lean, with big hands, and he moved about with the flexibility of an athlete. He may have been rough around the edges when it came to the social graces, but he had a nice face, a beguiling smile, and thick brown hair that sat there and looked model-good all the time. Patrick remembered Russell had always been a little vain about his appearance and was in demand with the girls. After some minor quibbling, they agreed the job was doable and agreed on a 60/40 split in Patrick's favour. Next they began to nut out the fine details of the venture.

"The way I see it, mate," said Russell, "is we grab the oldies and 'old them until we get the money – transferred via the internet."

"Well, they won't just give over their bank details, not just like that," interrupted Judy.

"No, of course not, but I suspect a few threats to the old girl will convince the old codger to cooperate, pretty damned quick," said Russell.

Patrick agreed.

"So, you're the computer genius, I hear," said Judy to Russell.

He nodded. "Sort of."

Judy said, "I don't want you guys to hurt Margaret. Hear me?"

The two men looked at one another and nodded. That part of the plan was between them.

Patrick continued, "So we launder the money and are on our way. Too easy."

Both men could also see they would have to have another discussion without Judy before they finalised their plan.

******

Day five, and the travellers arrived in Melbourne, mid-afternoon. The next day, most went   sightseeing or shopping, or, as a handful did, they visited the casino. Unlike the punter who allegedly scammed the casino for $33 million, these intrepid gamblers were led to the slaughter, but still managed to smile as they made their donations.

On day seven, just before they boarded the bus after breakfast, they all stood for a group photo next to the bus. They had taken one in a similar position when they left home a week ago, but they already looked different – so much happier and more relaxed and in little cliques and pairs that were not there before. Photo shoot over, they hit the road again, heading for Adelaide. It would be a long day – over eight hours travel time.

Once again, their travel agent had done them proud. To cater for the numbers, she had booked the group into three, beautiful, heritage listed B&Bs, all within a couple of hundred metres of each other. The lovely old homes had everything the travellers could wish for. The proprietors were all charming, the establishments well run, and the old buildings reeked of history. The food was excellent and the wines were some of South Australia's finest.

The independent bus tours for the wine regions picked the group up at their accommodation next morning, and first took them on a city tour including a lookout to view the city of churches and then to a chocolate factory where everyone got to sample the product with tea or coffee.

Rachael and Freya had started to keep a diary a few days out on the trip. Their entry for day eight read,

The next day it was on to the McLaren Vale winery where we all sampled the produce of Olive Oil making, cheese making and best of all wine making. It was at our last stop that two of the group, Peter Kaminski and Hank Fletcher got lost and there was an all points search for them. By the end of the tour, some of us (but not the writers) had done a lot of tasting and many had bought wine to take home with them.

Apparently, Peter and Hank decided to test their take home wine and they were finally found slumped behind a tree on the fringe of the vineyard, sound asleep, snoring with an empty bottle between them. With a little help they were loaded back onto the tour bus, then home to the accompaniment of either singing or giggling.

Gee whiz we slept well that night.

End of entry.

****

"I'm really glad to see Ralph enjoying himself so much" Di said to Jim, when they retired to their bedroom the same evening.

They had both been surprised and pleased as he started to come out of his shell. It is what they had hoped for but not really expected, as Ralph had been grieving for his wife who had died more than a year ago. He had slipped into prolonged grief and not been able to find his way out. That is why Di had suggested the trip to him in the first place. So, it was working and made any little inconvenience or discomfort worth it. Jim and Di sat up in bed chatting until late about the many changes they had noticed in the group. They saw a side of some that they would not have expected but they were delighted nonetheless.

"I've really enjoyed this trip so far, but I have to say that the next part is what I'm looking forward to most," said Margaret to Ethan, when they were on the bus next day.

"I agree. Central Australia holds more mystery for me, I have the feeling I don't even know what I want to see. Just everything and really soak it up, you know?" Margaret nodded.

******

On Wednesday, day nine, they hit the road later than usual, after more photos, and with a new driver. They had lined up for yet another group photo before they left, and the driver was anxious to get started. He had driven tours like this before but it was not his favourite thing. He found sticking to the highway a little boring. He would have liked to have been driving the four-wheel drive, cross-country tours. Nevertheless, here he was and he would make the best of it. He did the usual introductions and explained that the leg to Coober Pedy from Adelaide would have been too arduous, probably a ten-hour day allowing for breaks, hence the stopover at Port Augusta to break the journey. The party settled in for the relatively short drive.

That night, the bus eased into the designated parking area at a motel in Port Augusta.

"This town is the cross roads to the North, South, East and West of Australia and sits at the head of the Spencer Gulf," the driver said, as he turned off the ignition. "Tomorrow we head into the desert, so make the best of civilization while you have the chance."

They all offloaded again.

******

Next day was a longer haul to Coober Pedy, situated in the vast gibber plains where there were the largest opal producing mines in the world. They parked at a motel on the outskirts of town.

"I love this," said Di, when they carted their bags to their room in the dugout motel. The whole place was built underground, with all rooms dug out like the mines. The excitement level was rising, and that night Barry, the driver, explained the plan for day eleven. They would be free to wander the town and tour the mines, maybe buy opals to take home. The following day they would head for Engadoona, via the desert.

"I think this has been the best day so far," Robert announced to the assembled table that night. Quite a few agreed with him, but Ethan said Margaret had been a bit reluctant to enter the mine-like room.

"She obviously likes the open spaces better than the underground," said Ethan. "I hope it doesn't portend a sleepless night. A little sedation may be in order, do you think my dear?" He looked a question at his wife.

She nodded her head and said, "I think you may be right."

Despite Margaret's best intentions to get a good night's sleep there was a sense of tension and fear pervading the motel room where she slept with Ethan that night. One sleeping pill would normally send her into a deep, dreamless state within half an hour of putting her head to the pillow. Tonight was to be the exception, maybe it was the air-conditioned, windowless room or perhaps it was the full moon, but it was sometime after midnight, before Margaret drifted into a troubled sleep.

The sound of someone close to her face awakened her with a jolt. She became aware as a hand went over her mouth then stuffed it with a gag, quickly followed by a bag over her head. Margaret was pulled roughly from her bed and her hands pulled behind her back before she had any idea what was happening. She heard Ethan protest before his voice became muffled. They both struggled as they were taken from the room. Manhandled up to the entrance, they were dragged out to a waiting vehicle.

Chapter Ten

Early the following morning, Barry reminded everyone to change seats when they got onto the bus. They all agreed this was the best way for everyone to get to know each other; most complied.

"All aboard," he shouted, and the travellers filed past him and chatted while looking for a new seat. Finally, everyone settled down and Barry started up the engine. Before the door had closed, the motel manager ran out and stood on the step. He handed a note to the driver and waved to everyone. They waved back.

Barry read the note and stuffed it into his pocket. He pulled the microphone to his lips and said, "Your friends, the Doughertys, left a note under my door to inform you that they have taken a bus back to Adelaide, where they will be seeing an old friend who is very sick. They hope to catch you up again in Darwin." He closed the door, put the bus in gear, and hit the road.

The idea to change seats was a good one; everyone mixed in a way that they would otherwise not have done. Left to their own devices, most people would continue to reclaim the same seat each day and even become very possessive about it. As it was, some travellers changed seats but remained with someone, or in a little clique.

The desert was upon them. If they had they travelled this route in springtime, after a little rain, they would have enjoyed a fabulous wild flower display, but this was autumn and still quite hot, so they all appreciated the air-conditioning. Everyone was lost in their own thoughts as they travelled deeper into the desert and Barry told them a little of the history of the road from Adelaide to Alice Springs and the early explorers and settlers.

"The original mode of transport was by camel operated by Afghanis; nowadays you can hop on to the 'Ghan' in Adelaide and travel to Alice Springs in comfort. The railway has now been extended all the way to Darwin."

Barry took a swig from his water bottle and went on to talk about the early explorers of the Simpson Desert, the wilderness, the giant red sand dunes and interesting rock formations such as Chambers Pillar and Rainbow Valley. Most of the travellers had maps and information brochures open on their laps.

That evening they landed at a roadhouse at Engadoona, on the Stuart Highway.

Freya knocked on Di's motel door that evening, after dinner. "Di? I need to talk to you. It's about Lorna. I just saw her, and she's very sick again."

Before Freya could say more, Di nodded at her husband and slipped out to see Lorna.

Both women went in after knocking, and found Lorna sprawled on her bed. She had vomited on the floor and seemed unable to move. They helped her into bed and Di sponged her face and left the wet cloth on her forehead. Freya cleaned the floor as best she could.

"I think we need to call a doctor, Lorna" Di said quietly.

"No, please don't. I'll just have to go through all the explanations and talking again, and there's no more he can do that I can't do myself."

Profuse skin action soaked Lorna's nightie.

"You won't be fit to travel tomorrow, Lorna," said Di.

"I agree, I can't go on, I'll ring my daughter tomorrow, once I've decided what to do."

Di shook her head. She had a feeling Lorna may not get any better than this. *Why did I go along with this,* she thought, and stood and paced around the room.

"I'll sleep in here with you tonight, Lorna, and tomorrow we'll figure out the best course of action."

"No Di, it's not necessary. Don't feel you have to look after me, I can manage, honestly."

"I won't discuss it Lorna."

Di turned to the other woman. "Freya, can you give me a hand in the morning if I need it?"

"Yes, of course."

Di went over again what drugs Lorna had had and took inventory of what was available. She went back to her room to let Jim know what she planned and asked him to find out the best way to get Lorna home tomorrow.

******

Patrick and Russell wasted no time disappearing up the wobbly ladder in the mineshaft. They emerged from the entrance. Wind whipped little dust eddies across the desert. The two men jumped into their vehicle, revved the engine unnecessarily, and drove away in a cloud of dust.

Deep in the underground prison, Margaret said to Ethan, "I can't believe this. Why are they doing this to us?"

In the inkiness of the cave's darkness, Ethan found his voice while his eyes slowly adjusted.

"I know, I know. I can't believe it either, but I think we must be calm and try to think rationally about what to do next. You sound like you're breathing okay now. Are you hurt anywhere?"

Ethan's voice was still shaky but he tried to make it sound confident.

"I don't think so – no, I'm not." Margaret's voice ended with a small sob. "What are they doing this to us for?" she repeated. "We don't even know them, do we?" Once again, the tears dripped down her face as she sighed and, shoulders heaving, she bent to allow her tears to drip on her lap.

"I'm sure there's some reason we've been abducted," said Ethan, "and no doubt we'll find out when they come back. Did you hear them say they didn't want us to die, yet? Well, that means they must have some plan involving us. Maybe ransom? Yeah, that could be it. Maybe they know you have a very rich uncle, and we've been kidnapped for money. That definitely could be it."

They both thought about this possibility and continued to talk quietly for some time. "We should consider the possibility that the kidnappers are only interested in money, and not anything like torture or murder. But how could they let us go?" Ethan said.

This opened a completely new train of thought for Margaret and she became more subdued.

Eventually, they both dozed. They woke when they heard the sound of voices coming from the shaft.

A couple of minutes later, their captors appeared wearing their homemade masks and carrying several plastic bags.

"My wife and I need to go to the toilet" Ethan said looking up at the men.

"Smells like you've already been," the big one said, as held his nose and made his way around the back of the two, to check their bonds.

"We both need to go, now." Somewhere during the night, Ethan decided there was nothing to gain from being intimidated by the pair of thugs who were holding them. "Let us out, now!" he yelled. "You bastards will pay dearly for last night's work, I promise you that."

"Promises, promises," laughed the smaller one. Both men peered through the slits of the masks that had jagged holes cut for the eyes and mouths, making them look gruesome and freaky.

The big one led Margaret over to a bucket in the far corner of the cave after he untied her hands. He turned his back and took a few steps away. "Hurry up."

The smaller one was unpacking a bag near the opposite wall. He pulled out some paper and pens, a plastic bottle of water and a paper bag.

"Get out of there," the big one shouted to Margaret, and he walked toward her just as she lifted the bucket handle with her toe and kicked with all the force she could muster. She almost lost her balance, but quickly recovered and attempted to kick the man in the groin as he approached. He cursed and flicked urine off his face.

"You bitch." He grabbed her arm and swung her off her feet. He raised his fist and almost hit her when his mate called,

"No! Leave 'er. You'll get your chance later."

The big one backed off.

Margaret was shaking visibly but had a smirk on her face that Ethan could see, and he felt pleased for her.

The big one untied Ethan's hands and shoved him over to the wall. "Take a piss and be quick about it."

Ethan attended to his own needs, and as he returned to face his captor, he was shoved roughly to a sitting position again.

The smaller man walked over to the pair and handed one the paper bag and the other the bottle of water.

The bag contained sandwiches, and Margaret was about to hand them back when Ethan said quietly "Please eat, it's important, just try."

He drank from the bottle and handed it to his wife. She handed him a sandwich.

The two men were huddled in a far corner, talking.

"Don't go soft on me now. You 'ave to scare the shit out of 'em. That's 'ow it works."

"Yeah, mate, I know," replied the taller man.

The men turned back to Ethan and Margaret, and the smaller one handed paper and pen to Ethan. "Write you bank details 'ere. Do it right the first time and your wife won't get 'urt. Mislead me, and I'm going to take it out on 'er. The quicker you do this, the sooner we can all go 'ome, okay?"

Ethan stared at the blank paper then slowly took it from the proffered hand. He took the pen and started to write his details down. "I can't possibly remember my account number."

"Not a problem, I have that from your wallet. Just your password and customer number, please."

Ethan obliged and handed the paper back. He looked at his wife, "So now we know."

"Yes, so now we know."

Margaret and Ethan struggled against their retied bonds. The men disappeared up the ladder. The cave was hot and stuffy; Margaret and Ethan were aching in every joint and muscle.

"I should have known it was too good to be true that we could actually have money and enjoy it as well. Who the hell could it be?"

"I have a feeling that the bigger man is familiar, but from where, I don't know."

"Well, if you think of him, let me know." Ethan answered quietly.

Chapter Eleven

Most of the bus group went for a swim in the Engadoona Motel swimming pool but Hank and Peter thought they would investigate the local haunts, like the pub. They walked down the dusty, main road to the timber-clad pub. It's corrugated iron roof creaked in the late afternoon sun.

"Is this it? It's 'ard to tell if we've arrived in town. Maybe it's around the corner or somethin'," said Hank to Peter, as they looked around the cluster of buildings.

The pub was cooler than they expected and they both looked around curiously, as they passed through the opening hung with grimy, plastic fly strips. It was hard to guess if the strips were an attraction or a deterrent for the flies. There were several tables occupied in the main saloon. The bar ran along the far wall; the walls and windows were covered with photos of people and places. It oozed character. There was a large 'Smokers Outside' sign hung over the bar and salted beer nuts lay in saucers on the tables.

Peter and Hank took a good look around while they were scrutinised by the locals and other tourists at the same time. They made their way to a table in the far corner and sat down. The barman approached them. "Yer can't sit there fellers, its Bluey's table."

"What do ya mean? It's empty ain't it?" said Hank, not trying to disguise the belligerent tone in his voice.

"Yeah, but it's Bluey's table, and no one can sit there but 'im."

"Is he here now?" asked Peter, with a more conciliatory inflection.

"No. But still, no one sits at this table, 'cept 'im."

"You mean it's reserved?" Peter asked innocently.

"Somethin' like that, but there are any number of other places yers can park yer bums without sittin' there."

"Well, if this is a public bar," said Hank, "I can sit wherever I bloody want."

"Maybe where you come from mate, but not 'ere. This is my pub – my rules. Find another seat or piss orff."

"Hey, there's a good looking spot," Peter said to Hank, as he attempted to defuse the situation. He pointed to a table that two touristy types vacated in a hurry. They could see an impending argument.

"I like this one," Hank persisted.

A shadow fell across the three men. They looked up to see a policeman smiling at them.

"What's 'appenin' boys?" he asked.

"Can't convince these city mugs to not sit at Bluey's table," answered the barman.

"Well, that's easily settled. Stick yer 'ands out and I'll take yer to the best table in town. It 'as beds, bars, and lots of wall decorations. What about it, boys?"

Hank and Peter knew they had lost the argument. Peter walked toward the door but Hank stood, glued to the spot. He craned his neck to look at the policeman.

"Don't I know you?"

The policeman glared at Hank for a few seconds, before his mouth stretched into a broad grin. He said, as he stared and poked his index finger into Hank's chest, "Sunbury, 1972!"

"Yeah!" said Hank.

They both stared at one another, and then shook hands and backslapped each other. They both grinned from ear to ear.

The whole room was curious now; the cop waved to everyone to join in. "This is me old mate, 'ank," he said, "the world's top guitarist, accordin' to 'im, anyhow. We played in a rock band together at Sunbury, in Victoria – 1972. Can ya believe it?"

The policeman directed them to another table and they all noisily scraped out chairs. Hank explained to Peter that he and Tony, the cop, were old friends from the band they played in during the 1970's.

The barman, much relieved, brought over beers for all three. Back at the bar, he picked up a cloth and started polishing glasses, sort of, never taking his eyes from the threesome at the middle table.

"I can't believe me eyes. Get a look at ya. What the 'ell are you doin' out 'ere, mate?" asked Hank.

"Coppin', as you can see. Not too many want the job, and I've been here so long I don't know anythin' else. Actually, I 'ave to retire this year."

"You don't mean to tell me you've been 'ere since 1973."

"No, mate, since 95. I was transferred 'ere, sort of punishment, yer know, for bein' a naughty boy. They couldn't prove I was sellin' dope, but there were a few allegations flyin' around; nothin' proven o' course. But 'ere I am, and lovin' it. Ya can find me in any of the outlyin' stations, me and a couple a others."

"That so? Well, tell me what you did after we split up in '75. If I remember correctly, the last I saw of you, ya were headed back to Sydney to pick up with an old sheila. Someone about twenty-six, 'the love of yer life', ya said; 'just waitin' for ya return', ya said."

"Yeah, well, I did, but she didn't. Turns out, she 'ad more than just me on 'er list. Broken 'arted I was – fer 'bout three days anyway, and then I took off for parts unknown, namely the Northern Territory, where I joined up and I've been coppin' ever since. I got married and divorced – twice. No more o' that – got a girlie now and we're pretty 'appy. She works at the Road'ouse. I do a lot a relief stints – you know –

89

guys goin' on leave an' that – get posted anywhere from 'ere to just north of Alice and out into the desert, and down to Coober. Cover a lot a bloody territory, I tell ya – see a bloody lot a bare dirt. Ya been into the desert, mate?"

"Nah, mate, I 'aven't. This is me first trip to the outback an' me 'n' Pete 'ere are just beginnin' to see the wonders of it all. Mind you, we were rather partial to the wonders of the Barossa Valley. We did a little samplin' there, and now we've got a reputation to up'old till the end of the trip. Reckon we can 'andle that."

"What I remember of you mate, I reckon ya bloody could, too. Did yer ever get married?"

"I did. Let me get us another round and I'll tell ya all about it."

"Hold up, Hank," said Peter. "I think I'll cut out now. You blokes have lots to talk about and I could use a good night's sleep, so I'll toddle off and leave you to it. No offence meant, just better if you get on with it without me hanging around like a bad smell."

"Sure, sure," Hank waved to Peter, as he made his way to the door. "If I'm not back by mornin', come and check on me will ya, old son."

Peter waved back and continued on out to the motel and his bed. He thought about the likelihood of running into an old friend out here after all this time. He missed his wife, he missed his kids. Getting old had its drawbacks; best not to think too much. He looked around at the beautiful, starry night, the sky seemed endless and the air was getting cold.

Peter had promised himself a trip like this all his life, but in his dream, his wife was with him.

******

Hank and Tony were not the only ones burning the midnight oil that crisp, clear desert night.

"Can you take a sip of water?" Di held Lorna's head and put the cup to her lips. Lorna tried but was unable to swallow and she spat the fluid back into the cup. Di lowered her head to the pillow, then picked up the moist cloth, and gently wiped her mouth.

Di checked the time. It was past midnight. She leaned over Lorna and whispered, "Have you any pain, love?"

Lorna pulled a face, and then nodded.

"Can I give you some more pain relief?"

Lorna mouthed, "Yes," and then started to cough. It was a weak, feeble cough, but took so much of her energy the sweat rolled from her brow on to the pillow.

Di made a decision. She could not allow Lorna to suffer alone any longer, she was going to call a doctor and see if more medication could be prescribed. Di could see the pain in her face and guessed at the suffering Lorna was experiencing.

She picked up the phone but no one answered from the motel office. It was closed. Next, she dialled Freya's room number. Her friend picked up on the second ring. "I need you to go to Jim and ask him to organise a doctor. I don't feel I can offer Lorna the comfort she needs with what we have here. Please tell Jim he will have to get the help from the manager and organise an ambulance to Alice Springs. When Lorna is settled we'll have to notify her family. I'm afraid it looks like she has very little time left." Di hung up and walked back to the bedside.

Lorna's head was turning from side to side and Di picked up her hand and held it tightly.

"I'm getting you some more help, Lorna. You can't keep on this way. I think you'll be going to Alice Springs Hospital. We could go back to Coober Pedy, but I think it would be much easier for your daughter to get a flight straight to Alice Springs."

Lorna's eyes widened and a tear ran down her cheek.

"My dear, I don't have the drugs or help I need to do what's necessary for you now. I'll go with you; I won't leave you, I promise. Also, I'm ringing your daughter in a few minutes. I want to give her as much time as possible to get here."

Lorna sobbed softly. Di looked at her drug collection again and considered what would be the best possible drug combination to give and still keep within the realms of what had been ordered by her doctor before she left home. Di felt frustrated and angry with herself for allowing the situation to get so out of control. She should have just said 'no'. She should have been firm and contacted Lorna's daughter before they left home. However, she knew it was Lorna's decision; only she had the right to make decisions about her own life and death. She seemed to have given it all a lot of consideration and what right did anyone have to override a decision about how a person chose to die.

"Bloody hell." Di walked back to the bedside with another syringe to add to the cannula in Lorna's arm. "I'm ringing your daughter now, love. Close your eyes and take some big breaths, try to relax if you can."

Di used her mobile phone to ring Janie, Lorna's daughter, and she shuddered at the thought of being the bearer of such lousy news, especially in the middle of the night. She racked her brains for some words to soften the blow of what was coming. There were none, all she could do now was tell Janie the situation and offer her support.

Chapter Twelve

Both Ethan and Margaret slept fitfully for a few hours. Finally, they gave up trying and sat talking quietly about what they could do to escape. They now knew the men who abducted them were interested only in money.

"I don't think they'll just let us go when they have the money in their possession. They'll need time to get away. And they'll be worried about us being able to describe them to the police," Ethan said.

"So are you saying they'll have to kill us?"

"Possibly. If I were in their situation, I wouldn't be leaving a trail behind. But do they want a couple of murders to try to outrun? It all seems so senseless. How could money be worth risking a lifetime in gaol? It makes no sense at all."

"What can we do? There must be something, we can't just sit here and wait for them to come back and shoot us." The exasperation in Margaret's voice was evident.

Ethan said, "I think the only way is to get free of these ropes. I'm going to search for a sharp rock and maybe we can cut our way free."

For the next half hour, they both wriggled around and scratched the ground. There was a layer of dried mud with some whitish dust on top and numerous sharp rocks embedded in the surface. They were finally able to loosen several pieces of sharp stone, and then they sat back to back. Ethan tried to rub the stone on his wife's bonds. It was awkward, and his hand slipped on numerous occasions, each time slicing across the base of Margaret's thumb. The sticky blood ran on to the ground and they could both feel it.

"I'm so sorry," said Ethan. "If only I could control my hand better."

"Don't worry, with a bit of luck I'll get blood poisoning and not need to escape."

"That's hilarious, but if you'd rather stop, I will."

"No, keep going, I don't have a better idea. Oh, yes I do. I found that mouth gag on the floor when we were scrounging around before. Hang on, here it is. Can you take it and push it between my hand and the rope?"

Ethan successfully pushed the fabric mouth gag between the rope and the heel of her hand. "That's better. Let's see how that goes," he said. He went back to sawing away.

"Yes I think that is better, that's the right spot."

It was permanent night in the old mine, although their eyes had adjusted to the gloom. Ethan wondered if his wife felt the hunger and discomfort that he did. He sighed as he looked at her and thought how brave she was.

"Let's take a break", he said. Eventually they both slept, curled into foetal positions on the flattest spot they could find.

******

"Very good. Well done, Mr. Dougherty," the bigger of the two men said, as he stepped off the bottom of the ladder and strode over to where husband and wife lay huddled, half asleep. The smaller man followed and rubbed his hands together. They both wore their masks.

"I'm happy to say the first and second phase of 'Operation Outback' has been successfully completed and by tomorrow, this time, we'll be on our way," the taller man said, as he untied Ethan's hands.

"What's this?" the other man asked, as he held up the piece of cloth stuffed in Margaret's bonds.

"The rope was cutting into my wrists and causing it to bleed; I put that there to stop it rubbing."

The men were not really listening, so happy were they that their scheme was going well.

Margaret passed little urine into the bucket; she knew she was dehydrated, as was Ethan. They were both pushed down to the floor again and given the same amount of water and sandwiches as the previous day.

The two men stood together talking, while Ethan and Margaret drank every drop of water and ate every crumb in the paper bag.

"So, does that mean you'll let us out tomorrow?" Ethan asked, in his most forceful voice.

"The next day," said the smaller one. "I'll 'ave someone come along and untie you and you can be on your way."

"Will your friend drive us back to Coober Pedy?"

"Yeah, sure. Don't worry, gramps, you'll be fine. Now shut up."

The men checked around the cave making sure they had left nothing behind. The big one retied the wrist restraints, and to the relief of the captives, did not notice the fraying on Margaret's bonds. He then headed over to the ladder and disappeared up the shaft. The light from the men's headlamps disappeared with them as they exited the shaft. A few minutes later, he lowered a rope down with the couple's bags attached. The men had removed the luggage from the motel room and been carrying it around in their vehicle until now.

"Just to help you on your way, see?" said the taller of the two.

They piled the luggage near the bottom of the ladder then disappeared without another word or a backward glance. There was a sense of finality about this action that the captives did not miss.

The dark returned. Margaret and Ethan peered into the blackness and waited for their night vision to adjust.

After a few minutes, Ethan said, "I can see a faint patch of light. It must be the base of the shaft. I'm going over to the bags."

He dug his heels into the floor and dragged his bottom over slowly to where the luggage had landed. The exertion tired Ethan, but as he felt his foot touch one of the bags, a rush of adrenaline reinvigorated him.

"Ah, yes!" he yelled.

He leaned back on the suitcase and felt the fabric with the tips of his fingers. He ran his hands over the material and found the zipper on the side pocket. He recognised the loop of plastic tie attached to the pull-tab and knew it was his bag. He hooked his little finger through the loop and pulled gently. The zipper spread open all the way to the end stopper. That was the easy part. Next, he tried to get his hands inside the pocket; it was tight, and his hand would not fit down.

"I need you to come over here, Marg. Can you see where I am?

"Yes, just," said Margaret.

"I want you to tip the suitcase at an angle so I can slip my hand down inside and grab the wash bag."

"Planning to take a shower then, are we?" Her spirits lifted. "Keep talking so I can find you."

She wriggled closer and struggled until she had her back to her husband and the case was between them. She put her fingers under the bottom of the case and tilted it toward Ethan.

Ethan moved back a foot or so and stopped the case before it tipped right over. He held the case off with his shoulder then, by pulling his elbows in, he could slide his hands easily inside the pocket.

"I've got it!" he yelled.

He dragged the toilet bag out and dropped it on the floor. He allowed the case to return to the upright position and moved back to the wash bag. He fiddled with the zipper for a couple of minutes and he felt it slide open. He felt around for the scissors.

"Where the bloody hell are they?" he said, as he rummaged through the toiletries, shaking the bag. "Got 'em!" Ethan stopped and held the precious scissors in his hand. He heaved a sigh of relief.

"Good on you," said Margaret.

His wife made her way over next to him and they turned to face one another. Their eyes locked in the faint light and they shared an intimate moment of confidence and love. They had grown accustomed to the almost darkness and could see each other well enough to tell what was happening. They rested for a moment then turned back to back. Ethan started once again to dig away at his wife's bonds.

******

"So what else do we have to do now," Judy asked Russell, as she leaned over his shoulder at the computer.

"There's nothing else we can do. Just wait 'n' see if it comes out at the other end. I've done all the right things, so we should know by tomorrow if the last transaction 'as put us in the clear."

"So that's what's called money laundering, is it?" she said.

"Sort'a. In this case, it was all pretty simple. We 'ad to be sure this money couldn't be traced back to us. Next, we silence the Doughertys, and we can be on our way."

"But you're not going to hurt them, are you?" said Judy. She was concerned, and she glanced at Russell quickly.

"Course not, we've spoken to 'em today and they won't talk"

"How do you know?"

"Cause they've already 'ad a taste of what we're capable of and they're not prepared to risk what's left of their miserable lives for money."

"Threats you mean?"

"Exactly, just threats"

"And they believe you?"

"Naturally – they know we're serious."

"Are you?"

"Yeah. Now bugger off 'n' let me finish up 'ere." Russell turned back to the computer and was fully engrossed again.

******

Patrick had rented a cabin in the camping grounds at Coober Pedy. This was the best time of the year for tourists and the place was close to capacity. It was easy for the three to get lost in the crowd. Judy occupied the only bedroom and the men bunked on the floor and lounge. After Judy's light went off, the two men sat outside on the tiny veranda in plastic chairs. They drank beer quietly from long necks and smoked.

"We can drive out tomorrow night and lob a grenade down the shaft. It's so isolated, no one'll hear it," said Patrick.

"You're right, mate, and there's definitely no other way to be certain we can get away clear. Who's goin' to look under a pile of rocks in an old, caved-in mine. I think they'll be very old bones by the time anyone finds them. I feel pretty good about this. Its' been easy, quick and profitable. It's been good doin' business with you, mate."

"You too, mate. Maybe we can do another venture sometime. Good partners are hard to find. I think the red herrings you planted will make all the difference to the cops trying to follow the trail."

"Well, I'm a professional, aren't I. Worth every penny, you might say."

They both laughed and discussed the false leads they had created, like the note to the bus driver to say Mr. and Mrs. Dougherty were diverting back to Adelaide on the next bus to see an old friend who was ill. There would be more communication sent in Margaret and Ethan's names before the bus arrived all the way back at the resort. No one would be looking for the Doughertys, and a month would elapse before there was any possibility of questions being asked – maybe longer.

Russell thought about how he and Pat had first met in the Army Reserve when they were both 19. They had been given no choice about their time in the Reserve as both had been caught stealing and it was part of their rehabilitation. At that time, getting hold of grenades was not easy, but not that hard either – for a couple of thieves. They had caught up with one another on odd occasions since then, but this was the first time they had done a big job together. They both had souvenirs from their time in the Army, and these particular ones had come in very handy.

"Big day tomorrow. I'm off to bed," said Patrick

"Still shaggin' your sister?"

"Watch your bloody mouth. We aren't that friendly."

"Sorry mate, no offence meant."

"Yeah, okay, but I won't put up with that sort of shit. Right?"

Patrick disappeared into the cabin and threw himself on to the sleeping bag on the floor. Sometimes he wondered how he looked to other people, like Russell. He had not known anyone who had to grow up as he and his sister had, and beneath his casual facade, he was a very angry man. He hated the parents he could not even remember, and he hated the foster parents, all of whom had failed to be the ones he wanted so much. There were so many things he could not change, and the pain never went away. Patrick now dealt with life on his terms. He was old enough to take control and he did.

Chapter Thirteen

Sitting alone, Patrick allowed himself to drift back to a few weeks previously when he had first learned of the money his stepmother had come into.

After their discussion with Margaret's neighbour, Lillian Gossett, Patrick and Judy found the manager in her office. Patrick knocked loudly and barged in. Such were their manners, owing more to impatience than courtesy.

Sonja, a large woman, usually found in the company of her two dogs, as on this occasion, looked up from her swivel chair.

"Who the hell are you," she exclaimed, momentarily distracted from her right foot, poised on the edge of the manager's desk above a pair of nail scissors and a scattering of toenail clippings. Her right hand held a small brush, with which she was about to decorate the next toe with purple, sequined polish.

The dogs gave a perfunctory bark at the couple from under the desk.

"We want information about our mum and dad. We've been told they've gone off on some bus trip and we need to contact them urgently."

Sonja lowered her foot and carefully put the nail polish brush back into its little bottle. She looked up at the pair while screwing on the cap.

"And who are you?"

"Patrick and Judy Robilliard. Our mother was recently married to a man named Dougherty. I'm afraid we missed the wedding – we were overseas. But we're back now, and need to get in contact with them straight away."

Sonja swept the nail clippings into the palm of her hand and threw them into a wastepaper basket. She propelled herself around the desk in her office chair, castors spinning, and stopped in front of a filing cabinet. She pulled open one drawer after the other, slamming each shut in turn. She supported her chin with her hand in a pose of thoughtfulness.

"Check the computer, it's bound to be there." Patrick leaned over the desk to look at the dead screen. "That is, if you're not too busy," he added sarcastically.

The relief manager looked sharply at the man leaning over her desk. She detected something menacing in his demeanour and decide not to react.

At the same time, Judy made herself comfortable in one of the visitor's chairs and looked around the room, always confident Pat could sort anyone out; he was reliable that way.

Sonja looked for the switch to turn the computer on. She looked under the desk, on the keypad and ran her hand over the printer.

"Just a minute."

She looked up.

Patrick scowled at her, and said, "Let me sit there."

He moved to Sonja's side of the desk and almost pushed the big woman out of her chair.

She stumbled, then got her footing and walked over in front of the filing cabinet. She stood with her arms crossed over her ample chest, keeping an eye on the phone and wondering whom she should call. The temporary salesperson had gone home and so had the gardeners and handyman. She watched as the young man stared at the computer screen.

"What's the password?"

The woman fumbled in the top drawer, pulled out a notebook, and flipped it open. She shoved it in front of Patrick, on the desk. Moments later the screen lit up in front of him.

Sonja was quiet as Patrick scrolled through information until he found what he was looking for. He turned on the printer and soon had that information in his hand. He stood and walked toward the door.

Judy stood up.

"You know, sitting there with your filthy feet on the desk is not what my mum pays fees for. Why don't you do some work?" said Patrick.

Sonja took a step toward the pair. She trembled and clenched her hands.

"How dare you!" she said. Her face was red. Sonja almost took another step forward – then thought better of it. The door slammed before she could think of anything else to say.

Outside, Judy smiled up at her brother. "You sure gave that fat bitch something to think about."

He laughed and they strode off to their car.

The relief manager flopped into her chair and began to tremble, as much from anger as embarrassment and fear. A tear formed in the corner of her eye and she brushed it away. She gathered up her nail polish, files, scissors, and cottonwool into her little pedicure bag and drew the string. She stood looking around the room; as if afraid her afternoon visitors may have left some trace of themselves behind. Satisfied, she locked the office and walked back to the residence. The dogs skipped happily around her feet.

When she walked into the manager's residence lounge, she headed straight for the cocktail cabinet that Jim had left well stocked. Not for her consumption of course, but she did not care. She poured brandy into a glass. At first sip, she shuddered and pulled a face, then sipped again. She took her drink to the kitchen, found her lemonade, and dashed about half a glass on top of the brandy.

"That's better," she murmured to herself, and walked with the drink into the lounge. She rarely drank alcohol and the effect was swift and pleasurable – so pleasurable that she followed it with another – and another.

The shrill scream of the resident alarm did not wake Sonja. Her dogs ran around in circles, barked and jumped up and down next to the unconscious form of their mistress. She was out cold. Having found brandy and lemonade was not only a good taste but also made her feel great, she had exercised her insatiable appetite on the almost full bottle Jim had left in his cabinet. It now lay empty on the lounge room floor and Sonja's snores drowned out the urgent repetition of the resident alarm.

Alfred and Greta lived next door to Elaine Steinberg and Greta dashed round to the unlocked front door when she heard the resident alarm. She called but got no response. She opened the door and called as went in. Greta found Elaine on the floor. There was no sign of the manager. Greta rang the ambulance.

Elaine was unconscious and began loud snoring when Greta leaned near her face to check her breathing. The ambulance arrived within ten minutes. During that time, Alfred had joined his wife for the vigil, and they had turned Elaine's head to the side to give her an airway.

"Looks like a stroke," said the paramedic, as they lifted Elaine on to the trolley and adjusted the oxygen tube in her nose. They checked all her vital signs and had her away to the hospital as soon as she was stable.

Greta said she would ring Elaine's son and let him know what had happened. No one knew where the relief manager was.

******

On day thirteen, Jim waited near the door of the bus. When everyone was aboard and seated, he stood on the first step and asked Barry for the microphone.

"Morning, all," said Jim. "I just wanted to let you know that Di and I are accompanying Lorna to Alice Springs in the ambulance, so we'll be missing the next legs to Uluru and Kings Canyon. We'll wait for Lorna's daughter in Alice Springs, so we'll catch up with you all there." Jim waved and stepped out of the bus.

Jim had been looking forward to seeing Kata Tjuta and Uluru, but reluctantly accepted that it was not meant to be. When the ambulance arrived at the motel a short while later, Lorna was only semi-conscious. She was stretchered into the ambulance. Jim and Di then sat in the front seat with the driver and they set off to the Northern Territory town of Alice Springs.

Before the bus moved off, the driver addressed his passengers. Well known as the great, natural wonders were, the bus driver always enjoyed talking about the sights the tourists had come to see and marvel at.

"I know it's a long day today, hence the very early start, but it will be worth it." He went on to tell his passengers of the sights they would experience that day. "We'll see Kata Tjuta first – gigantic rocks standing like silent sentinels in the desert. We'll back track from there to Uluru, our next overnight stay. We'll get there for a late lunch, and then get ready for the stunning sunset viewing of that magnificent monolith. By the way, if any of you are trivia fans, you can amaze your friends by knowing that while Uluru is commonly described as a monolith, it is more correctly known, geologically, as an inselberg – but I digress. Both Kata Tjuta and Uluru are on the traditional lands of the Anangu, who are the custodians of that World Heritage Property. A variety of accommodation and facilities is available for tourists, as well as the opportunity to buy souvenirs and take photos. As I said, we'll overnight at Uluru, so you'll have the added bonus of a sunrise viewing as well."

The bus set off.

******

On arrival at Alice Springs, Lorna was transferred to the acute care unit. A doctor examined her as soon as she had settled on the bed. Fortunately, Di was able to give the doctor a good account of Lorna's story so far, and he was later able to contact Lorna's home doctor.

"I'm going to book us into the hotel and take a shower. I'll be back shortly and we can have some dinner together," Di said to Jim, when he made himself comfortable in the visitor-waiting lounge.

"Take your time." Jim kissed his wife and hugged her. "You're doing a great job. I'm proud of you."

"You too, my darling." She left the hospital to find a cab to take her to the hotel.

******

Hank and Peter sat together on the bus to Kata Tjuta. Hank held his head as still as possible on a small pillow.

"I gotta stop doin' this to meself ya know, mate. Me head feels like an egg about to explode, under pressure like."

Peter tried not to smile because he believed Hank did not know how to stop drinking. It was part of his way of life, as familiar as breathing.

"Well, mate, I'm glad you caught up with your old friend anyway, are you going to see him again?"

"Yeah, sure, I'll be in touch after we're 'ome. I wish I 'adn't come along here today though, I should be in bed."

Hank put his hand out for the paracetamol tablets Peter offered him. He swilled them down with a big gulp from his water bottle. He put both hands to his head and closed his eyes.

"Just let me sleep, please God, let me sleep."

Late in the morning, the bus arrived at Kata Tjuta. Peter made sure Hank was not disturbed when they parked. He lifted his friend's feet up on to the seat and left him there to sleep it off.

"Yes, well, I sure as hell don't want anyone passing out on me today," said Barry, when Peter explained his friend should remain undisturbed.

The rest of the passengers swarmed off eager to stretch their legs. Some of the fitter travellers set off on the one hour walk to Walpa Gorge.

Hank was still asleep when Barry fired up the coach and turned east, towards Uluru.

******

"You must pay up sir" said Penny to Harold.

She stood with hands on hips and a smile on her lips, demanding the girl's reward following the end of the race.

From the start, there were only two real contenders, Robert and Lottie. Penny and Harold had fallen behind within minutes. They had found a great deal to talk about as they strode along discussing, music, art, antiques and travel. They also discovered both enjoyed a similar ironic sense of humour and perspective on life. The four had chosen to walk around the base of the Uluru and wager that night's restaurant bill - the men against the women.

The pace was set from the beginning. All four elbowed their way good-naturedly into the best position, pushed into arms and ribs and took long strides in the dust. No running was allowed, only fast walking, 'power walking' Robert called it, and they were bunched up together as each jockeyed for a spot that gave them the advantage.

It was not long before Harold and Penny lingered behind to enjoy the fresh air and sunshine. It was at a leisurely, companionable pace that they completed the walk. A little over an hour later, they had caught up with the others at the finish line only to discover each claimed victory.

"Well, I bet Harold that Robert would win, and Harold bet me that Lottie would win. Now, you two can't decide who did win. Surely it wasn't that close?"

"As a matter of fact Ma'am, it was," said a drawling American accent from the sidelines. They all looked up to see a tall man wearing a cowboy hat. He stood next to a small woman in a similar hat. They both smiled and introduced themselves, and the man added, "We were close on the heels of this pair; they inspired us to step it up a bit, anyway. I do believe it was a tie." They all looked at one another and began to laugh then the American man looked at Lottie and Robert saying, "I wonder, sir, if you're good wife and yourself would join us for lunch. He then turned to Harold and Penny and made the same invitation.

They all accepted, however the American couple discreetly raised their eyebrows at each other in a mutual recognition that the four Australians shared some secret joke to which they were not privy.

Chapter Fourteen

"I have it! That's it!" Margaret was ecstatic – her hands were free. She tried to wriggle to Ethan but realised it would be easier by far if she untied her feet. She picked and pulled and her feet were soon free.

"Darling, take it easy, slow down. Take a couple of deep breaths and concentrate."

"Yes, yes."

With effort, she crawled to Ethan and began to untie his hands in silence, too afraid that something would happen now to prevent their escape.

"I'll do my feet," he said, as his hands came free of the bonds.

Margaret leaned over and stretched her back; she could feel the tension and pain gathered there and in her hips. She stood up slowly, and regained her sense of balance while she strained to look around from a standing position. It was so dark, but her sight must have improved because she could make out shapes and solid objects.

Ethan stood up next to her and put his arms around her. He walked over to the bags, which lay near the ladder. He reached down, pulled open the zipper, and lifted the lid.

"We're going to need clothes and shoes, better hurry," he said.

They dressed quickly and Ethan rummaged in the darkness for a watch and a compass. They also found Margaret's small first- aid kit, two aluminium-cased LED torches, and their wallets. There was no money, nor credit cards. Suddenly, Ethan gave a shout.

"What's wrong?"

"I just remembered, look at this." He shone his torch and reached down to the base of his large bag. He scratched around at the lining. Seconds later, he withdrew a credit card. "I learned that trick when travelling years ago, to always be prepared in case my wallet was stolen or lost." He waved it around his head then pocketed it. "Let's get out of here," he said.

Ethan turned and started up the ladder, but with trepidation. Margaret followed. They were almost at the top when Ethan froze and said, "Listen!"

Margaret heard it at the same moment, opened her mouth to speak, but remained silent as she tried to steady the ladder.

Car doors slammed in the distance and faint voices announced that the men were back, undoubtedly heading for the shaft. Margaret and Ethan quickly retreated down the ladder. The unsteady rungs threatened to dislodge their grip and they struggled to retain their footing. They hit the bottom and pulled the torches out of their pockets. They shone the beams right and left, desperately seeking a place to hide.

"Pssst! Margaret, look." Ethan trained the beam of his torch to his right. It lit up the passageway leading away horizontally from the chamber. "Let's go down there," he said, quickly but quietly. "It seems to be quite long – it looks like a solid wall at the end, but they may have tunnelled left or right and I just can't see it from here."

"No, no, they'll only come looking for us down there. Pretend we're still tied up," said Margaret, with a sense of urgency. "They may be here to release us, but if not, we might be able to put up a fight. Quick, sit down where we were. Keep hold of your torch. It's not big but it's solid and heavy for its size. We may be able to use them as a weapon. We'll look like we're asleep."

They rushed back the few steps to the far wall of the chamber and resumed the positions they were in when the men had left, feet drawn up and hands behind their backs. They were both sweating when they heard the voices at the edge of the shaft entrance. Margaret had tears in her eyes and Ethan was on the verge of hyperventilating. They both sat waiting, hoping beyond hope that the men had returned to release them.

A voice Ethan and Margaret recognised as that of the taller of their captors screamed, "See you later alligators!"

His companion yelled out, "But not in a while, crocodiles."

There was a burst of maniacal laughter from both men, a few seconds silence, then, "Sayonara, suckers!"

As the sinister words echoed in the chamber, Ethan heard a thumping sound somewhere in front of him. He whipped his torch out from behind his back and shone it in front of him. What he saw made his blood run cold. A hand grenade had bounced off the top of a suitcase and now rolled toward him.

"Shit!" he yelled, as he lunged. In one continuous motion, he grabbed the hand grenade, jumped to his feet and hurled it down the side shaft, just off to his right. He aimed high, and the grenade flew many metres down the shaft before Ethan heard it land, bumping two or three times on the floor of the passageway.

As he threw the deadly object, Ethan knew what was coming. He immediately turned around, grabbed Margaret, and rolled both their bodies to her left. He lay on top of Margaret and covered his ears with his hands as he did so. His subconscious mind counted – *one thousand and one – one thousand and two – one thousand and three – one thousand and ...* There was a flash of light. Rock, dust and shrapnel blasted up the tunnel. Its long, narrow profile funnelled the flying debris into a concentrated, malevolent shower of deadly projectiles, which spewed out of the mouth of the passageway like the spray of pellets from a shotgun. A pressure wave shook their bodies.

Lumps of dirt and claystone, large and small, dislodged by the tremor of the explosion, rained down on the couple.

Debris fell from the entrance shaft as parts of the sides caved in. The ladder lay in a mess on top of their suitcases, tangled among the rocky rubble that had fallen with it. The only escape route was rendered useless. Choking dust hung in the air. Black silence returned.

******

Without exception, everyone from the bus went to the sunrise viewing of Uluru. The 'Ooohs' and 'Ahhs' prompted comparisons with the previous evening's sunset spectacle. Opinion amongst the travellers split as to which had been the most spectacular, and the debate continued at the breakfast tables on their return to the motel. Some were still good-naturedly debating the issue as they set off for the next leg of the journey to Kings Canyon. As the kilometres rolled by, the Uluru excitement gradually subsided and was replaced by the anticipation of their next destination.

"Kings Canyon is located in Watarrka National Park and is best known for its rugged landscape and 100 metre high sheer walls." Peter read out the description to Hank, as the coach entered the last half-hour of the drive to the next overnight stop.

At almost the same moment, Barry flipped a switch on his microphone and said, "We've made good time, folks, so we'll hit our target just after eleven. That'll give the more adventurous of you time to do the rim walk, but you won't want to take too long over lunch. You'll want to get cracking if you want to complete the walk before you lose daylight."

Hank and five others wasted no time after they arrived, and after a quick lunch, set off on the rim walk. Most of the others were content to do the shorter walks and settle down with a cool drink afterward. Some took advantage of the cloudless sky and experienced the thrill of a helicopter flight over the Canyon and Watarrka National Park. That night, the dinner table conversation buzzed with the recounting of the afternoon's activities.

The next day, after two weeks on the road, the travellers were all excited to see Alice Springs approach.

"This says it is the second largest town in the Northern Territory and lies at the geographic centre of Australia. It is equidistant from Adelaide and Darwin and was established in 1872." Lottie continued to read aloud to her sister and anyone close enough to hear. "Many aboriginal people live in the town and on the outstations and surrounding communities. This is the country of the Arrernte people and the town is bordered by the McDonnell Ranges many water holes and gorges. All this creates a variety of natural habitat and certain areas are set aside for conservation where various flora and fauna are protected. It was not until 1887 when alluvial gold was discovered 100kms east of the town that a significant European settlement was started."

This information, and more, was filed away in the tourists' memories when they set off on excursions later that day.

"I feel like our little group is shrinking" said Lottie to Penny, as they walked toward the shops in search of a few souvenirs.

"Well," said Penny, "we haven't caught up with Di and Jim yet, and Lorna, of course, and then Margaret and Ethan went to see their sick friend. I wonder if we'll lose anyone else before we get home. Probably Hank will drink himself into a coma again and miss half the sights."

Penny shrugged and they entered a shop displaying all manner of Aboriginal artefacts and hand painted lengths of cloth.

******

Janie, Lorna McDonald's daughter, arrived late the same day as the tourists hit the town. Di and Jim had taken turns to keep a vigil at Lorna's bedside, and Di was glad to see Janie as she entered the private room where her mother slept quietly.

"She's been sleeping for about 24 hours; actually she's unconscious and hasn't roused in that time," Di explained. "They're giving her intravenous fluids but I know she specifically did not want that, so I agreed only until you arrived, and can make the decisions from here."

Janie nodded and then spoke to the doctor. They agreed that since it was her mother's wish, according to her Advance Health Directive, that she not receive any form of life support, it would be discontinued. Di sat with Janie for a while and then Janie expressed a desire to be alone with her mum. Di left her and made her way back to the hotel, where she fell into a deep sleep.

The phone awakened Di and Jim a little after midnight. Lorna had just died and Janie was weeping on the phone.

"I'll come in and we'll decide what's to be done next," said Di. She took a cab to the hospital, where they stayed and prayed together and then made the necessary arrangements to fly Lorna's body back to Brisbane.

By morning, both women were exhausted and they returned to their hotel rooms for a sleep. Di woke after only a couple of hours and noticed Jim was gone. She picked up the phone and rang Janie. She was already up and getting ready for her journey home. She was very grateful for all the love and attention Di and Jim had lavished on her mother and expressed as much to Di before she said her farewells.

Di rolled over and went back to sleep. She woke when Jim returned in the early afternoon.

"How are you feeling my darling?" he asked.

"Much better thank you. Janie has taken her mum home and I'm starving. What's to eat?"

"Get dressed; I have a surprise for you."

Half an hour later, Jim smiled as he slid an envelope across the restaurant table to his wife.

"What is it?"

"Open it and see."

Di tore the flap open and pulled out two ocean cruise tickets to the Fiji islands.

"We'll be on that ship in a couple of days. I was very lucky to get us on at such short notice, but it just goes to show what can be done if one really tries."

A smile spread across Di's face and she sat there nodding. "I can't believe it." Her face took on a more serious, questioning look as she said, "How come? What about the bus trip?"

"I've had enough of you pleasing everyone else at your own expense. You're still hobbling from the ankle damage and you need a rest, both physically and mentally. We leave here day after tomorrow, and fly out to Sydney. We'll board the ship there and will be lost at sea for ten whole days. What do you think?"

"I think yes, but seriously, Jim, what about the bus trip and all the residents? What will they think?"

"I'm so glad you asked me that, Mrs. Watersen, because I have the answer. I spoke with our mob earlier today at the motel. I gave them the news about Lorna and told them about our departure from the tour. They all agreed, nay, encouraged us to get away on our own. Mrs.den Ronden didn't look all that pleased, but several of the women said they will keep their eyes on her."

"Oh, thank you, you lovely man." Di stood and walked around to her husband and hugged him.

******

Ethan lifted his head up and said gently into his wife's ear, "Marg, Marg?"

He gingerly moved his arms and legs and heaved his body off the still form of his wife. Debris fell off his back as he raised himself on all fours. A chocking coughing spasm shook the dust from his head. He wiped his eyes with his fingers and felt the grit bring tears.

He started to remove the rubble from around Margaret's body and cried out, "Margaret, can you hear me?" He heard no reply. His coughing became interspersed with sobs as he kept removing the rocks from around where his wife's body lay.

"I'm okay, love," said Margaret, as she raised her head and turned her face toward Ethan. "What about you?" she asked.

Jim saw Margaret's lips move but heard no sound. He panicked. He thought Margaret must be so badly injured she could only mouth the words she was trying to say, but the ringing in his ears snapped him into the reality of his situation. *Oh my God*, thought Jim, *the blast has deafened me.*

"I think I'm alright, Marg. Got a few scratches, I think," he said, as he wiped his palm across the back of his head and felt what he assumed was blood, "but nothing broken and all my parts seem to be here. Can't hear though, love – hope it's only temporary." He ran his hands over his body then made a lunge for his wife.

"Thank God you're okay," he cried.

"I won't thank him," said Margaret, "he could have avoided this whole mess in the first bloody place."

Ethan shrugged and said, "Don't know what you said, love, but I'm sure you're right." He looked around despondently.

Margaret held on to Ethan but sat motionless for a moment, as if listening, and then slowly she turned and said, "I feel a draft that wasn't there before. There, look at that." She could see Ethan still struggling to hear, so she pointed her arm in line with the beam from her torch. Through the settling dust, they saw a faint patch of light reflected off the wall at the end of the tunnel. They stood, and with arms outstretched, began to feel their way along what was now a rock-strewn tunnel. They reached the wall at the end and stood unsteadily on top of a jumble of debris. Their hearts sank. There were no side passages. It was a dead end. They embraced and sighed in defeat.

Margaret suddenly let go of Ethan and said with a strong voice, "Can you hear me, love?"

"Yes – yes – it's very faint, but I can hear you now. The ringing in my ears has almost subsided."

"Ethan, I can feel that draught even more now, and look how the dust is moving. Turn off your torch for a minute."

The white light of the LEDs clicked off and the sparkle of the dust motes disappeared. As they stood on the pile of rubble, holding hands, they let their eyes adjust to the dark.

Margaret felt the wafting of cool air rising up her bare legs, past her arms, then past her nostrils. It was no more than a zephyr, but she felt the soft curls on her forehead ruffle in the gentle current. Slowly, with her eyes wide open, she lifted her head; as if she could follow the airflow on its journey.

"Look, Ethan, look up!"

Ethan raised his downcast head and craned his neck. Starlight twinkled through a small aperture in the tumble of rocks above them. Margaret switched on her torch and Ethan followed. They shone the beams up.

"See how the dust is moving up in the current?" said Margaret.

"Yes, I think this could be another entrance," said Ethan. "Maybe it was blocked until the explosion. Well anyway, while the blast has put the other shaft out of action, maybe it's opened up this one enough for us to work our way out. Look, see how the rocks have fallen mostly on one side of the shaft. We may be able to shift enough of them to work our way to the top."

Grinning, Margaret said "I do believe you may be on to something this time old boy." Ethan shook his head in amazement at his wife's never ending positive attitude.

"Right, now let's think," said Ethan, as he stepped cautiously onto a more stable piece of rubble and held Margaret's hand. "Those buggers who dropped that grenade down the shaft will obviously presume we are dead and buried, along with all traces of our ever being here, so they've probably already gone."

"Of course," said Margaret, taking up his train of thought. "It must surely be in our interest to continue to let the bastards think we're dead. When we get out of here of course," she added more soberly, and then took several deep breaths as she again looked up and attempted to judge how far they would have to climb.

"Agreed," answered her husband.

"Let's take a closer look," said Ethan, as he walked up to the wall and the pile of rocks stacked next to it. He started to pull loose rocks away but that started a small landslide. They both jumped out of the way and watched as the slide settled. Ethan stepped up again and tried this time for a foothold. He reached slowly upward and fumbled for a firm handhold.

Slowly he began to pull himself up. Margaret watched, mouth agape, as he climbed two, then three tentative steps, all the time testing the foothold before grabbing a grab rock a little further up. He slowly lowered himself back to the base.

"I think we may be able to do it. Well, it's our only chance anyway and so I'm going to give it a go." Agitated, he looked around for some of the equipment they had gathered for their escape.

"What do you mean you're going to give it a go? I'm going with you; don't think for a second you can leave me here."

"I just thought I could climb out and then maybe find a rope or something to make it easier. We could both get halfway up and the whole bloody thing could collapse, and we could both die."

"I prefer that option," Margaret said.

Ethan could see his wife was adamant. Both or none. "Okay, let's see what we can find to take with us. Our survival stuff."

They began to rummage around where they had been sitting when the bomb was dropped and found the compass and first aid kit and Ethan felt for his wallet in his pocket. They filled their pockets and Ethan looked at the luminous numbers on his watch. "It's 3.22, that's am. I wonder which day?" They returned to the new shaft and slowly began to climb.

They had cuts and bruises on their hands within a few minutes and the rocks under their feet gave way and resettled every time they stepped on them. It was two steps forward and one step back, but they made slow but steady progress and stopped every few minutes to rest themselves and consolidate their position. It was getting more and more precarious as they ascended and they knew that to fall back now would be disastrous. They could bring the whole pile on top of themselves. They continued cautiously.

By 4.00 am, they were still climbing, slower than ever. A few feet separated them but they were making progress simultaneously. While the gradient was climbable, it was the looseness of the rock pile that made it all so unstable. Several times one of them put their weight on what seemed a secure foot hold and then it all gave way, sending them back down the pile, leaving precious skin and confidence behind. Ethan had reached out and grabbed Margaret's hand on several occasions as she attempted to ascend and moved too quickly, causing a mini rock fall and general subsidence.

"I can't go any further," she said in desperation, after one such occasion.

"Sure you can," he answered reassuringly, but at the same time wondering if his own strength would give out before they reached the top. "Just keep going" he said, as he reached for his wife's hand and squeezed it in encouragement.

They kept going.

The outside light and the rim of the shaft were quite clear now.

"Only a few metres to go, Margy. I want you to go up first, and then I'll be right behind you."

Ethan glanced at his watch and noted it was past 6am. They had been climbing for almost three hours and now Ethan was beginning to think that they were going to make it. *Thank God,* he kept saying, over and over, to himself.

Margaret stumbled as she approached the top and a small avalanche fell beneath her. She screamed, then quickly adjusted her footing and scrambled to hold on, her face pressed against the rock. Ethan reached for her arm but almost lost his balance. He could not get a hold for a moment and she was scratching at the air. Then she stopped. Clinging like a limpet to the rock face, she held on and froze. Once again, tears fell from her eyes and splashed off the stones in front of her.

"I'll go first. Don't move." Ethan now made a gigantic effort to bring his head up level with the top of the shaft; he could not see how he could make the final stretch to get his body up and over the top. He knew that had he been younger he would have had the strength in his shoulders to haul himself up. Then suddenly he was doing it. He had no idea where the energy came from, but with an almighty effort, he used his arms he hauled himself up and over the top. He landed face down in the dirt.

Without further thought, Ethan turned and called for Margaret. He was momentarily blinded by the light and could not see her. Alarmed, he leaned ahead and almost fell back into the abyss, and then he saw her white hand reaching upward. He lay flat out on the rim of the crater and stretched down with both his hands, but could not quiet reach her. "Just a little more, love, a few more inches. You can do it – come on – just a little more."

Tears rolled down his cheeks and sweat ran down his hands as he stretched every sinew. At last, he grasped her arms. With every ounce of energy in his body, he pulled his wife to the top of the shaft and dragged her to freedom. They lay side by side, in total exhaustion, as the first rays of sun hit their backs and their ravaged legs.

Chapter Fifteen

Elaine Steinberg survived the first twenty-four hours of her hospitalization. She had had a stroke and one side of her body was paralysed. She could not speak. Her son had been informed of her condition and was at her side when Greta van der Leer visited the next day. She told him how she had called him, then the ambulance, and he wanted to know why the Resort management had not responded.

"I have no idea, but I will certainly be asking some questions," she answered. "We have a relief manager at present and I get the feeling she is not up to the job."

"I will also make enquiries," Elaine's son said. "I have been led to believe that Mother has been living in a reliable situation. Now I have my doubts."

******

Sonja scraped food into her dog's bowls and stood up, wincing with the pain in her head. Never in her whole life could she imagine such a headache. The act of bending brought her stomach contents up again, just when she thought it was empty. She raced for the kitchen sink and heaved up. She rinsed her mouth out and stood leaning on the kitchen bench, waiting for the dizziness to pass. She pulled out a kitchen chair and flopped down.

There was a knock at the front door, and at first, she thought it better not to answer it. However, it was insistent and Sonja finally dragged her body to the entrance and opened the door. Through blurred vision, she noted a tall man in a business suit.

"Good morning," he said. "May I speak to the manager?"

"I am the manager."

In broken English with a European accent, the young man introduced himself. "My name is Joshua Steinberg. My mother is a resident here, in number 12. Last night, she was taken away by ambulance having had a stroke. She apparently had engaged her personal alarm before she fell unconscious. She may still be lying on the floor if another resident had not come to her aid. The neighbour called an ambulance and then contacted me. Unfortunately, the time lapse meant that the damage to my mother's brain is extensive. Had she been the recipient of a quick response, she may now be sitting up and talking to me. As it is, she is paralysed and unable to speak. What do you have to say to this, madam?"

Wide-eyed and open-mouthed, Sonja stared back at the young man. She spluttered, "Sir, I have been unwell myself.

Unfortunately, I was too sick last night to attend anyone else. I'm sorry to hear about your mother but I was not able to leave my own bed. I'm very sorry. What is your mother's name again?"

"I suspect from what I can smell exuding from your person that your ill health may have been caused by an excess of alcohol. I'm putting you on notice that this is not the last you will hear of this issue. I will be in touch with my lawyer. Good day." He turned and walked back down the path.

Sonja belched, groaned, and covered her face with her hands. She gave the door an almighty slam. "Shit, shit, shit," she mumbled, as she staggered back to a chair.

******

Margaret lay spreadeagled on the ground, feet still on the rim of the mineshaft, her face to one side, and taking great gulps of air. Her eyes were closed.

Ethan struggled to his feet, and then crouched to put his hand on his wife's shoulder. He spoke to her as he gasped, recovering his breath. "Still with us sweetie?" he asked.

She put one finger in the air to respond, then for the next few minutes lay waiting for normality to return. *I may never feel normal again,* she thought. Slowly she pulled herself into a sitting position, and then sat upright. A few moments later, she made her way back over to the shaft and peered down into the evil blackness.

Ethan joined her, and they crouched close to one another, truly amazed at their own achievement.

"I wonder if anyone will ever believe this," he said.

The thought of talking about their experience made them both shudder; in unison, they turned and faced one another.

"What now?" Margaret said, in a muted voice.

Ethan looked around. It was like an alien landscape, with almost no foliage, just sparse clumps of tussocky grass and a great flat expanse of dirt. He put his hand into his trouser pocket and pulled out his compass. He walked around, trying to make an educated guess as to which direction he would find the town.

"I have a feeling it's this way." Margaret pointed east.

Ethan shook his head and continued to concentrate on the little instrument, walking this way and that. Margaret sat down on the ground and began to examine the damage to her arms and legs. She pulled the first aid kit from inside her blouse and examined what might be useful. For the next ten minutes, she cleaned and patched her skin, then walked over to Ethan.

"Just stand still a minute, love, I don't want you getting an infection."

She did what repairs she could to the cut on Ethan's scalp, then looked around for a private spot to go, before she could say she was ready to travel.

Ethan finally decided they must travel south and then west. "There are some tyre tracks here, fairly recent I would say. They're leading off in that direction," he pointed.

"So will that bring us out near town do you think, Ethan?"

"Actually, darling, I have no idea. This is a guess. Since I have no idea in which direction we travelled when we were taken from Coober Pedy, then I have no idea in which direction we need to travel in order to return. We must go one way or another and these tracks are our only lead. There doesn't seem to be any kind of cover for us to remain hidden either. Once we start walking, we will be completely exposed from every direction. I hope we'll run into a prospector or miner, or maybe a tourist. Anyone at all."

"Well, I think the men who took us will try to get away quickly. The longer they hang around town the more people will remember them. They have our money, so now they will want to go and spend it."

"This is true. Let's go, are you ready?"

"Ready."

Margaret had brushed herself down and now she adjusted her clothing and pulled on a cap. She tightened her shoelaces and they set off with the sun on their left and the wind picking up behind them.

******

After Russell threw the grenade down the mineshaft, he and Patrick ran for cover. After a couple of minutes they returned to inspect their handiwork. Completely caved in, ladder gone and shaft filled with rubble.

"Looks alright to me," said Russell, as they walked back to the four-wheel drive.

"I hope they died in the blast and don't live to die of thirst or suffocation. That doesn't bear thinking about," said Patrick.

"Look, mate, no one could survive that. Rest your mind on that account."

They drove back to the cabin in the tourist park.

"Ready, Judy? We're 'ittin' the road," said Russell.

"What's happening, have you let them go?" she asked.

Patrick answered before Russell could speak, and said, "No, of course not. We have someone else to do that tomorrow, after we've left town. But they won't talk, I guarantee that. They think we'll be back for them if they do. They're scared shitless. Come on, are you ready?"

The three drove out of town without a backward glance. They planned to stop overnight in Port Augusta and then make their way across to New South Wales, thence to Sydney where they would lie low, and decide what their next move was.

Russell passed a stubby of beer to Judy and then passed another to Patrick. They toasted their success and then started to talk about what they might do with their money.

"I'm definitely going to invest mine," said Patrick. "I think property, always wanted to be a property developer." He took another swig from his bottle, one hand on the wheel.

"Oh, mate, that's not gonna buy you much property. Think 'ow long it'll take to double your money."

"Not as long as you might think. I've given this a great deal of consideration and done my research."

"That's true," said Judy. "He spends half his time on the computer doing research. I think I'd like to own a house or maybe an apartment on the Gold Coast." Judy started to fantasise about walking a dog on the beach in the afternoon and waving to lifesavers, maybe an 'ironman' for a boyfriend. She often wondered what it would be like to have a boyfriend, someone completely different from her brother. She also knew it was out of the question as long as Patrick was around, and she could not imagine that changing.

Chapter Sixteen

Margaret and Ethan paced themselves from the outset, stopping about every ten minutes to rest their muscles. Fortunately, they were not too out of condition as both of them normally enjoyed a daily walk. They both considered they were reasonably fit. Ethan was a regular golfer and Margaret attended aerobics twice a week. Their ordeal had weakened them however, and the emotional stress was taking its toll. Now, inadequate food and fluid was fast using up what little reserves they had. Both quietly feared for the other and desperately hoped to find water soon.

They had been walking for almost two hours, when suddenly Ethan stopped and shouted, "Look!" He pointed straight ahead and Margaret shielded her eyes to peer in that direction. It was a cloud of dust, obviously stirred up by a vehicle.

They both became excited and walked faster in that direction.

"Oh, but they won't see us; we can't get there in time," Margaret moaned.

"But it means we're headed in the right direction, toward a road. Where there's one vehicle, there'll be more. Come on, let's hurry."

They both broke into a run. Despite the rocky and uneven ground, they were closing fast on the road ahead.

Ethan looked over his shoulder and saw his wife was falling behind. He stopped, turned, and ran back to where she stood, bent forward, hands on her knees, breathing hard.

"It's a stitch, a cramp," she said.

They both looked up again and saw a truck disappear away from them on the rough road.

"Don't worry, there'll be more," Ethan said, "the main thing now is, we stick to the road. It will have to lead us somewhere."

"Maybe into the desert," said Margaret, as she wiped sweat from her forehead with the tail of her T-shirt.

"No, my dear, I know the desert is east or west and north, and we are travelling south. We could end up in Adelaide, who knows."

Margaret tried to laugh but could not quite manage it. They trudged on toward the road and stopped at the edge.

"Which direction now?" she asked.

"That's exactly what I was about to tell you," Ethan said, but at the same time realised he did not have a clue. He decided not to let his wife know how unsure he was. He would simply rely on his intuition.

The road ran northwest to southeast and, hoping his luck would not let him down now, Ethan pointed to the northwest.

"We'll be home in no time, wait and see," he said.

They both picked up the pace again and strode out along the road. Ethan noticed they were getting sunburnt and were as dry as a chip He felt his cracked lips as he ran his tongue across them and he had a salty film on his skin, which was already ravaged by sharp rocks and dirt. The wind blew dust into their faces and there was no shade. He guessed the temperature would have to be about thirty degrees centigrade.

"Just as well it's winter, eh love," he said.

Margaret could not raise a smile.

******

Patrick walked up silently behind Russell, grabbed him by the collar, and swung him around. Russell's eyes were as wide as saucers when he saw Patrick pull his fist back then drive it into his face. Patrick let him go. He hit the floor with a thud.

Judy screamed.

"Go and get something on," Patrick barked.

He kept his eyes on the man on the ground, as Russell felt for his nose. It was covered in blood that ran freely down his chin. Patrick looked over his shoulder to see Judy slip her arms into a dressing gown over her nightdress. She stared at the man sprawled on the floor.

"Get up."

"You bastard." Russell scrambled to stand up and was about to lunge toward Patrick.

"Get out of here," Patrick yelled at Judy. "We haven't finished this yet."

Russell staggered to the table and flopped on to the chair. He grabbed a bunch of paper serviettes and held them to his face. He winced as he touched his nose, then got up and went to the sink and turned the tap on. His hands shook as he gently washed the blood off, grabbed a tea towel, and held it firmly against his nose. His face screwed up in pain.

Patrick had come into the room and found Russell with his hands on Judy. He king hit Russell in a way he normally reserved for the most dire of circumstances.

Judy shouted, "He didn't do anything. You overreacted. Don't you think I can look after myself?"

"Obviously not, or he wouldn't be here with his hands all over you."

Russell stood and walked to the bathroom.

Brother and sister could hear him moaning in pain as he tried to adjust his nose.

"I'm taking him to the hospital," said Judy, as she changed to jeans and shirt. She picked up the car keys and took a step toward the bathroom.

Russell emerged, still holding the towel in place. "You rotten bastard," he said, "I wouldn't touch your sister if she was the last female on earth."

Patrick clenched his fists again and was about to come at the other man.

Judy shouted, "Stop, for shit's sake. Stop. Russell, go and get in the car." Judy made to follow him but Patrick grabbed the keys from his sister and walked outside. He slammed the back door then made his way to the car.

The other two followed and Judy got into the back seat and Russell slid into the front next to Patrick.

"What's your problem? All we were doin' was talkin'."

"With your hands?"

"She was upset, and I was tryin' to explain somethin'. That's all."

Patrick took a deep breath as though actually considering the veracity of what the other man said. "Yeah, well next time you keep your distance."

They drove in silence to the Mildura hospital; the only sounds were Russell's cries of extreme pain.

The hospital waiting room was crowded and they had a long wait. An hour and twenty minutes later, Russell was called in.

"Oh, wow, you look as if you've had an altercation with a truck," the doctor said, as he gently removed the towel Russell held to his face.

"Yeah, that one sittin' in the waitin' room, my best friend."

"I see," said the doctor. "Let's hope you don't meet any more enemies on the way home." He set to cleaning up the mess and gave Russell an injection for pain.

"So," asked the doctor, "you're not going to have him charged with assault?"

"No, mate, I'm as much to blame. Just do what ya can and I'll leave you to get on with yer sick people."

"Go to your local G.P. when you get home and he will refer you to an E.N.T. specialist, where you can arrange to have your nose reset. Don't leave it too long, I've done what I can for now, but it needs surgery."

"Sure, thanks, mate." Russell was out of there feeling so much better after the injection. With a packet of pills in his hand, he returned with the others to the small unit they were staying in overnight.

Russell considered his situation now with Patrick and his sister; he knew that his friend was obsessive and had a hair-trigger temper and he began to wonder if they should split up now.

"I'm sorry mate," Patrick turned to Russell as they drove into the parking lot. "I think I did overreact a bit. Judy's right, I've got an evil temper and I suppose I expect every man to make a pass at her."

After a childhood of brutality and unhappiness, with no one to depend on, and handed from one foster parent to another, Patrick did not trust anyone. Also, because of his responsibility for his sister and his need to protect her, he was aggressive and had little understanding of anyone's feelings.

Their world had been insulated; there was no room for anyone else.

Silently, Russell got out of the car and the others followed him into the unit. They sat down in front of the TV and stared at the empty screen.

"What do you want to do?" asked Patrick.

"I dunno," replied Russell.

"In that case, let's all get some sleep and decide in the morning," said Judy. She could be relied upon to make sense.

They all went to bed.

The next day they took their time wandering around town, buying things they needed, and indulging in a few things they did not. A little after two in the afternoon, they hit the road.

Chapter Seventeen

The manager's phone rang early on the day after Sonja had the visit from Elaine's son. His mother was now languishing in hospital and contemplating a lifetime in a wheelchair and the exasperation of never being able to speak again. It was the Keeala Resort head office in South Australia, investigating a complaint against the relief manager.

"Yes. I have spoken to Mr. Steinberg and explained to him that I was unwell myself, on the night in question, and unfortunately unable to attend the alarm system."

Sonja was informed that she had been negligent in her duty because she did not get a replacement for herself and fulfil her responsibility. They were sending the area manager to relieve her until the regular managers returned. They said she should remain where she was until he arrived and be ready to leave at that time. If the area manager confirmed her culpability then she would get no reference from them and be black listed. If the son decided to sue the company, then she would be held responsible.

She listened to all this in astonishment, then hung up the phone and sat down on the lounge chair. *Mongrels, they can all get stuffed. I'm not taking that shit.*

Unfortunately, the head office had broken their own rules and not checked her qualifications, time being short and understaffed. They too, would be held responsible for not verifying Sonja's claims.

I'm going to call a lawyer, she thought to herself. She turned to the phone directory, and scrolled through names. *I'll open the office when I'm good and ready, and not before.*

******

Matthew Weatherlee had been the best sales representative Keeala Resort ever had and was now at head office training to be the next area manager for South East Queensland.

When his boss called him in, he was surprised to hear Di and Jim Watersen were away on extended leave. He listened to the story and complaint about the relief manager and was happy to agree to act as replacement manager until the return of the Watersens. He had not finished his training, but since he knew the village and most of the residents, he had a head start on anyone else. He was looking forward to seeing his mother and some of his old friends again. With a sense of anticipation, he packed up that evening, prepared for the early flight to Brisbane the next morning.

After having experienced Adelaide's cool weather, Matthew was happy to land at Brisbane airport and be welcomed by blue skies and soft, fluffy clouds floating in the gentlest of breezes. The weather alone was worth coming home for.

"May I come in?" asked Matthew, as he knocked on the manager's door and put his head around.

Sonja looked up from her desk and her mouth fell open. For a moment she stared, then realised her lapse. She stood and said, "Come in. Could you be Mr. Weatherlee?"

"I am, and you must be Sonja Steele. Please, sit down, Sonja."

Courtesy was something that Matthew enjoyed affording people. Having been a salesman, he knew it was all part of the con, and he never forgot the adage that had been drilled into him at so many sales courses, 'You catch more bees with honey than vinegar'. It did not take long before Sonja was at her ease and Matthew became her confidant.

He had put the 'Do not Disturb' sign on the office door and made them each coffee before he sat and listened to the relief manager's story of woe.

She sobbed out the last few words of the events leading to her present situation.

"I really think anyone, including a court of law, would understand that when a woman is stricken so unwell and so suddenly, that she could not be expected to act rationally. It's a shame you didn't call a doctor, but that's understandable. Also, I feel very sorry that you were left alone yourself at the

145

time. A 24 hour virus can be vicious," Matthew said, with a consoling voice.

When Sonja packed her suitcases and dogs into her little car that afternoon, she left Matthew standing on the front porch of the manager's residence. He turned and walked inside. He looked forward to a good night's sleep before he came to grips with the resort affairs and books the next day.

Walking in, his eyes widened at the sight that confronted him. The place was a mess. There was dirty crockery and cutlery piled in the kitchen and the half-loaded dishwasher stood open. Dog hair covered the furniture, and there was rubbish on the floor. The furniture belonged to Jim and Di and from what he remembered of them, they would be disgusted to see their home in such disarray.

Matt shook his head. He did not have time for this. He decided to make up a clean bed for himself and call the cleaners in tomorrow. He was sorry now he had even been nice to the woman that left this appalling mess for him. After seeing what she was capable of, there was no way he would report to head office in her favour.

Matthew went out for a burger and came back to ring his mum.

******

"Hi, I'm Terrence. I'm your new driver," said the tall, weather beaten man as he welcomed the travellers to the coach. "All enjoy the Alice?"

There was a chorus of consent.

"Ready for beautiful, downtown Tennant Creek?"

Yells of 'Yeah, mate' and 'Let's move 'em out' and 'What are we waitin' for?' greeted Terrence's question.

"I'll take that as a 'Yes' then," he said, and laughed as he pulled out of the exit of the motel parking area.

On the road again, Terrence proved to be the best driver so far. Full of information, he gave a running commentary to the travellers and interspersed his narrative with firsthand accounts of outback experiences. Such interwoven facts and yarns, it was generally agreed later, certainly beat reading the dry facts from a tourist information pamphlet.

Terrence said he had lived in the Territory most of his life and he loved it. His enthusiasm to share some of his personal experiences and his obvious love for the land allowed him to give everyone a deeper understanding of the physical environment and the people who have inhabited the land for more than 40,000 years.

The intrepid travellers headed up the Stuart Highway to Tennant Creek, had a comfortable night's rest, and next morning settled in their seats for the long haul north to Katherine, further up the highway.

As the huge diesel engine kicked into life, the driver adjusted his microphone and began the information session, which took place at the beginning of each day's drive.

"Until recent years," said Terrence, "there was no absolute speed limit on the highway and travellers could drive at any reasonable speed according to conditions. Now, there is a limit of 130 on the highway, except for a trial section north of Alice, but Barry probably mentioned that as you passed through it. You couldn't have missed it anyway – you would have noticed the thrill seekers low-flying past you. There have been some spectacular accidents on the road over the years. On certain occasions the Flying Doctor Service does also use the highway as an emergency landing strip, after the police temporarily block the road to traffic."

There was wildlife to see on the roadside and Terrence had to stop for kangaroos on the road several times. They saw wedge tail eagles feasting on road kill and large herds of wild brumbies grazing. Incredible termite mounds pointed toward the sky. At one point, they stopped for a cup of tea on the roadside. Terrence broke out the picnic basket and the travellers all alighted, looking around with great interest. Suddenly the cry went up and everyone began swatting at the flies and insects, stamping and smacking themselves.

"Where the hell did they come from?" Harold shouted to Robert, as he swatted them left and right. "It's amazing how there is no sign of insects driving along, but the minute you stop, they find you. They seem to come out of nowhere."

Robert swiped his arms and legs and face. He saw them settle all over Harold's back and almost fell over waving them away. They were all back in the bus and on the road again in the time it took to swallow a quick cup of tea. In the comfort of the air-conditioned bus, they all laughed at their own panic about the insects but some still swiped and slapped at some stowaways who had managed to sneak aboard.

Katherine was a welcome sight after nearly nine hours on the road and an early night suited most of the crew. Bright and early next morning, Terrence fired up the diesel and set course for Pine Gap, where they would leave the Stuart

Highway and strike out on the Kakadu Highway. On the drive toward Kakadu, Terrence explained where the National Park lay in relation to the rest of the state.

"Arnhem Land, which was named by the early Dutch Explorers, extends from Port Roper on the Gulf of Carpentaria, around the coast to the East Alligator River and adjoins Kakadu National Park. The early explorers confused crocodiles with alligators. The major centres are Jabiru on the Park border, Maningrida at the Liverpool River mouth, and Nhulunbuy, also known as Gove, in the North East of the Gove Peninsula. Gove is the site of large scale Bauxite mining with an associated alumina refinery. Its administrative centre is the town of Nhulumbuy and this is the fourth-largest population centre in the Northern Territory."

The travellers listened with interest while Terrence explained how both the indigenous people and the Commonwealth of Australia jointly manage the Park.

"As a World Heritage listed area," he said, 'the lands, birds, mammals, insects, plants and freshwater species are all protected, as are the many forms of indigenous and ancient rock art. The area is best known for its isolation, bark painting, and the strong continuous traditions of the aboriginal people. One or two days is not a long enough time to take in the magnificence of the beautiful waterfalls, rock pools and rock formations, the landscape, the sunsets, the profusion of rare flora and fauna. Despite this incredible natural wonder, you can also find the Ranger uranium mine located in the park. There is a variety of accommodation, a police station, a medical clinic a shopping centre and a small airport. Tourists can trek or go on one of the Yellow River cruises, photograph rare birds, or swim in crystal-clear rock pools. Let me warn you though, most of the waterways have crocodiles, so do not, I repeat, do not swim anywhere unless you have checked with a responsible local resident. Just recently, a man was taken when he walked into the river to unsnag his fishing line. You have been warned, so take these animals seriously."

The coach arrived at Kakadu National Park in time to settle into their camping site where they enjoyed a great feast from the campfire and then retired for the night to tents. There was much attention paid to securing each tent from intrusion by anything that may visit on more than two legs. The travellers finally fell asleep to the sounds of the wild and the snoring reverberating from a couple of the tents.

To the great relief of the driver, there had only been minor incidents for him to deal with, such as bruises, scratches and an assortment of insect bites. As they had approached their Kakadu destination, Terrence had reminded everyone to protect their delicate skin from injury and invasion. Most had complied.

After two days, it was time for the Keeala Resort group to move on. Luggage was stowed and the intrepid sightseers boarded the bus and selected travelling companions for the three-hour drive to Darwin.

Terrence had the big diesel idling while he made last minute adjustments to the coach's mirrors. He swore under his breath as he saw the figure of Helga den Ronden looming large in the internal rear view mirror. "Oh, God," Terrence said, perhaps not as quietly as he could have, 'this is all I need."

A few seconds later, Helga stood beside Terrence with her hands on her hips. "I need to know when the managers will be back," she said, "there are several things I must discuss with them."

"I'm sorry about that Mrs. den Ronden, but they aren't coming back to the bus. They have left the tour and you will not see them again until you return home."

Appalled is the best word to describe Helga's response. "But they must. I am depending on them to help me with personal issues that I cannot possibly discuss with anyone else."

Terrence had the measure of Helga from the moment he had taken over at Alice Springs, but had managed to contain himself until this moment. He looked at her and smiled benignly. "I think you'll find you'll be alright. Take a seat now and let's be off." He closed the driver's window.

Helga stared at the closed glass. She almost fell backwards as Terrence put the bus into gear and moved a couple of metres forward in a false start. Thick as she was, Helga got the message and started to make her way back to her seat, which she did not share with anyone now, since no one wanted to sit next to her.

Just to add a little more emphasis to his displeasure, Terrence announced over the intercom, "Sorry, ladies and gentlemen, we are unable to proceed until all passengers are seated."

Sniggering and barely repressed laughter erupted.

Helga pursed her lips and looked around accusingly, but most of the travellers were already looking out the window.

"Alright for you," she mumbled. "Humpf!"

Chapter Eighteen

The sun slowly rose in the sky as the two escapees trudged along the seemingly endless road. Suddenly, Ethan shouted and almost fell backward on to his wife when something slithered away from where he was about to place his foot. She too jumped, and they clutched one another as they watched it disappear into the dust in front of them.

"For God's sake be careful of those things, it just shot out from nowhere." They both looked around in fear of more before setting off again.

Margaret was already nervous. "I can't imagine how awful it would be to escape a couple of murderers and an underground explosion," she said, " then a trek across a desert, to then be bitten by a snake, and take my last breath desiccating in the sun."

"True." Ethan had little energy to make conversation. The day wore on slowly and they saw no more cars, trucks, or anything else on wheels.

Ethan looked at his watch. It was a few minutes after four o'clock in the afternoon and the pair were exhausted. Ethan looked up and cocked his head to one side. A distant rumbling disturbed the silence. Ethan and Margaret stood frozen, listening. They turned in unison to look in the direction of the noise. Then they saw it. A road train coming full pelt toward them. They both immediately began to wave, and shout, then jump up and down, using energy neither of them would have believed they had. A smile spread across their faces as they heard the giant horn blast it's acknowledgement of them. The giant rig slowed as it approached.

"Thank God," said Ethan, as he slid to a crouch and watched as the great truck came to a halt before them. The truck driver opened his door and climbed down.

"You blokes have picked a hard way to get to Coober Pedy." He smiled as he walked over and took in the desperate appearance of the couple. He handed them a bottle of water, telling them that no matter how thirsty they were, they were only to take sips of it for a while.

Margaret drank first, and then handed it to Ethan. They both drank and splashed the precious liquid down their chins.

The driver watched, waited, and then directed them to the truck cabin. They climbed up into the blessed coolness and sank down on to the front seat.

"So tell me how you came to be out here on such a lovely day."

Ethan spoke "We broke down, a long way back, couldn't find the road again, and have been walking since sunrise."

Margaret looked at her husband and realised immediately that he had his reasons for the story.

"I haven't seen any cars on the road. By the way, I'm Josh."

"I'm Ethan Dougherty, and this is my wife Margaret. We made the fatal mistake of leaving the road, then we got lost, then we broke down. I feel completely foolish for doing such a stupid thing, but there you are; if you hadn't come along just now I don't think we would have lasted much longer. Thank you so much."

"Yes." Margaret was nodding and leaning forward with her head almost in her lap.

The driver turned around and grabbed a hand towel from behind. He tipped some cold water onto the cloth and handed it to her. She covered her head and neck and just sat there, luxuriating in the incredible coolness. Next, she wet the towel again and handed it to Ethan. "Thanks," Ethan said.

He dabbed at his sore face and burnt neck. He held the cloth to his eyes then finally looked up at Josh and started to explain how he had hired a car in Coober Pedy and set out on the most disastrous excursion of their lives.

Josh listened, nodding at Ethan, who hoped the truck driver believed his story.

They travelled along Seventeen Mile Road which linked up with the Stuart Highway and then on to Coober Pedy. Within ten minutes, the pair was asleep. Josh wondered how two people of their age could make such a deadly mistake. He also wondered if he had heard the true story. When the driver pulled into a roadhouse on the edge of town, Margaret and Ethan woke up with a start.

"I think I should take you both to the hospital. What do you reckon?"

"I think we'll just check into our motel and take stock first thank you. We would like to give you something in appreciation of your kindness," Ethan reached into his pocket then realised he had no more than an empty wallet. "Oh, I don't have any cash on me. Sorry about that, can I please have your address and I would really like to send you something for you kindness."

Before Ethan could finish what he was saying, Josh waved his hand. "I definitely don't want anything, thanks. It was my pleasure to help out. I'm sure, given similar circumstances, you would do the same for anyone."

"True, but I would still like to contact you at a later date and perhaps explain a little more than I can just now."

"Sure." Josh leaned over, grabbed a small card from the console, and gave it to Ethan. "I'd be happier if you would be seen by a doctor at least."

"You're right, of course, we will. Thank you again."

Margaret took Josh's hand in hers and squeezed it.

"Thanks," she said. She smiled and said, "You are a life saver and we will never forget you."

The truck driver smiled back and nodded his acknowledgement.

They all stepped down from the truck cabin and walked into the roadhouse. Ethan and Margaret seated themselves, looked around for a waitress and watched as Josh spoke to the attendant and left. He waved as he walked out the door.

"I think all I want is another drink and a bed," said Margaret.

"Me too, but I'll grab something to eat later," said Ethan. He used his credit card and they set off down the road to a different motel from the one they had stayed in previously. No taxi service meant they trudged wearily to the last motel in town and finally stretched out on a bed.

"I'm sure you had a good reason for concocting a story for the truck driver, Ethan, but please hold that thought until I wake, I'd love to hear more."

No luggage meant no clean clothes, so they both showered and left wet clothes to dry while they slept.

"I can't believe we're back, it all seems like a dream now," Margaret murmured, but all she heard was snoring and she rolled over and went to sleep herself.

Down the road, the truck driver had stopped at the police station.

"G'day, mate," said the policeman, as he looked up from a pile of papers on his desk. "Ow can I help you?"

"I just wanted to let you know about a couple – man and woman – I picked up on Seventeen Mile Road. I'm not sure what the real story was with that pair, but I'm certain it's not what they told me. I just dropped them off down the road. I actually picked them up about half an hour out from town. They were walking, said their car had broken down. Thing is, I didn't see any sign of it – bit bloody hard to miss out there, eh. I'm not sure I buy their story. They didn't look in too good condition and not young either. I thought I should let you know they went to one of the motels in town."

The policeman asked Josh for a description of the pair and asked a few other pertinent questions. He took Josh's name and contact details and thanked him.

Josh drove out of town, satisfied he had done his good deed for the day.

******

Matthew looked around the manager's residence and gave a nod of approval. *Much better,* he thought. He had already made his rounds and let the residents know that he was on board now, and would be in the office if anyone wanted to speak to him.

"It's great to be back, I've actually missed this place," he said to Alfred and Greta van der Leer, when they came to welcome him back. They told him about the incident involving the relief manager and Elaine Steinberg, and added their own assessment of 'stupid Sonja', as she had been quietly known around the resort.

Matthew spoke to lots of people that day and he had the feeling they were glad to see a familiar face, and one they trusted. He was about to leave the office and go home for afternoon tea when the phone rang.

"Hello." At the end of the line was another old friend, someone he had not spoken to since he had gone to Adelaide for his managerial training. "Yes, Detective Pekalski, I just got back here yesterday, a bit of a surprise for all of us. How are you going?" Matthew listened, then said, "Why don't you come over later today, when you've finished work, we could have a drink and you could bring me up to date?"

Frank Pekalski arrived at the resort just after 5.00pm and they took a drink up to the balcony of the manager's residence.

"I'm surprised to find you here," said Frank. "I heard you were in Adelaide training up for a job."

"True," said Matthew, "but I was asked to come back and fill in here following a complaint from a resident's relative – just until Di and Jim return. It seems the relief manager wasn't coping."

"I see. Well, it's good you're here because now I won't have so many gaps to fill in for you. You remember the previous gardener here, Kevin?"

"I do, what's he up to these days?"

"Well, I'm not sure to be honest, but I had a call from Jim before he went away, to say a resident saw Kevin throw Ben, the poodle that used to belong to Jessie Thornton, into the pool to drown. Ben was saved, but Kevin got away and I'm still looking for him. My interest isn't really in the actual incident with the dog, but it's to do with the reason Kevin

159

would come back here, some unfinished business possibly. He's still the most likely suspect for tripping me on the path and breaking my leg."

"How's it going, by the way?"

"Aches a lot and I won't be doing too much running in the future, so I have my own score to settle with Kevin."

"I can imagine. Why do you think he came back?"

"I think you may be able to answer that better than I, Matt."

"Yeah, well, selling drugs probably - not to the residents, but he may well have kept his stash here."

"Just what I thought. Got any ideas where?"

"Not off the top of my head, but I'd be happy to give it a little thought."

"Good." They drank in silence for a couple of minutes.

"When will the Watersens be home, do you know?" asked Frank.

"About a week or ten days I think. I bet they're having a great bus trip, lucky buggers. I always wanted to see the red centre; still plenty of time I guess."

There was another pause in the conversation as both men took a couple of sips of their drinks.

"And how's our mutual friend, Allen Sinclaire, getting on in prison?" asked Matthew.

"Not too good, I'm afraid. Got his own private accommodation. A couple of the heavies have a score to settle and they think killing Allen will do it for them."

"I see," said Matthew, and he thought how close he had come to being in there with the ex area manager.

At home later that evening, Matthew thought a lot about where a miserable little drug runner like Kevin would hide his stash. As he drifted into sleep, he knew he would have a few ideas to check out in the morning.

Chapter Nineteen

"Can you see it yet?" Harold asked Robert, who leaned against the window looking toward the approaching built up area.

"I can. There's the Darwin sign"

They both looked down at their travel information, just as Terrence began his spiel on the approaching city.

"Here it comes, folks. In a few minutes we'll be in the northern-most stop in your journey. The capital of the Northern Territory, Darwin, has a varied population with many different ethnic groups including a large percentage of Aboriginal people. The climate is either wet, in summer, or dry in winter. The temperature rarely drops below 30 degrees centigrade and the humidity is high. This, the most northerly of Australia's harbours, is the cosmopolitan city of Darwin, named after the scientist, Charles Darwin, and founded in 1869. The city played a large role in defending Australia from the Japanese in World War II. It survived Cyclone Tracy in 1974 and now is Australia's most multicultural city. No one should get bored here, there's plenty to do. You may wish to visit one of the many natural parks like Litchfield National Park and swim in the cascading waterfalls, or perhaps the Berry springs Nature Park, where you can swim next door to the Territory Wildlife Park. I'm sure the crocs don't slip over during the night – well I'm pretty sure."

There were a few giggles and muffled laughs at this; most of the travellers had begun to enjoy Terrence's sense of humour.

He continued with an enthusiasm that belied the fact that he had done this speech hundreds of times.

"There are the jumping, saltwater crocs that propel themselves from the water while you cruise the Adelaide River. Keep your hands in please. Why not visit Melville or Bathurst Island. Known as the Tiwi Islands, you can buy local arts and crafts and see the indigenous culture. You can go fishing or hiking, or hell, you can do just about anything you want."

A small hotel on the outskirts of town provided a comfortable stay that evening. Following what most agreed was a most satisfying meal in the motel restaurant, the travellers, almost without exception, opted for an early night. They all wanted to be in top form to make the most of the three full days ahead of them in Darwin.

"This 'ole place is one big theme park," said Hank, to the group gathered at the table for breakfast.

The consensus was that everything was expensive, but since all the accommodation and main meals for the trip were pre-paid, the only out of pocket expenses each had to bear were for their extraneous activities, and everyone had a different idea of what that was.

Rachael and Freya had taken Helga under their wing, since she was in such desperate need of company and support. They took off to see the city and harbour sights.

Hank said he and Peter were, 'Goin' ta do a little prospectin' of their own'. Peter liked Hank's adventurous spirit, if not his propensity to make the same mistake of overindulging in alcohol on a daily basis. They always had fun though, and Peter had not had much of that for a long time prior to the trip.

Joy Rayne and Martin Judd had definitely become 'an item', and disappeared every day to return late in the afternoon looking flushed and happy. They were going to Kakadu Mango Wines in Palmerston and planned to stay for lunch and then, in the afternoon, go to the open-air Mindil Beach sunset markets.

Penny and Lottie had once again paired up with Harold and Robert to hire pushbikes and see the sights from the network of bicycle and walking tracks that follow the coastline. That evening they were planning to go to an outdoor, deckchair cinema.

"Be sure to take the insect repellent," Terence reminded them.

That evening Hank came home, once again supported physically by his now, best mate, Peter. He brought the inhabitants of Castaways Hotel to a complete standstill, retelling the adventures they had while travelling on the river cruise and almost becoming the crocodile bait. He and Peter both laughed so much the rest of the guests simply laughed at their laughter.

After four days, still no one wanted to move on, but advanced bookings meant move ahead they must. They packed their bags again and prepared to board the bus on Tuesday morning. They all had souvenirs that threatened to overload the baggage department, and even Terrence could not see the need for so many didgeridoos, considering they nearly all lived in the same place.

"Why didn't you just buy one for the community centre and leave it at that?" he had asked, when he saw the extra baggage arriving. Comments came from everywhere about how there were grandchildren and friends to think of, all of whom must surely want one of those delightful musical instruments standing in their lounge.

"Oh, well, I guess it keeps the wheels of commerce turning, doesn't it," said Terrence resignedly. "On a serious note though, folks, I will have to ask you all to be conscious of the space we have left. We are pretty well chock-a-block in the baggage holds."

They took off for the long trek to Kununurra, just over the Western Australian border. At the end of a long day in the coach, they were all ready to have an early night, but not before they all enjoyed the delights of great restaurant food from an Australian menu, and drank wine from the Western Australian wineries.

"Our next stop will be Halls Creek." The driver addressed the passengers as the coach set off next morning. "The Bungle Bungle mountain range, in the world heritage listed Purnululu National Park, is only accessible by four-wheel drive and our schedule won't allow time for land based tours, however, I can highly recommend the flights from Halls Creek."

Terence again proved to be a great source of interesting local information and personal anecdotes. "Halls Creek is a small township with hotels and motels and anything a tourist may need. Originally, a town was established because gold was found there but the first town was moved in 1948 when the water ran out, and by 1954 there was no one left in the original site. There is a large aboriginal settlement, and the township also supplies the pastoralists in the vicinity."

It was at Halls Creek that a handful of the travellers, including Harold and Robert, had pre-arranged a scenic flight over the Bungle Bungles. As they flew over the area, they marvelled at one of Western Australia's most fascinating landmarks from the air. Gorges deep in shadows, pools like mirrors, and amazing palms clinging to crevices, held them spellbound. The rock formations and the colours astounded them.

As they disembarked, Robert said, "I think this is the highlight of my trip. It's so exciting and comfortable and such an easy way to get in touch with such an isolated part of the country." A chorus of agreement confirmed Robert's assessment of the flight.

That night, the joy-flyers shared their experiences with the others in the group, who had their own activities to report on. Their stories were perhaps not so exciting, but nevertheless very interesting and varied.

******

She did not have a clue where she was when she woke. Margaret looked around through glazed eyes at the bed and little room. Slowly it all came back to her and she looked across at Ethan, sleeping quietly. She tiptoed to the toilet, then sat on the side of the bed drinking water from a tooth mug. Still dehydrated, she drank deeply as she cast around for the bag of food, and pulled out a donut, filled with jam. Then she ate some cake, followed a banana. She began to feel satisfied and turned around to see Ethan watching her from behind.

"Can I have some of that?" he put out his hand.

"What do you want?"

"Anything."

She handed him a jam donut, then filled up another glass of water and handed that to him.

"I've been thinking," he said.

"When? I thought you'd been sleeping."

Ethan smiled. He rubbed his face with both hands as he sat up. He swung his feet to the side of the bed. "I mean when we were walking." He locked both hands together in front of his mouth and leaned his chin on his fists. "Since the guys that abducted us now believe we are dead, we should let them keep thinking that until we can catch them."

Margaret was nodding and waited for more.

"Since we're not detectives we can't catch them ourselves."

"Agreed," she said. "I had a feeling then, you were going to say we should chase after them."

"No, that's not my forte, and anyway, we've had enough excitement to last this lifetime. No, Margy, this requires a professional. I'm afraid if we go to the police, the media will get hold of it, the criminals will go to ground, and maybe we'll never catch them – not to mention get our money back."

"I guess that's true. So what then?"

"We need advice. I'm going to ring Keeala Resort to get the number of the detective inspector who solved the case of those drug runners, and the murder of Jessie Thornton."

"Hmm, well, in the absence of anyone else, I suppose it's as good a place as any to start."

Ethan picked up the phone and dialled. His call connected on the third ring.

"Keeala Resort. Matthew Weatherlee speaking."

There was a moment of stunned silence. Ethan knew Matthew; he had arranged the purchase of their new home and was selling the resales.

Finally he spoke, "Hello, Matt, this is Ethan Dougherty, and I'm sort of on the bus trip on the road to nowhere."

"Huh? What did you say?"

Ethan explained that they had left the bus trip because of illness, and now he had a situation that required police help, but was he loathe to go to the local police and would rather get some advice before proceeding with the matter. It all came out as a confused jumble, but eventually, on the third go, Matt cut in and said, "As a matter of fact, Detective Inspector Pekalski is here this afternoon. He came to see me and was about to leave. Would you like to speak to him now?"

"I'd love to." Ethan breathed out in surprise and relief.

Ethan gave an outline of the situation he and his wife were in, and when he finished Detective Pekalski asked him to repeat it all again.

"Just bear with me, I'm taking notes as we speak," said the detective. Lots of 'ah huh's,' and 'Yeah, got that,' followed, with plenty of head nodding.

Matt sat on the sideline listening to the one sided conversation.

The detective said, "I want you to go to your local police station and ask to see whoever is in charge. In the meantime, I will make contact with whoever it is from this end and confer with them. I think you were right to lie low and a disguise would not go amiss at this point. You're only presuming the perpetrators have moved on and that they don't live in town. Since you have no idea who is involved, you should be cautious and not let them know that you are still alive and kicking."

Ethan agreed and said he would wait for a call from Detective Pekalski later that night or maybe in the morning.

Margaret rummaged around amongst their clothing. She had washed their clothes in the shower and hung them over the shower screen overnight to dry.

"We won't win the best-dressed traveller awards but at least I've got most of the dirt off," said Margaret.

"Don't worry, love, it's good enough to pass muster until we can buy some new outfits."

They dressed and walked to the roadhouse, where they each bought sunglasses and hats, then walked on to the police station.

Brisbane was a million kilometres away, or so it seemed now.

Chapter Twenty

Di's ankle had improved enough for her to be able to dance, albeit a little restricted, but dance they did till all hours. Having made friends with several couples, they were never short of good company or things to do.

"Would you like to join us when we go ashore tomorrow?" Jim asked one of his new friends as they made their way to their cabins at 2am.

"Why not, roll on tomorrow!"

They went ashore when the ship docked at yet another tropical island, where they enjoyed swimming, sightseeing, shopping, and eating. They soaked in the local culture and could not resist souvenirs and island clothes no matter that they may never wear them again once they got home.

"So isn't this better than rolling along on the bus, day after day, surrounded by faces you see every day of your life?"

Di smiled at Jim, and had to concede that it was a great idea. "Yes," she said, "We should take a cruise every year."

They had been at sea for eight days and were on their way home. Both looked a picture of health; tanned from playing deck games, fit from attending the gym each morning, and doing something that resembled power walking around the decks after dark.

"I hope the bus trip will all be okay and everyone will forgive us for deserting them."

"Doesn't matter, you did the best you could and we have needs too. You're the one always telling me we have to take better care of ourselves."

"True, though I'm actually looking forward to seeing our family and catching up with how things are going at home."

"Soon enough, my dear."

They heard the band start a new bracket and they got up together to join the other couples on the floor. They were soon lost in the music.

******

"What are you two doing in the back there? Why are you whispering?"

Judy and Russell looked up together from the back seat of the vehicle, and saw Patrick following their movements in his rear vision mirror.

"Just talking," said Judy.

"Well, why are you whispering?"

"Ah, jeez, mate, just didn't wanna to disturb you while driving, that's all – fair suck of the sauce bottle, eh? You're definitely soundin' paranoid ya know," Russell said.

For a moment, anger gripped Patrick. He fought the urge to turn around and grab Russell by the scruff of his neck, but, with great effort, settled himself and thought again how much he overreacted these days. For the next half hour, he tried to ignore them and think about what he was going to do when they got back to Sydney. They would arrive in Blacktown in a few hours if all went well. They had taken turns in driving and covered a long distance in three days, including the time they spent in Mildura.

"How are you getting to the coast after you leave us?" asked Patrick, as he looked in the rear vision mirror again.

"I'm gonna buy myself a car," said Russell, thinking to himself that the sooner he was on his own the better he would feel.

"Sure," Patrick said and wondered what he and Jude would do, first up.

They travelled in silence for a while. Judy broke the lull in the conversation and said, "How long do you think before Margaret and the new husband get home?"

There was no immediate response from the men, but then Patrick responded. "I have no idea and care even less. I don't even want to talk about them," he said.

"Well," said Judy, "I can't help but wonder how they're going to feel when they get home and have no money, you know, they'll feel safe and could go to the cops. I mean how

173

would you be? I think there's going to be a big splash on the TV and everyone could descend on Coober Pedy looking for the abductors and you know, start tracking us down and all."

"Not likely I say, not likely." Russell started to chuckle and then broke into laughter.

Russell's levity goaded Judy and she immediately responded with, "Well, I don't see how you can be so sure. What can we do, on the run, hiding out? Actually, I've been having my doubts about how they are going keep their mouths shut long after we've disappeared. It just doesn't make sense. They're not senile, just old. I'm worried."

"Oh shut up, Jude. Give us a break. They don't know who we are and I told you they won't blab," said Patrick.

"That's easy for you to say, but don't you see what I'm saying? They won't have any reason to shut up, once they're released."

"For Christ's sake, Jude, they're bloody dead!" Patrick shouted.

He pulled over to the side of the road and sat with his hands on the steering wheel. He looked straight ahead, furious with his sister for pushing him, and furious with himself for having such a short fuse. His shoulders moved up and down with his frustrated breathing.

"Cat's outa the bag now," came from the backseat, followed by more chuckles from Russell.

Judy stared ahead, eyes wide, her brain trying to take in the significance of what she had just heard. Patrick turned around and faced his sister.

"Look, we had absolutely no choice," he said. "They wouldn't agree and in the end it was them or us. I knew you wouldn't want to spend the next twenty years rotting in prison."

Judy's stare bored into her brother's eyes and he looked away, unable to cope with her unspoken condemnation. She shook her head slowly as she turned her head to face Russell. He fidgeted on the seat beside her.

"Bloody 'ell, Judy, Patrick's right," he said.

He nodded in agreement with his mate's comments. A grin spread from ear to ear, and he launched into what he obviously thought was an attempt at levity.

"Just look at it this way, luv, we did them a favour, saved them from old age and just witherin' away in the old people's 'ome, sufferin' from arthritis and not bein' able to do anythin' and wettin' themselves and all that stuff. Mind you, the other day I saw this old bloke drivin' around in a bloody sports car with the fuckin' top down, looked bloody ridiculous 'e did, silly old fart. Anyway, now you know they're 'appy up there with God an' all, lookin' down at us and bein' really 'appy to see us enjoyin' the money they left behind. See, they won't 'ave to make fools of themselves now, not like that other silly old bugger I saw – they'll be better off where they are."

Judy turned her body and slapped Russell hard across the face. He grabbed his bandaged nose and shouted in pain. She faced the front again and looked down at her hands. They shook uncontrollably.

"So now we're murderers," she said, as she raised her eyes and looked at the back of Patrick's head. She said, "Well, aren't we, Patrick, aren't we?"

"Yeah, so shut up, or you're next."

Patrick started the car again and pulled out onto the road. His face flushed and he was thinking, for the first time, just how much his sister's opinion meant to him.

"Shit, shit, shit." He banged on the steering wheel with both hands.

The other two looked at the driver and stayed silent; Russell frustrated at not being able to get away from this pair quickly enough, and Judy, still trying to accept that they had committed murder, and that Margaret, the only foster mother she had even the slightest regard for, was dead.

Judy knew, in her heart, it was true; killing her foster parents was the only way the three conspirators could hope to pull off this deal. The reality started to sink in. If they were apprehended, and convicted of the crime, she would go to gaol, probably for life. She put her elbows on her lap and her head in her hands and cried. She sobbed and withdrew into herself, curled up as she had done when she was a child, and alone.

"Margaret," she sobbed.

******

They drove on in silence. An hour and a half passed, still without conversation. As he stared at the black strip in front of him, Patrick saw a sign indicating a rest area, five hundred metres ahead. He slowed and pulled into a parking space near a barbecue area. He picked out a street directory from the door pocket, flipped over a few pages, opened the book out flat on the passenger seat, and traced a route with his finger.

No one spoke.

In the back seat, Judy was all cried out. She looked fixedly into the distance through the windscreen.

Russell snored softly; his head flopped to the side.

Patrick closed the book and pulled back onto the road. A few minutes later, he rolled into the driveway of a suburban house in Blacktown. He turned off the motor and got out.

At the same time, Judy stirred, fumbled for the door handle, and slid out of the vehicle. She walked around slowly and dragged herself lethargically into the front passenger seat. As Patrick walked up the front steps of the rental house, he flexed his neck and began to rub the weariness from his shoulders. He took a key from a magnetic key-case, which had been stuck to the back of a metal light fitting beside the front door. He entered and started to check from room to room. As he moved through the house, he began to reminisce and wonder how he had ever arrived at this place in his life. Had he started out differently in life he may well have been a very successful businessman or manager, he thought. He had foresight and was good at keeping focused on the issue. He believed his mean, hair-trigger temper was surely the result of his early treatment by a very abusive father and an absent mother. He had managed to bring his sister up and had never failed her. She was the one constant thing in the life that he struggled for, and the only person he had ever loved.

The sound and flash of the hand grenade explosion sent a disturbing memory to the forefront of his consciousness. Patrick bit his lip in response to the guilty intrusion. How could he now reconcile what he had done to Margaret and her husband? Judy had not really known the rejection and pain that her brother had lived through. He had protected her from as much as he could. She had been the reason they had survived so far, simply because Patrick wanted a better life for her and himself. Patrick was twelve and Judy ten when they went to live with Margaret and her previous husband. Patrick was unable to trust them or anyone, and could not recognise their goodwill. He rejected their love and was suspicious of anything they offered them, like an education and attending sport and music classes. After an argument with his stepfather, Patrick had taken Judy and disappeared when he was sixteen, and she only fourteen. He had provided for his sister and although they had lived 'rough' much of the time, he had always held down a job and put a roof over her head. He always planned that he would do more, much more. However, there were not any quick ways to success and he was an impatient young man.

Patrick walked back to the car and slid into the driver's seat. He made no comment about Judy's change of position to the front of the vehicle. Russell, he noticed, was still asleep.

"You know, Jude," he said quietly, both hands gripping the steering wheel, "I don't like having killed two people. But they were old; they really didn't have much time left anyway. They didn't suffer. The explosion killed them instantly. In a way we did do them a favour."

Judy turned to look unflinchingly into her brother's eyes.

"You can't really believe that," she said, shaking her head. "She was good to me, and to you as well. She never hurt anyone in her life. I wish I'd never agreed to any of this and I can't believe how you lied to me. Now I'm wondering how many other lies you've told me. How I trusted you and believed everything, I feel as though you've treated me like an idiot. And what if we're caught? We could go to prison for life."

"Well, you won't. I made sure you were not involved and I'm taking full responsibility for the whole deal."

"Huh! For a start, no one will believe that, and how do you think I'm going to feel if you go to gaol? For one thing, I'd have to manage without you and what sort of a life would that be for me. And, I'd know how bad it was for you and spend the rest of my life worrying about you. Really my life would be over anyway."

Patrick looked at his sister's profile and saw how beautiful she was and how distressed he had made her. It was not meant to be like that; he wanted to bring happiness into their lives, get some of the things they both deserved and would never have without money.

"I'm sorry. I really am. The last thing in the world I wanted to do was hurt you anymore. Somehow, I'll make it up to you and I promise you right here, right now, we will never do anything illegal again. Well, not much anyway," he said, as he tried to coax a smile from the girl staring at him.

He put his arms around her, and pulled her head on to his shoulder and rocked her while she cried. After a minute, he lifted her face up and kissed her on the lips.

"I promise I'll make it up to you, maybe by settling down with this money and getting a proper home, and maybe we can even adopt an old lady with no home. How would that be, hey?"

For the first time she smiled, then sighed. "Well, let's get started. What do you want me to do now?" she asked.

"Take a look at the house. I've rented it for three months and that should be enough time to see how the land lies and put our plans into action. We won't be staying here after that and we can decide where we want to live and so on. What do you think?"

"Great, let's go."

They both got out of the car and slammed the doors. Neither had looked back to see Russell unbuckle his seat belt and look after them. He had heard the whole conversation and had shaken his head in amazement, never had he known such love and loyalty. He felt a great sense of admiration for both of them.

"So, we're 'ome are we?" he asked, as he strode up the driveway behind them.

Chapter Twenty-One

No longer did the travellers change seats regularly. They all knew one another well enough and wanted to sit next to their favourite companion. Harold and Robert were still enjoying the company of Lottie and Penny and they could be seen huddled together over maps and local literature, discussing the things that most interested them.

Freya, Rachael and Helga also stuck together when they explored the towns and tourist spots. With a few days to go, the trip would soon be over and become the topic of conversation at the clubhouse for months to come.

******

Only a small police force was responsible for law and order in the very large area of the outback centred on Coober Pedy. On the day Margaret and Ethan entered the police station, they were met by young Gerry, and old Tony.

"Come into me den 'ere an' take a seat," Tony said. He directed the couple to a separate room, with a desk, covered by lots of messy papers, as its centrepiece. They each found a chair. Tony nodded and smiled as he said, "What can I do for ya?"

They explained that they had been on a recent bus tour, with a group from their retirement resort in Queensland.

"Strike me roan!" said Tony, "Are youse from a place called Keeala Resort?"

"Well, yes, we are, but how would you know that? asked Ethan.

Tony quickly jumped in with his explanation, saying he had met up with an old friend from that bus group, while he was in Engadoona overnight. His mate had given him his contact details and Tony said he remembered the name of the place, because it had a nice friendly ring about it.

Ethan wondered for a moment if he was baring his soul to the right person, "Yes, well what I'm about to tell you, I've already discussed with a Detective Inspector from Brisbane, and he suggested I come and see you and tell you our story, and then he will contact you and discuss the next step."

"That so? Please continue." Tony sat back, eyebrows raised and with his arms crossed over his chest, looking them both up and down.

Ethan could see from the policeman's body language that he was a little resistive, but he ploughed onward and told their story. He raised his eyebrows at his wife, to see if she wanted to add anything, but she shook her head. They focused on the big policeman, now sitting with mouth agape, but looking much more receptive to their story as he stared at them.

"Strewth, that certainly explains the visit I 'ad from the truckie 'oo'd picked you up."

"Oh, he came here?" asked Ethan.

"Only to say 'e 'ad picked youse up and 'e wondered if there was more to yer story than ya told him. He was just concerned that there could be a problem, and so now, I see there was. Right?"

"Yes, that's right."

"Well, havin' come through what you blokes 'ave been through, you're a couple a 'eroes."

The phone rang. 'Ow well timed, Inspector. I 'ave the couple in question sittin' in front a me right now and I've just 'eard their rather amazin' story."

Tony listened for the next five minutes or so, only acknowledging Detective Inspector Pekalski's monologue with the occasional, 'Uh huh – yep – sure.'

Ethan got up and walked around the room, imagining what the inspector may be saying.

"Okay. I'll be talkin' to 'em right now. Yeah, bye." Tony put the phone down and looked at the two people watching him. "Seems you 'ave friends in 'igh places and they believe ya story."

"Does that mean you don't?" Ethan was quick to ask.

"Nah. It just means I've 'eard a lot a crap in me time and I know better than to jump to conclusions."

"Does Detective Inspector Pekalski suggest anything we should be doing?" Margaret asked.

"Sure does. Sounds okay to me, too. First, I want youse to go over a few o' the finer points that need some clearin' up. Like, where did youse say youse're stayin' now?"

"The Sunset Motel, in the side street, west of here."

"That's fine. Ya say you'll be wantin' to do a bit of shoppin' before you go home?"

They nodded.

"Well, t'morrer, I'll send Gerry 'ere with ya, and keepin' a low profile, like, pick up what youse'll need. Then, I'll need to see this mine shaft and get a few more things straight before youse hit the road."

"Actually, we plan to fly back home, I believe there's an airport here in Coober Pedy," said Margaret.

"Yeah, there is. You'll be sellin' yer story to the Women's Weekly when this is over, I'll wager."

Margaret and Ethan looked at one another and smiled, almost laughed. At this point, they both were wondering what to make of this man, but they both knew that they liked him.

"So what does Detective Inspector Pekalski suggest we do after tomorrow?" asked Margaret, hoping to leave Coober Pedy a little more informed than when they arrived.

"Talk about that t'morrer, eh?" Tony stood up, walked to the door, and held it open. "I'll send Gerry around at nine, and you can buy some clothes and then back 'ere and we'll take a little drive, eh? After that, we'll 'ave a chat about our next move. 'Ow's that sound?"

"Fine thanks, Sergeant."

"You can call me Tony. See youse t'morrer."

With hats and sunglasses in place, the pair walked back to their motel room. It was going to be another long night.

******

Surprisingly, they both slept well and were ready when Gerry knocked on their door at 9am sharp.

"Morning, Mr. and Mrs. Dougherty." Gerry, early twenty-something, had a broad smile and revealed soft spiky hair when he took off his hat. He had the lean, hardened country-boy look and the good manners to go with it. "Ready to go?" he asked.

"We certainly are." Ethan pulled the door shut behind Margaret and pocketed the keys. They walked to the police 4WD. Ethan hopped into the front seat and Margaret belted up in the rear.

"Where first, Mr. Dougherty?"

"Well, this is your town. Where would we go to buy clothes and toiletries and some luggage?"

"If you're happy to wear what other people around here wear, I'll take you to a couple of places; one better for women's clothes, and another one for blokes. We'll pick up the other stuff at the supermarket."

"Fine, let's go," said Margaret, "and please, my name is Margaret, and this is Ethan."

"Oh."

Gerry's upbringing made him hesitate. He had an ingrained respect for his elders, and found it at odds with his natural instincts to call the Doughertys by their given names.

"Sure," he said, as he accepted their invitation, "and, likewise – Gerry – please."

Gerry and Ethan stood back while Margaret selected several sets of undies and nightwear and then slacks, blouses, a jacket and some practical shoes. Ethan added the same basic items for his wardrobe then selected a couple of suitcases and two smaller carry bags. They stocked up on a few toiletries at and were on their way out of the shop in a little over an hour. They made their way back to the police station and were pleased to sit down and have coffee with Tony by ten thirty.

"The way I see it," Tony said, "is you guys are best to stay out of sight, and the perpetrators will relax and eventually bob to the surface. Oh, 'scuse me." Tony looked over Ethan's shoulder.

A tall, middle-aged, scruffy, but friendly looking man knocked on the open door of Tony's office.

"G'day, mate," he said, as he winked at Tony.

"G'day, Johnno," was Tony's warm acknowledgement. "Come in, mate. Take a seat," He waved a gnarled hand in the newcomer's direction. "This 'ere is John Stitson. John, this is Mr. and Mrs. Dougherty."

"Margaret and Ethan, please," said Ethan, as he shook hands first with the newcomer.

Bloody hell, thought Ethan, as he withdrew his hand from John's iron grip, *I may never play the piano again!*

Ethan had already noticed on this trip, that the further into the outback he went, the firmer the handshakes became.

Margaret followed with her outstretched hand, but the handhold was surprisingly gentle.

"Pleased to meet you both," said John. He turned around, picked up a chair from the outer office, and squeezed it into the tiny inner space beside Margaret.

"Johnno's our forensic man and e'll be comin' along with us today, and 'opefully, if ya friends 'ave left any clues, we'll find 'em."

Ethan and Margaret nodded.

"Can ya just fill 'im in on a few details?" said Tony.

John pulled out a notepad and started to scribble as Ethan spoke about the circumstances of their abduction. When he had finished, Margaret added what she could think of that may be pertinent.

"Gerry," said Tony, "Can ya go and rustle up some lunch to take along, and plenty o' water, oh, and top up the fuel will ya, please? Sandwiches okay with everybody?" Tony acknowledged sandwiches with any sort of fillings were acceptable to all and added, "Oh, and Gerry, chuck in some meusli bars, some fruit, and maybe a few cans of stuff, just in case. Ya know what we need. Thanks, mate."

Gerry nodded to his superior and squeezed out of the room, while John continued to question the couple on some finer details of their escape.

A few minutes after eleven, they all piled into the police wagon and headed out of town. The truck driver had given

Tony a description of where he had picked up the walkers, and Ethan agreed that it had been an accurate account.

The police vehicle was well along Seventeen Mile Road when Ethan's voice startled the others.

"Stop! This is it. Look, see the tyre tracks heading off past those three trees. Remember, Marg, I said to you that they were the only living things we'd seen taller than us? And over there, there's that flat-topped hill with the sawtooth profile on one end. Now, if I'm correct, there should be three mounds of mine tailings off to my – now, wait a sec, while I reverse this in my mind – yes, they were on our left as we walked out, so off to my right now, a few hundred metres in."

"Yep, your spot-on, mate," said John, "they're out my side, a couple of hundred metres up. But hang on a minute, there are thousands of mounds in opal country. How can you be so sure these are the ones you saw."

"Because the mine we were in was the only one we saw. We didn't see any others until we walked past those three there. I'm sure this is the place."

"Ya probably right, Ethan," said Tony, "This area is really marginal country for opals. Gamblers, or fools, call 'em what ya will, sink speculator 'oles well away from the main fields. Maybe one in a hundred find colour. We 'aven't seen any others for at least ten minutes. And another thing, these tracks look pretty fresh, so I'd back your judgment, mate."

Ethan peered out of the 4WD's windscreen as Tony followed the tyre tracks into the barren landscape. The policeman did well, and they covered the ground quickly. In less than half an hour, they had reached the mineshaft site.

Margaret was reluctant to get out of the vehicle; she felt afraid and watched from the open door as the group made their way past the original shaft to the one that had opened up with the explosion.

John carried an aluminium case containing his instruments and other paraphernalia of his profession, as well as bags in which to collect samples. He took a powerful torch from his case and shone it down the shaft where the pair had so recently crawled out.

"Bloody amazing, mate," John said to Ethan. "You and your wife really are very lucky to be alive."

Margaret finally got out of the car and walked over to look down the hole again. She stepped back and shuddered.

Ethan put his arm around her. "We are very lucky," he said, "but it didn't feel that way at the time."

"I never want to see this place again," said Margaret. "I never really knew what fear was until we ended up here." She sobbed, and dabbed at tears as she snuggled close to her husband.

"I can understand how you feel," said John.

"Do you think you can get down there," asked Ethan.

"I'm just going to have a squizz at the original entrance as well, Ethan. I don't doubt your word that it's blocked, but I'll check it out. I need to get a few photos of it also, to send to Adelaide. I think I'm going to have to get some reinforcements up here – a special team to get us down there safely. It looks unsafe for us to attempt it on our own," John said quietly, as they all walked back to the car.

Tony pulled an insulated box onto the tailgate of the 4WD, and handed around sandwiches and bottled water.

Ethan took a swig of water and asked, "So how much longer will you need us, do you think?" Ethan had anticipated his wife's next question.

"Well, I'll try to set everything up for day after tomorrow," said John. "I'll probably need you back again, once we establish safe access. I'll want you to identify things; we need to see what there is to find. Do you think you'll be up to it?"

Ethan paused for a few seconds before he nodded his assent.

John caught the hesitancy in Ethan's reaction and said, "I'm not casting doubt on your nerve at all, Ethan, because I fully understand how traumatic the experience was for you and Margaret, so if you have any reservations, please don't be afraid to say so. I can work around it."

"No, I can see you're a cautious man and don't want to take any unnecessary risks, so I'll trust your judgment on the safety issue. Just remember that I'm not as young as I used to be, and I was probably supercharged with adrenaline last time, sort of like a geriatric Incredible Hulk!"

When the laughter subsided, they finished their lunch and then John made a big sweep of the area with Gerry and Tony. They combed the vicinity for anything the abductors may have left behind, but found nothing, apart from some footprints. They were too indistinct to be of much value. At about four that afternoon, they headed back to town.

Tony sat next to Gerry, who was driving, and John squeezed into the back seat with the Doughertys.

Tony turned halfway round and said over his shoulder, "We'll 'ave to keep a lid on all of this, of course. It'll be tedious for the time bein', but I need youse guys to stick to the motel room until youse leave. Yer gonna 'ave the same restrictions when you get 'ome, accordin' to D I Pekalski, so youse might as well get used to it now. Until we find these blokes, youse are supposed t' be dead. You might want to join a good library." He looked at the pair with a smile. "If there's anythin' youse need, you'll 'ave to call the station, and me or Gerry 'ere will get it for ya, or drive youse wherever youse want to go, but the less youse are out and about, the better, okay?"

"Yes, understood," answered Ethan. "We've had enough excitement for two lifetimes, haven't we, love?"

Margaret nodded, but could not suppress a shudder.

"There'll also be someone on watch, undercover, and I'll give youse an emergency number to use if need be. This'll be stretchin' our resources o' course, so we'll be 'andin' youse over to your detective friend as soon as possible."

"Yes, thank you Tony. I must say that we're really pleased with all the help and understanding we've had from everyone. We couldn't have asked for more."

"My pleasure," said Tony, as they drove up outside the motel room. "I've arranged for youse to get a day's menu sent over from the cafe. One of our fellers will deliver it to ya when youse want it."

"Thank you again," Ethan and Margaret both said, as they got out of the 4WD. They went down to their room and locked the door behind them. They just stood and looked at one another for a moment, before they flopped on the bed. Ethan lay on his back with his hands clasped behind his head.

"I'm really pleased," he said. "It wouldn't have surprised me if no one had believed us, and we'd been fobbed off. However, this is all as it should be. What do you think, love?"

"Oh, I agree. While I'm not looking forward to what's ahead, I would dearly love to find out what sort of people could do this to us. How did they even know we had any money? Who would have had access to our financial details, and who would've known we were here anyway? I know this place has a reputation for having some rough and ready characters amongst the population, but I find it hard to believe we were just targeted randomly by some local yahoos."

"Yes, I've been thinking about that too," Ethan said.

Margaret stroked her chin and said, "You know what's niggling me though, love?"

"What?"

"There's something about the taller one – his voice certainly – but something else about him. I just can't put my finger on it."

"I've felt the same thing. It makes you wonder, doesn't it?"

Ethan got off the bed, walked over to the TV and picked up the remote.

"Might as well see what's happening to the rest of the world," he said, with a sigh.

Chapter Twenty-Two

Matthew Weatherlee was enjoying being home again. He felt full of energy and really wanted to get stuck into something. His first responsibility was to call a resident's meeting and let everyone know that he was now managing Keeala Resort until the Watersens returned. He tidied up lots of loose ends and swept through the unfinished work Sonja had left behind; mostly paperwork, but also ordering supplies, arranging maintenance and following up correspondence.

He had access to Rachael Ross's house with his master key, and since she was away on the bus trip, it was an opportunity for him to enter Unit 27. This was the unit where Jessie Thornton had died last year and Kevin, the ex-gardener, was seen lurking around her premises at the time. Matthew was aware of a slight trepidation about entering Rachael's home in her absence. However, it would be to her benefit if he uncovered Kevin's hidden stash of illegal drugs somewhere on her property. Her little dog, Ben, had attacked Kevin more than once, and this may be why Kevin had thrown Ben in the pool. Maybe it was just payback because Kevin had actually ended up with a bad limp when an untreated infection followed from a bite to his ankle by Ben.

Matthew let himself into Rachael's house. He searched inside for more than half an hour, but found nothing. Disappointed, he locked up and walked around to the tiny back garden at the rear of the unit. A small, steel garden shed sat in the corner of the yard. Matthew slid the sliding door open and drew back; the smell was unpleasant; more than musty and damp, but he dipped his head and entered, and began to poke around behind old garden tools and potting mix. Blood and bone fertilizer, mixed with rat droppings, fanned out on the floor below a hole chewed in a plastic bag. *No wonder it stinks*, thought Matthew. Another small, dark patch on the floor in the opposite corner caught his eye. The gap between the pavers in this area was bigger than the rest of the floor and one paver stood proud of the others. Moist dirt had squeezed through. Matthew's interest was aroused immediately. He looked around for something with which to lever the corner paver. He found a flat bladed screwdriver hanging on the wall above his head. He pushed the blade into the gap and pulled back on the handle. The paver offered no resistance and Matthew was able to lift it out with little effort. He used the screwdriver to poke around in the soil and a gasp left his lips when the tool touched what felt like a buried metal object. Matthew got on his knees and started to dig around it. A sense of excitement rose in his chest as he saw a handle on the lid of what looked like a cash box. He pulled on the handle, but the container would not budge. He loosened the soil around the sides of the box with the screwdriver, and finally lifted out the container. It was a little bigger than a shoebox. Matthew thought it was probably was a cash box; it had a catch on the side but was unlocked.

Matthew carried it out into the light and squatted down on the ground to open it. He looked around nervously, as though he thought someone may be watching him, but there were fences on three sides and no one hanging over any of them. He returned his attention to the box as he lifted the lid. Money, and what looked like packets of cocaine, filled the tin. Matthew's eyebrows flew up and he sat back on his heels and whistled. *I wonder what Pekalski will say about this?* He went back into Rachael's house and put in a call to the detective.

Matthew was quiet excited when he told Pekalski how his intuition had led him to the loot.

"Just stay where you are, I'm coming over. Don't touch anything."

Matthew went back outside and looked around, hoping no one had spotted him moving around in the yard. All was quiet, so he sat down on an old chair to await the arrival of the police officer.

******

Although the drive through Carnarvon and Geraldton was picturesque, and totally different from their home landscape, the intrepid travellers were beginning to show a little fatigue. With another new bus driver, James, they were only a week from home and their enthusiasm was beginning to flag. Happy to see the skyline of Perth as it slowly came into view, they were all anxious to relax in the luxury of the next hotel. From there they would explore the city and distant wineries, markets and dockside.

"I would like to see some of the historic Aboriginal sites," Peter confided to Hank, who listened intently and nodded as he wondered if there could not be something with a little more action to get involved in. They agreed to start with a trip to Rottnest Island. They left on a ferry from Fremantle and sailed out into the wonderfully blue water off the mainland. Their plan was to snorkel in the waters off the island and stay overnight in the hotel, to return the following afternoon.

They discovered the crystal blue bay, with a view of the white sandy beach and the native West Australian bush in the background.

"Are you sure this is all right?" asked Peter, as he adjusted his snorkel and face mask.

"Looks good to me," answered Hank, as he pushed off and started to kick his way round the far side of the boat. The two old men splashed around in the water, trying not to look stupid. Peter had never tried to snorkel before, and after a few preliminary instructions, Hank left him to his own devices. Twenty minutes on, he had had enough and he swam over to the back of the boat and waved for a hand up.

"How was that" said the young assistant as he reached toward Peter.

"Great, but I'm not really much of a snorkeler. I'm happier with dry land under my feet."

They all sat back and watched Hank's antics as he chased after something underwater. They lost track of him several times then up he came to the surface again. When they finally hauled him up he said he was done in, and he lay panting on the deck for several minutes before he sat up and started expounding the beauty of the deep and how at home he felt there.

"Listening to you, mate, anyone would think you were the first person to explore the underwater world." Peter laughed at Hank.

Lunch on board followed, and then the men were dropped off further around the island, near the amenities. They waved goodbye to their friends on the boat. They shook their heads and laughed as they headed back to Fremantle, with a couple of good stories to tell their mates about, over beers that evening.

Hank and Peter checked into the hotel then set off to explore the island on pushbikes. There are no privately owned vehicles on Rottnest so anyone can ride around freely and enjoy the scenery.

"I noticed a bunch of Quokkas under a bush back there, did ya see 'em?" asked Hank, as he peddled hard to catch up with his mate.

"I did. They're very cute, and I suspect, protected."

"I'd like a photo with some. If ya see more, can you stop and I'll sneak up and you can snap a picture for me."

"Right," said Peter. He kept peddling. A few minutes later, he heard a shout and turned to see Hank waving madly at a small group of Quokkas huddled in dense shrub and blending into the background. They were about the size of a cat and looked a bit like a tiny kangaroo.

Peter rode back to Hank. They left their bikes on the roadside. Peter had his camera hanging around his neck as they both crept forward slowly, trying not to alarm the little animals.

Hank lay down on the ground and continued to edge closer while Peter stayed back and readied his camera. Just as Hank stretched out toward the nearest animal, they all took fright and started to run in every direction.

Hank was up, chasing one he had his eye on, and a moment later he was scampering after it across a manicured grass expanse. Peter ran after them.

Neither noticed the wedding party, posing for photos, with the bride and groom in position on a mound and the ocean in the background.

Hank lunged and Peter stood up and snapped his photo. "A classic!" he shouted, as he slowly looked around and saw they were in the middle of the photo shoot and the guests were all watching in amazement at what looked like a Benny Hill movie chase.

Then the crowd started to clap and laugh; even the bride and groom. They all walked into the centre of the lawn and some took snaps of Hank holding onto the little Quokka. The wedding photographer agreed to take a snap of the intruders and their little captive and add it to the collection. Peter apologised profusely for interrupting their wedding, while Hank laughed and took his leave with a wave and he blew a kiss to the bride. They made their way back to the bikes and said goodbye to their furry little friend, who looked scared stiff. They put him back under a tree and mounted up for the ride back to the hotel.

"We've sure had a great day, haven't we?" said Hank. Peter agreed.

******

Russell looked around at the lounge room, and noted that it was fully furnished.

"Not bad," he thought. He heard voices coming from the kitchen. He went to the back of the house and joined Judy and Patrick. "This place seems okay, what do you guys think?"

"Yeah, we're happy enough with it," said Patrick. "Only be for three months and then we'll be out of here. What about you, you've got something planned, haven't you?"

"Yeah, yeah, sure. Not as good as this o' course, but I call it 'ome; not everyone can call Byron Bay that."

"So where are you going to stay when you leave here?"

"Tomorrow, I'm goin' to buy myself a car. Nothing fancy, maybe a small four wheel drive, you never know when you want to go off-road, do you?"

"This is true," agreed Patrick. He thought of all the times he and Judy used their vehicle as their home and slept in out of the way places – definitely off road. "And then?" he prompted Russell.

"Oh yeah, then I'm goin' to head north to Byron Bay, I got a few friends there and I'll be glad to see them. One especially."

"I hope these friends aren't too high profile, if you know what I mean. And I also hope you remember you can't say a word about our job. Right now, if a word gets out, we're gonners."

"No worries there, mate. I know when to shut up. Even when I've had a few, I keep my mouth shut. It's my head too, you know."

"Good. Let's get some food in here. After dinner we can make some plans."

"Right," said Russell. He went out to the car and brought back his kit bag, which he dumped on the dining room floor.

Judy brought in her bags and put them in the master bedroom. "You can put yours in there," she said to Russell, and pointed to a small second bedroom. Judy helped Patrick clear out the car and then they went shopping, leaving Russell behind, sitting in front of his laptop computer and tapping away madly.

******

"It's pizza," said Judy, as she put two cartons on the bench. "Help yourself," she said, as she put the other supplies away, either in the walk-in pantry or the refrigerator.

"God, I 'ate fuckin' pizza," said Russell.

"What?" replied Judy.

"Nothin'," said Russell. "I'm just thinkin' about startin' a diet – now we're 'ome. Count me out and I'll just eat fruit tonight, gotta get this old gut back into shape."

After they had eaten, Russell pulled his computer round to the side of the table so they could all see. Patrick sat at the table beside Russell. Judy stood behind them both, watching over their shoulders.

"As I see it, we'll be right to divide the money now. Better too, in case anythin' 'appens to one of us," said Russell.

"I agree," said Patrick, "but can it be done now?" He was referring to the fact that the money had gone to various accounts to make the tracking much harder to follow. Bringing it all back together took a great deal of expertise, and that is why Patrick chose Russell in the first place. Russell had a reputation for being a professional; both with money laundering and computer hacking. Those two talents were essential when money was moved from one account to another. Illegally, that is.

"Let's see where we are now," Russell said, and the screen lit up with rows of figures as his fingers blurred across the keyboard.

"Now fifty per cent for you, and the same for me."

Patrick turned and grabbed the front of Russell's shirt.

"What the hell are you playing at mate? We made a deal, 60/40 our way, and you bloody well know it."

"Yeah, yeah, but I figured since I took as much risk as you, and my contribution doin' all this stuff just about balances out the fact that it was your idea. I'm entitled to an equal share. And your sister here did nothin' as well."

Patrick stood up, still holding Russell by the shirt. They were eye to eye and the look on Patrick's face was fierce, getting redder by the minute.

Russell was not going to be intimidated again.

"On top of that, mate, I'm gonna have medical expenses gettin' this bloody nose fixed when I get 'ome, unless you want to pay for it. You and your shitarse temper 'ave a lot to answer for."

Patrick held the other man there and stared at him. His eyes bulged and his hands still shook Russell's collar. Russell could see him thinking. With an audible sigh, Patrick slowly relaxed his grip on his partner.

"You might be right." He turned to look at his sister. She agreed with a nod of her head.

"Okay, done," said Russell. "I think this is fair. We both contribute equally and we both benefit equally. This is a better deal, I think."

"You would," Patrick mumbled.

They all turned back to the computer screen and watched, mesmerised as Russell tapped away. Numbers appeared and then disappeared, and somehow in the process, he was making them rich. Judy finally went to bed and left the two men to finish the fine details. They were each going to be three hundred thousand dollars richer. They had stripped the Dougherty's account clean; left them with nothing.

"They won't need anythin' where they are now, will they?" laughed Russell.

Patrick was not amused. He had a lot to live down with Judy, and she would be there constantly, a reminder of his very guilty conscience.

They completed their transactions and turned the computer off. They now had healthy balances in their accounts and did not need to see one another again if they did not want too.

"What time are you getting away in the morning? asked Patrick.

"Can't leave without a car, can I?"

"Oh, sure. I'll drive you around and see if we can get you something nice. I may come in handy for you now - there's not much gets past me when it comes to wheeling and dealing in cars. Just you wait and see." Patrick's temper had gone and now he was all smiles.

"Oh, great" said Russell.

"What?" Patrick had not missed the sarcasm.

"Nothin'. Good night."

Chapter Twenty-Three

Ethan was the first to wake to the knock on their motel door.

"Your breakfast, sir." A middle aged, neat looking police officer in khaki uniform handed him a tray. Ethan took it and turned to place it on the table. "My name is Snr. Constable Ian Lange and I'll be your contact today until four. If you need anything just ring this number." He handed Ethan a piece of notepaper.

"Nice to meet you, Snr. Constable."

"The sergeant will be over later today to talk to you. He sends his compliments. Oh, he also said to remind you not to go out."

"Thank you." Ethan turned to the room as the police officer walked off.

"I could develop a liking for room service," Margaret said, as she wrapped a light gown around herself and went to the bathroom.

Ethan laid out the breakfast things then picked up a newspaper from the tray. He quickly scanned it for anything of interest, found nothing, and threw it on the table when his wife re-entered the room. She sat down. Ethan disappeared, and when he returned she was already buttering toast.

"The one thing that cannot be served cold is toast, have you ever noticed that, dear? Whenever I'm away from home, the only thing I always miss is hot, crisp toast. You simply cannot cook it, then hold it over for longer than three minutes."

Ethan heard his wife's displeasure at having cold toast, but simply mumbled, "Hmm, bloody thing's got to be here somewhere." Ethan was looking for the TV remote.

"Are you looking for anything in particular, love?" Margaret could see her husband was preoccupied this morning.

"Bloody remotes, they have a mind of their own. I'm wondering how long it will take for us to go mad in this room though. I do hope we can finalise things here today, at least when we get home we can catch up with friends and move around."

They ate in silence. Both wondered what would await them when they got home. They had no money now, and the credit card was great until they had to pay for it. Ethan was wondering if they might be able to prevail on Margaret's uncle again. He was a very generous man and he had a soft spot for his niece; that much was obvious.

Ethan had rung his bank as soon as Josh had rescued them and dropped them back at their motel. The bank balance was zero so he knew the men had been successful at transferring their money. Ethan and Margaret both knew what it was to be poor, but they should not have to be now, and it distressed Ethan terribly.

He had not been able to protect his wife from the loss of all their money, or the incredibly painful experience they had gone through. He looked at her now and thought that she was more resilient than he had given her credit for. He wished he had married her when they were young, and had children together. He remembered Margaret, the schoolgirl; the one that was driven to be successful and was always competitive. She was not complicated, not like his previous wife, and she was not devious either. Margaret was easy to live with and had a happy, positive attitude. He loved her very much and knew he must do whatever he could to return her to the stress-free life they had just begun together.

About two o'clock that afternoon, Ethan answered the door. He was expecting Sergeant Tony. He stepped back to let him in. Tony got straight to the point.

"So, folks, it's all arranged. If youse come with me now we can go down the shaft. I'm 'appy to say we set it up quickly and the boys 'ave been workin' down there all mornin'. The shaft is safe to enter with care, and once down there, I don't expect we'll need you again after that. Margaret, ya won't be needed if ya don't wanna come." He looked at her questioningly.

"I'll come for the drive, anything to get some fresh air – if that's okay?"

"Sure, no problemo."

Margaret grabbed a bag and put on her sunglasses and hat. Ethan followed.

******

Margaret sat in the hot 4WD with all the doors open. She watched as two very strong looking men were lowered by winch, one at a time, down the shaft she and Ethan had climbed out of. After this, John, the forensic police officer went down, then Ethan, and finally Tony. There was a small group still standing around on the surface. They laughed and chatted among themselves.

Margaret could imagine the scene that awaited the men when they reached the bottom. She shuddered whenever she thought of that cave, and the fear and sense of hopelessness she had felt down there. *How could anyone do that to another human being?* she wondered, and her heart filled with sadness at the thought of someone wanting money so much that they would commit murder to get it.

Down the shaft, the team had scoured the floor and had moved a lot of rock to try to recreate the scene as Ethan described it. There was very little to be found at first, but then a cheer came from one man who stooped over a pile of rubble. He held up a pen. "Is this yours Mr. Dougherty?" he asked.

"Let me take a look," said Ethan. He picked his way across the rubble to the man with the pen. "No, it's not mine. It's the one they gave me to write down my bank details with, so I guess my prints will be the most obvious?"

"What about this?" He bent again and picked up a water bottle by the neck with his gloved hands.

"No, that wasn't the one we used. Ours was two litres – that's only about half a litre."

The police officer dropped the bottle into a plastic bag and sealed it. They continued to scratch around and moved more debris. The original shaft with the ladder had gone completely and would need much labour or another explosion to free it again.

"This folding chair. Is it what you sat on?" asked another man.

Ethan looked up, "No, we sat on the floor, and they brought that down to sit on when they entered information on the computer. It was theirs."

The chair was bagged as another potential source of fingerprints. They found the suitcases and old rags used to stuff Ethan and Margaret's mouths, and these also were enclosed in large plastic bags, along with rope and bucket. In fact, everything that had been taken down was brought back to the surface and taken away for forensic examination.

Ethan smiled as he emerged from the mineshaft. He walked over to his wife and gave her a big hug.

"We found things that only the men had touched, so maybe we can get fingerprints and that'll be a start. It was also a good opportunity for these forensic people to see the scene of the crime and get the idea of what had happened."

His wife nodded and made space for Ethan to slip in next to her in the back seat of the 4WD.

Tony climbed into the driver's seat. "Quite a sight, I must say, youse guys really do 'ave a story for the Women's Weekly, maybe even for a current affairs show on TV," he said.

They all laughed at that and the tension eased.

"Can we go home now?" Ethan leaned forward and put his hand on the front seat, looking at Tony.

"Yeah, there's nothin' more youse can do here now. I'll be in contact with your Detective Inspector Pekalski, and if all is well, youse'll be on ya way t'morrer. Make your bookin' when we get back. Ya do know youse'll have to change planes, there's no direct flight, but youse'll soon be on yer way 'ome to Keeala Resort."

******

At Keeala Resort, Frank Pekalski was busy conducting a search of the shed where Matthew had found the drugs and money the previous day. He had come straight over. What Matthew had found looked very interesting to him. The next day, he had his own forensic team go through the shed but they found nothing else. They took away the box and its contents and Pekalski finally joined Matthew in the manager's office.

"So things are really beginning to pick up here," said Matthew. "We have the Watersens expected home later today.

That was an interesting turn of events, them leaving the bus tour. The Doughertys are on their way home as well, but they won't be coming here, I gather. And we're going to have an investigation into this recent find. I don't think the bus people are due for about a week, but they can look forward to a bit of excitement when they return. They'll no doubt catch up on the gossip about the sacked relief manager and they'll have Kevin to watch out for. We can put Ben 'on guard' in the backyard for that duty. And, of course, Lorna McDonald won't be coming home; they'll have a memorial service for her I think, depends on the family. It'll give the residents a chance to pay their respects, even though she is already cremated."

"The Watersens will wish they'd never come back when they hear all that's been happening," said Frank. He grimaced as he imagined Jim's expression when he hears about all the goings on while he and Di had been away. He was fond of Jim and Di and would be glad to see them again. Pekalski could see himself managing a place like this, not that most places attracted anything like this much trouble. He chuckled.

Matthew regarded him quietly. He too could picture the face of Jim Watersen when he got out of the cab.

******

Ethan looked down and saw the city of Brisbane below.

"What a great sight," he said.

He squeezed Margaret's hand as the jet descended on its final approach. When Ethan flew, he usually took an interest in the landing. This time was different. He was totally distracted by the reality that as soon as they landed, they would have to face the daunting task of trying to continue their lives with their life savings gone. They had already agreed that Margaret should contact her uncle and tell him her story. They hoped he would lend them some money until their own was retrieved, if ever. Ethan felt uneasy, even guilty, that they would have to rely on Margaret's uncle; he had already been far more generous than either had a right to expect. The plane touched down. The jolt brought Ethan back to the present. When the pair emerged from the exit, a plainclothes policeman quickly attached himself to the couple and introduced himself as Silvio Agostini. He told them he would be their main contact with head office.

There had been few passengers on the couple's flight, and they did not have to wait long at the luggage carousel. Within ten minutes, they were on their way to a safehouse in Kallangur, not too far from the airport. Agostini told them Detective Inspector Pekalski would come to see them later in the day and he would answer any questions they had. The house they pulled up at was a duplex. No one occupied the left unit and they had the right side – a safe house. They found the interior comfortable and clean, the fridge lightly stocked with essentials, so they would not starve for a while. As soon as they settled in the detective took his leave and Margaret wandered around, touching things, wondering how long they would be there.

"Are you going to ring your uncle, love?"

"Yes, I'll do it right now," and Margaret walked to the phone with the tiny diary she had taken from her bag when they were still in the mine. After being put through a couple of extensions and hearing unknown voices, Uncle Roderick finally came to the phone.

"Well, how nice it is to hear from you, my dear. I thought you would be still on your round Australia hike."

She asked if he had enough time to listen to a long story and he said, "Of course." Margaret told her uncle to sit down, and then she spent the best part of half an hour going through their saga of woe.

"I'm absolutely stunned! If it was anyone else who told me this story, I just wouldn't have believed it."

On the other end of the line, Margaret shrugged. She was all talked out.

"What can I do my dear? You must need some money – well of course you do – and I'll have some sent to your account as soon as I get off this phone. What else can I do? How are we going to catch these buggers? What about the cops, are they doing all we expect?"

"First thank you, we could use some money to tide us over, just a loan of course, until things are sorted out. The problem is, we are undercover and can't use our name on anything including a bank account. The men who abducted us have already hacked into our account; they have all our details. We have used another account in Ethan's name, a credit card, but when we came home the airline bookings were made by the police and we can't be seen to be operating any accounts, since we are supposed to be dead."

"Oh dear, I see. Well what about I open another account in my name and give you the details so you can operate it?"

"Well, that sounds possible. I'll run it past Detective Pekalski when I see him. The cops have been great. It wouldn't have surprised me if they hadn't taken us seriously, but they did, right from the start, and they have really looked after us."

"Good, good, nice to hear something positive about the constabulary for a change. Do you think a private investigator would be called for here?"

"I really don't know Uncle Rod. I believe there is always a shortage of staff, but I will mention it to Detective Pekalski when I see him this afternoon."

"Good, good. How are you in yourself? You are so lucky to be alive. What a monstrous experience. Would you be able to come and live with me here in Sydney for a while?"

"What a lovely offer, Uncle, and I don't know. I'll get back to you on that also, if I may?"

They chatted on a few more minutes. Margaret felt exhausted when she finished and went to lie on the bed. Ethan followed her in and she told him about her uncle's response. They both wept tears of joy for the generosity extended to them.

Ethan's voice choked with emotion. "We are so lucky," he said.

"Yes, we are. We certainly are." She turned over and closed her eyes. It was time for Margaret to let her guard down; the whole thing was taking its toll. The tears rolled down her cheeks.

Chapter Twenty-Four

On a crisp, sunny Monday morning, the round-Australia travellers pulled away from their luxury stopover in Perth. The mood was buoyant.

James, the driver, cleared his throat and delivered the obligatory spiel about the day's activities.

"We've a fair haul today, ladies and gents. We should hit Kalgoorlie just in time for a late afternoon glass of lemonade."

"Bugger the lemonade, mate!" someone yelled from the back of the coach.

Laughter and convivial chatter followed, with one-upmanship the order of the day, as individuals and little cliques vied to regale the others with accounts of the wonderful times they had at their chosen attractions.

"Say goodbye to the City of Lights, folks," said James, as they left the city limits. "Full steam ahead to Kalgoorlie."

Twenty-five minutes out from Coolgardie, light rain started to fall. By the time the bus reached Coolgardie, the rain fell heavily. James switched his wipers to high-speed. The travellers watched from their windows, as water filled the drains along the sides of the road. James pulled back his speed to compensate for the deteriorating conditions. A few of the group became concerned about the extreme driving conditions and the chatter subsided. Gradually, everyone settled down, and the conversation hushed as they mentally drove with James. A few looked out of their windows and simply trusted that the driver was extremely competent and used to such conditions.

"Seems like we may have a slow trip the last few k's into Kalgoorlie," announced James, over the PA system. "Looks like the heavens are going to open up ahead."

A couple of minutes later, the downpour became torrential. James wondered how far ahead he might find a reasonable place to pull over. The gravel shoulders were wide, but in this weather, they would be treacherous. He slowed the vehicle as much as he dared but could not stop, as he feared any driver behind him might not see the coach in the atrocious conditions, even with the hazard and taillights activated. The responsibility for all these people weighed heavily on him, and he was beginning to wonder whether to make another announcement.

James saw it seconds before they hit. A torrent of muddy, debris-laden water flooded across a dip in the road, barely twenty metres ahead. A huge tree trunk, tumbled along by the force of the water, rolled from left to right into his path. James pulled on the steering wheel in an effort to avoid it, but the front wheels ploughed into the deluge and aquaplaned. James felt the loss of traction as the steering wheel spun, light as a feather, in his hands. He had no control. The vehicle started to slide sideways onto the wrong side of the road. James felt the weight come back in the steering wheel and he fought to bring the vehicle back under control. *Thank God*, he thought, *that was close*.

His relief was short lived. The rear wheels of the bus hit the same wall of water and slewed violently to the right, into a metre deep washout in the road shoulder. The body bucked and the bus shuddered, as the log slammed into its side at the same time. The log acted like a battering ram, powered by the pressure of the water behind it, and the weight of its irresistible force triumphed. The bus teetered for a moment, and then started to roll over, ever so slowly, as the heavy vehicle's momentum still carried it forward. The driver's side of the bus took the full brunt of the impact, as the length of the bus scraped along the rocky sides of the high-sided drainage channel. Metal and glass screeched and cracked and mud and gravel and rocks poured in through the breaches in the bodywork. As the bus slowed and slithered on its side, the offside wheel rode up a small rocky outcrop. The impact jerked the vehicle upright. It slid a few more metres, before it came to rest with its wheels straddling the muddy ochre stream raging under it. But for the rev limiter, the engine would have blown itself to bits. It screamed in protest, the throttle jammed to the floor by a bloodied boot. Its wheels spun uselessly in the mire. The spray flew out of the wheel wells for metres, as if flung from a centrifuge. Seconds passed and time seemed to stand still for the occupants. Unrestrained luggage fell haphazardly, the noise of the diesel engine continued and screams rent the air.

James reached for his seat belt and tried to release the clip. That was when he realised his legs were trapped. He heard the screaming and banging and searched for his C.B. radio with his left hand, but it was beyond his reach. He fumbled in his pocket for his mobile phone, grabbed it with two hands, lifted it to his face, and dialled 000. He tried to look around to see what the situation was behind him but could only get a glimpse of people and things falling in a blur of confusion.

"Which service do you require – Police, Fire or Ambulance?"

"Police and Ambulance, maybe Fire."

"What is your emergency?"

"A crash! A bus crash with twenty people. I'm the driver and my legs are trapped."

"What is your location?"

"About ten k's west of Kalgoorlie – travelling east."

"Are there any other casualties?"

"I ... I can't see ... but there's a lot of screaming and moaning."

Within a couple of minutes, the emergency vehicles were dispatched and on their way to the site of the accident.

"Help me, please, help me." James tried to turn his head to see the extent of the damage and injuries behind him, but he could not twist that far.

"It's alright, we'll get you out, mate," said Peter, as he scrambled up the aisle to the driver's cabin and assessed James's situation.

"I can't move my legs," James said. "But how are you? Are you injured?"

"Nah. Well, nothing to speak of. Couple of scratches, that's all. Now, let's have a look here."

"Before you do anything, switch the engine off, will you. I can't reach – there, see, behind the wiper stalk."

Peter turned the key. A shudder shook the vehicle as the engine died down. He gave his attention to James's jammed legs. It was difficult for him to see. The driver's cabin was like a capsule, and, at the best of times, was a snug fit for most drivers. A deformation such as it suffered now, turned the space into a prison.

Peter put his hand on James's shoulder, and said, with as much reassurance as he could muster, "As you can see, James, the steering wheel has your thighs pinned, but it doesn't look as if there's all that much pressure on them. The console is a problem. Your lower legs are hidden by it, and I can't get my hand in there to check."

"Can I help?"

Peter looked up. He had not realised Martin was at his elbow.

"Oh yeah, Marty. Good man."

Peter turned back to James and said, "James, I assume the steering column has height and reach adjustment?"

"Yes. I did try to move it but I couldn't quite reach it. My arm's pinned. It's a black lever on the right hand side of the column – about half way down – it pulls up to allow the adjustment."

"Okay, mate, we'll see what we can do."

Peter looked up at Martin and said, "I'll try to reach it. If I do, can you pull the wheel up?"

"Gotcha."

Peter leaned across James's chest and felt for an opening in the tangle of materials. He found a small gap and worked his fingers along the side of the steering column. He felt the indentation holding the folded handle. He grasped the rubber grip on the end of the lever and pulled. It did not budge. He tried again, but to no avail.

"Bugger," he said, 'the column must be bent. I can't shift it."

"See if you can pull the console away," said James. "It's only a moulded plastic casing. There's probably nothing substantial internally, mostly wires for the electronic stuff and radios inside, I'd reckon."

Try as they might, the console proved immovable to Peter and Martin. It was distorted by the intrusion of the dash. It, and the driver's footwell, was stove in by the impact of the bus's front offside with the rocky protrusion on the embankment. It was a no go. No human hands would shift that twisted mess of plastic and metal.

"Can you reach your seat adjustment lever," Peter asked James. "You may be able to lower the squab,"

"No, the bodywork has been pushed in, hard up against the side of the seat. I can't get my hand down."

"Bugger. Well look, we rang the emergency services," said Peter, "and I think a few other people did too. I think you may have to bide your time, James, until they can cut you out of here. I'm sorry, mate. It looks like they'll need the Jaws of Life to cut this stuff away. How is it, anyway? Is it painful?"

"As a matter of fact, it's not, and that's what worries me. I can't feel a bloody thing. Maybe that's a good thing - for now. Guess I don't have a choice about waiting, eh. What about you two? You seem okay."

"Yes, a lot better than some," Marty said.

"What's happening back there, anyway?" asked James.

"Some, like us, seem relatively unscathed. Maybe it's because we had our seat belts on. I know a few have been travelling without them fastened – said it was too restricting on a long trip. There are some, though, who don't look too good. The other walking wounded are doing what they can for them."

"Yeah, well, we can't do much else for you now, mate," said Martin. "We'll leave you be and see what we can do back there. Is that okay?"

"No wuckin' furries, mate." James's sense of humour was still intact. "By the way, I phoned 000 as well. Let everyone know we're only about ten clicks out of Kalgoorlie, so the emergency services shouldn't be long. Oh, and there's a small first-aid kit in a compartment on your side of the console – may be of some help."

Peter took the kit and he and Martin started to make their way back up the bus. Each row was checked. Some of the passengers had released their seatbelts, others sat dazed and needed assistance.

Hank sat beside Helga den Ronden and put his arm around her shoulders. He tried to console her. He wanted to find out just how badly she was injured, if at all. She shook and sobbed uncontrollably. *Bloody woman*, he thought, *'asn't stopped whingein' since we left Brisbane.* As soon as he had thought that about Helga, Hank regretted it. She had been a pain in the arse for the whole trip, he knew, and he was aware he was not alone in that assessment, but now, as he thought about the situation they were in, Hank realised Helga was probably in shock. He looked around and saw a throw rug hanging from an overhead locker, which had sprung open in the impact. He reached for it and spread it over Helga's shoulders and upper body.

"How is she?" Peter was stumbling up the aisle, trying to get a firm foothold among the debris scattered up the walkway.

"She's okay, probably in shock," Hank replied. "Maybe we should get some a these people outside."

"No, no. We have to do this better. You can't just put them out in the rain. Don't send anyone out until we fix up what we can here." He turned around to see Martin behind him. The two men began to evaluate who was in the most acute need.

"You look up there," said Peter, and he then turned his attention in the other direction. He could see Rachael and Freya, huddled together, waiting with their seat belts in place.

"Are you girls alright?"

Freya put her hand up. "We're fine, help the others and tell me if there's something you want us to do."

Peter next saw Joy Rayne, Penny, and Lottie. They were helping each other get free and seemed to be unharmed.

In the other direction, Martin was helping to free a couple of the passengers who were not from Keeala Resort. They seemed to have injuries but it was hard for him to tell what. As he asked one of the women if she was injured, he heard Harold scream. He saw him lift Robert's head and call out to his partner, "Robert, look at me, open your eyes."

Martin made his way to the desperate man and nudged him aside. He took Robert's hand and felt for a pulse.

"He's alive, unconscious. I'll check for wounds." Martin ran his hands gently over Robert's torso and legs.

Harold put his hand on the back of Robert's head to support him. He found it covered with blood.

"It's here, his head, oh God, no. Robert, open your eyes." Harold placed his mouth close to Robert's ear and spoke quietly and pleadingly, but the man did not move.

"He's breathing. May be concussion; you stay with him Robert. I'm going to help get the rest of these people."

They all heard the sirens, long before the emergency services vehicles came into view. Cheers erupted as the passengers realised professional help was almost there. A couple of minutes later, a cavalcade of vehicles arrived, all coming to their rescue. The rain stopped.

******

Ambulances, police vehicles, and rescue unit trucks lined the roadside. A fire truck was the last to arrive, but only a minute or so after the others. The rescue squad vehicle spewed out its personnel and a roadblock was set up. Ambulance men and women ran to the bus. Within minutes, the emergency service teams had split into small groups, each carrying out their allotted tasks. A senior ambulance officer triaged the injured and supervised the orderly evacuation to the officers waiting outside with the trolleys. Two rescue squad members cut through the seat behind the driver's module. The occupant squeezed up against the panel that formed the rear of James's capsule, unable to free himself from the twisted seat. Two other men from the rescue squad cut and pulled at the console which trapped James, making space to accommodate the hydraulic ram with which they would lever the deformed panel which trapped James's legs. Hank, Peter, Martin and Jimmy O'Brien climbed out of the bus and lined up to help, but were quickly ushered to the sideline.

A man in a uniform directed most of the procedure and the unhurt passengers were quickly separated from the injured. Those with obvious or suspected injuries, but able to be moved, were taken outside and put under the protection of a field hospital tent. They were assessed quickly and efficiently, and those worst injured were loaded into the ambulances.

Some, including James, the driver, remained trapped in their seats. Rescue squad personnel struggled to operate cutting equipment in the confined space of the bus interior. Outside, another group had the Jaws of Life cutting into the A pillar of the bus.

One team worked on the driver while another stabilised Robert and transferred him to a trolley waiting outside the bus. Two other teams worked on trapped passengers and carried those who could not walk, to the waiting trolleys.

"We've got another one back here," said a paramedic, as she moved from seat to seat searching for anyone else. "No, it's two," she said, as she bent to reach between the seats and found a man and a woman piled on top of each other.

It was Ralph and Salina.

The waiting passengers identified them when they were carried from the bus. Salina was not a resident at Keeala Resort and had come on the trip alone. Ralph was a quiet, gentle man. He had many friends among the music group at the resort. They were both dead. The news spread instantly. Cries and sobs rose above the hubbub of the rescue activities.

Huddled in groups, shoulders draped with blankets, those with none, or minor injuries, waited patiently as a commuter bus made its way through the scattered tangle of rescue vehicles. The driver manoeuvred, forward – back – forward – back, across the width of the road, careful not to place the rear wheels on the slippery, muddy edges of the road. He faced the bus the way he had come, toward Kalgoorlie. The able bodied climbed aboard. Eight minutes later, they arrived at the Emergency Department of Kalgoorlie Health Campus for a more thorough medical examination.

A long afternoon and night followed. Some passengers were discharged soon after arrival, and were taken to accommodation for the night. Others remained under observation overnight. A few would spend longer, specialist treatment required for their injuries.

Then police interviewed each passenger and even James, who was in acute care. By that next afternoon, most of the people involved in the accident were free to go home. The bus company offered them a new bus to transport them back to Brisbane, but without exception, they all decided to either fly home, or go by train.

Harold stayed at Robert's bedside, as he lay unconscious in acute care. Next to him was the bus driver. He had gone to surgery immediately they had assessed his injuries. The surgeon had been standing by, ready to operate. He repaired James's deep wounds and saved both his legs.

The remaining passengers made their bookings to go home. Penny, Lottie and Helga flew out the Wednesday morning. The rest went by train on Wednesday afternoon. They wanted time to sit and mourn before they arrived home to face their friends. It would be a long trip, but it would give them time to think about the tragic circumstances of the accident, and the sometimes ephemeral nature of man's existence.

Chapter Twenty-Five

Russell left. He collected his few personal belongings, said 'ooroo' to brother and sister, and left Blacktown as if it was on fire. He could not get away fast enough. Patrick had been as good as his word and found him a Toyota Rav 4 with low kilometres, in excellent condition, and at the right price.

"You're spoilt for choice in Sydney," said Russell. With a smile at Patrick, he drove away in his new vehicle.

Bloody glad to see the back of you, Patrick thought, as he walked back into the house. *Now we can make some plans.*

Judy watched TV with glazed eyes, her feet up on the coffee table.

Patrick leaned over and turned off the TV, which brought a shout from Judy as she grabbed the remote control. He immediately snatched it back.

"Who died and made you the boss, eh?" she said

"We have to talk."

"When I'm good and ready." She stood up and faced him.

"Now, Judy! While I provide the money, I'm in charge. It's that simple."

"Well what if I don't agree with where the money came from? I wasn't consulted."

"Don't friggin' start that again. You're eating the food that was financed by my hard work."

"Bloody hell, what do you want to talk about?"

"I've decided to invest in a restaurant in Brisbane."

"What happened to real estate?"

"Too slow, so I emailed an old buddy last night and he's pretty anxious to take me on as a partner."

"Out of money is he?"

"He's actually doing very well, but any business can be enhanced by a cash injection. We're good mates - sort of doing each other a favour."

"So his business is doing so well that a tiny $300,000 will make a difference. Why can't he borrow some money?"

"He's given me a chance to make some money without waiting until I'm fuckin' sixty – and why all the bloody questions?"

"If you don't know by now that you get nothing for nothing, then you are more stupid than I thought."

Patrick raised his arm and balled his fist.

"Go ahead. If you cared about me, we wouldn't be here now."

He grabbed her by the shoulders and shook her until she felt her head would fall off. When he let his sister go, she flopped on to the lounge and cried.

"Oh, for shit sake, shut up will you, or I'll give you something to really cry about." Patrick walked out of the room and slammed the back door.

******

A few of the residents of Keeala Resort noticed Pekalski's car coming and going and wondered what was up now.

"We don't have the manpower at the moment to stake out this place, so we're going to have to play it by ear." The detective spoke to Matthew when they met up in the manager's office. It was the morning of the Watersen's homecoming. "Let's hope Kevvy boy comes back for his stuff and is spotted by you, or one of the residents. I don't want to tell anyone what's going on. It'll only start the rumour mill and we've had enough of that."

"Yeah, I have a feeling Jim will be none too happy either."

"I've put the drugs and money away as evidence and replaced the tin in the shed. He may have moved on, but I think it unlikely that he would want to leave anything of value behind. We did forensics and he is a match. He has a record. He's a minor drug runner and operator, but he's only good to us if he leads us further up the chain. As you know, his old

229

source has dried up, with all the big fellas in gaol. As for him, we normally would not bother. I'd like to know though, if he's found another supplier. The problem here is we suspect he may be a danger to the woman living in Unit 27, and we still think he was the one that could easily have killed me when I was tripped in the garden. If we can get extra men, we'll stake the unit out, but in the meantime the management will have to keep their eyes peeled."

"Did you hear about the bus crash in Western Australia yesterday?" Matt asked.

"I did, two dead, one from here, and several staying behind with injuries. You'll have your hands full when they return."

"Yes, and three ladies will be back today. The sisters, Penny and Lottie, and everyone's friend, Helga den Ronden. I'm sure it will be an upsetting homecoming for Di and Jim."

The phone rang and Matthew picked up. "Oh, hi, Di."

"Matt, how come you're manning the phone?"

"Long story – I'll explain when you get in."

An hour later, the managers drove in and got out at the residence. They put their bags into the lounge and marvelled at the lovely clean house. Fresh flowers brought a cheery touch to several rooms.

"What a kind thought. I may have misjudged our relief manager. She's done well, hasn't she?" Di said, as she looked at her husband.

"Yes, I'm surprised, that's for sure."

"Let's go over and see what Matt is doing here anyway." Di led the way down the path to the community centre and office.

"Well, well, well – Detective Pekalski," said Di. Her face lit up as she opened the office door. "What a lovely surprise. To what do we owe the pleasure of your company on this seemingly ordinary day?"

"Just came to wish you both a happy homecoming and watch your reaction when Matthew gives you all the latest news. I also have some surprises in store, but let's all sit down with some coffee before we get into that."

Jim and Di looked at one another with a quizzical expression. They pulled up a couple of chairs, and waited while Matthew went to get some freshly brewed coffee from the machine in the community centre.

Matthew returned with the mugs on a tray, and set it down on the desk. Each took a mug and listened as Matthew started with, "So, your story first. Why did you leave the bus and where did you go?"

Jim realised he wasn't going to get any answers until he told them his story first, so he explained about Lorna McDonald's illness and death and how he decided it would be best if he took Di on a holiday, away from any obligation to be helpful or useful to others.

"So you sound like you had a really good time and it was the right decision."

"Absolutely," said Di. "I'm going to let him choose all our holidays from now on." She squeezed her husband's hand and they both smiled.

"But where's Sonja? I thought she'd be here now?" said Di.

"The short answer to that is she wasn't very good at her job and she was sacked by the management in Adelaide. That's why I'm here now. I'm filling in until you get settled again. I'll tell you more about her later. I've taken the liberty of having your place professionally cleaned. Hope you approve?"

"Yes, the place looks lovely, thank you. And the flowers?" asked Di.

"Ah, just to welcome you home." Matthew continued, "But on to more serious things. I wonder if you've heard any news since you docked this morning."

"No, been travelling all day. Why?"

"There was an accident on the highway from Perth to Kalgoorlie, day before yesterday. The Keeala Resort mob was involved."

Jim and Di sat with mouths agape, waiting for more.

"Their bus left the road in very bad weather conditions. The majority of the passengers are okay, but there were two deaths, one of ours and one from outside the resort. A couple of ours have serious injuries. They're in acute care at the Kalgoorlie Hospital."

"Oh, my God." Di's hand flew to her mouth. "It could have been us!"

Jim shook his head in disbelief.

"Who died?" he asked.

"Ralph Johnston. The other was a woman not from here. Her name was Salina something."

"Ralph – shit – yeah – quiet sort of a bloke, but solid, dependable, got on well with everybody on the trip," said Jim. "Next of kin been notified, do you know?"

"Yep, spoke to his son this morning. He's organising the return of the body; said he'll get up from Sydney in the next couple of days to sort things out here."

"I remember Salina, a really nice lady," Di said. "And who was injured?"

"We'll get a report on that later today, but one person was Robert Wieland."

Di and Jim gasped in unison.

"Harold rang yesterday and said Robert was still unconscious, but they were hopeful he'd make a good recovery. Harold said he will ring again today and speak to you."

Di and Jim looked at one another. "I should have been there. It was my idea to go, and then I wasn't even there to help in the emergency," said Di.

Jim shook his head, "No, Di, don't even think that."

"Di, you cannot possibly take any responsibility for that situation," Pekalski said.

The others looked at her, and she nodded, just so they would all look away.

"It's hard to take this in, but we will, and hopefully everyone will recover." Jim began to be optimistic.

The phone rang and broke the silence.

Matthew answered, listened and then said, "Yes, they're home, but I wonder could they ring you in about an hour? ... Fine, bye." He scratched a phone number on a note pad and pushed it across to Jim. "It was Harold. He said Robert is conscious and looks like he's going to be alright. You can ring him when you have a minute. Don't worry, guys, I'm going to hang around here for a couple of weeks yet. Give you time to get a handle on all this. It's sanctioned by head office."

A few moments of silence ensued before Detective Inspector Pekalski stood up and walked to the window.

"This brings us to why I'm here. I know you have enough to burden you right now, but there is more. You remember Kevin, the ex-gardener?" The detective paused, but did not really expect a response. "Matthew here found why the fellow was hanging around from time to time. He had drugs and cash stashed in the shed in the backyard of Unit 27. Now, we hope to catch him if he should come back to collect his stuff. You'll have to keep your eyes open as we simply don't have the manpower at the moment, to stake this place out for a small time crim like him, and he may never come back anyway. But, if things change downtown, we will try to do more in that direction."

"I'll have a word to the neighbours around 27," said Jim. "Get them to keep their eyes open."

"No, look, I'd rather keep it between the four of us, if you don't mind, Jim. I don't want any loose talk getting back to him and frightening him off." Pekalski looked at his watch. "Ah, I'd better get going," he said, "but before I do, could you and Di slip out to the car. There's something I want to check with you. I'll catch you later, Matt."

Jim gave Di a quizzical shrug of his shoulders as they followed Pekalski out to his car.

Pekalski opened the boot of the vehicle and he took out a briefcase. He opened the lid, pulled a piece of paper from an envelope, and pretended to examine it. He looked back at the office window and could see Matthew typing on his computer keyboard.

He turned back to the couple and said, "Look, there's something I have to tell you. I didn't want to speak in front of Matt about it, hence the subterfuge. Now, I want your word that what I'm about to tell you stays strictly between the three of us. Do you agree?"

"Absolutely, Frank," said Jim.

"Do you remember when you were on the trip and you were at Coober Pedy?

"Sure," Di answered. They nodded and looked at their friend, and wondered what they would hear next.

He told them the whole story of Margaret and Ethan's abduction, their escape and return home. He finished by saying, "So now, they're in a safe house close by, and we are going to catch the culprits."

Jim and Di were stunned. They did not say a word, just stood and tried to digest the indigestible.

Pekalski went on, "Our main concern, obviously, is finding the guys who tried to kill Ethan and Margaret Dougherty. We also want to recover the money. We may need your cooperation in this case as well."

Still the Watersens said nothing. They stood shaking their heads in silent disbelief. The only sounds were the children's voices at play in the primary school down the road, and the hum from the motorway.

Jim finally looked at Frank and nodded. "I find that story hard to believe," he said, "but of course we'll help in any way we can."

"Yes, yes," Di said. "Oh, poor Margaret; poor Ethan. What an awful experience. And they got out! They are both so brave. So brave."

"But what can we do, Frank?" Jim asked.

"Look, both the Doughertys thought there was something familiar about one of the men. They couldn't quite put their finger on it, but it may be someone they've come into contact with in some way. It could be someone they've done business with, perhaps – maybe someone in a bank, who knows, but it may be someone who is familiar with their lifestyle and their financial situation. The circumstances make it too coincidental for it to be a random act. There was planning and personal knowledge behind this. What I'd like you to do is keep an eye out for any activity concerning the Doughertys – phone calls, visitors, anything at all that crops up concerning them. Remember, these guys think Ethan and Margaret are dead at the bottom of the mineshaft. We have to keep it that way, so mum's the word, eh?"

Chapter Twenty-Six

When the remaining travellers from the bus crash boarded the train, it was with heavy hearts, but as the Indian Pacific rolled across the country, the sombre mood dissipated with each click of the wheels. It was a different experience from the bus travel of course, but in many ways more relaxing, and certainly it felt safer.

The travellers started to put the thoughts of the crash behind them as they clocked up the kilometres and swayed in their seats to the momentum of the train. Rachael, Freya and Joy started playing scrabble to pass the time and Jimmy, Marty, Peter and Hank started a card game. It kept them increasingly engrossed as the day disappeared in a silver ribbon behind them. As the wheels clacked inexorably eastward, all overt discussion of the accident and its aftermath gave way to introspection, as most of the group processed his or her trauma internally. Each took a different path to the resolution of the anguish inflicted upon them by the accident. A small number continued to sit silently, as they had since the event. Their release from the torment would come later.

A sombre homecoming awaited Penny and Lottie. They were dropped outside their house in Keeala Resort, and Liela, the sisters' next-door neighbour, saw the taxi drive away. "I'm so sorry to hear about the accident and Ralph not coming home. How are you?" she said, as she went to them and hugged each in turn.

"We're fine, thanks," said Penny. "It's good to see you Liela. When we've had a little time to have a shower, I'll put the kettle on. Please come and have a cup of tea with us. There's so much we'd like to talk about and at the same time so much we don't want to talk about. However, we are home now and that's a great relief."

"Why don't you both come to my place when you're ready and I'll take care of afternoon tea? I'm sure you both must be exhausted after your terrible ordeal."

Leila returned to her own garden and picked a small bunch of flowers and took them inside to the little crystal vase on the dining room table. She set out her best tea set and lifted down a fruitcake from the pantry. The radio, tuned to ABC Classic FM, played softly in the background. A sense of comfort and tranquillity permeated her little house.

******

I'm havin' trouble digestin' this," Tony, the sergeant at Coober Pedy police station, said to DI Frank Pekalski. "Are you tellin' me that the suspected abductors are actually the foster son and foster daughter of the victims?"

238

"Yes, we have a positive match here with the prints you got from the mine and the holiday park. I believe the unit they used had been cleaned, but not the chairs outside on the veranda, and no one else had used the unit, so that's a good result. Your guys did well, Tony."

"Yeah, and they did even better, mate. Did ya get that information about the explosive? They identified it as an old, army issue, fragment grenade."

"Yep, our boys jumped straight on it. People joke about the Army keeping documents in triplicate, but thank God they do. Our boys were able to get them to trawl through their records. They ran a check and we came up trumps. The two male suspects are ex-Army reservists and would have had access to the munitions, but you've probably already seen that information." Pekalski was speaking to Tony on a long distance call. They were working in collaboration, following Margaret and Ethan's return to Queensland.

"Yeah, jumped right on that. We 'ave a few sightin's and a witness, the caravan park manager, willin' to swear 'e recognised both Judy and Patrick Robilliard from the shots we showed 'im. 'E's a bit vague on the other bloke, but 'e thought it was your Russell Mills when we showed 'im the army mug shot. The park guy says the three of 'em checked into the park at Coober Pedy the day before the couple were grabbed, and they checked out the day of the explosion. He remembers 'em particularly 'cause it's unusual for two blokes and a sheila to book in together."

"And the other sightings?" asked Frank.

"The service station attendant, 'e gave us a description of the vehicle. Apparently, the two blokes had an altercation over the fuel bill when they were there, and the servo guy described them and the car. It was a Toyota Prado, and 'e said there was a female waitin' in the car."

"Thanks, Tony, this is coming together nicely. So, as far as we know, they drove out of town the day of the explosion. We have no idea which route they took?"

"Yeah, south. Well, the servo guy thinks so."

"That's a good start. Thanks mate. We'll be in touch, and the Doughertys have been singing your praises, by the way."

"Really? Well that's a nice bloody change, ain't it, eh?"

Pekalski chuckled and finished the call.

Tony wore a self-satisfied grin, but then became serious as he realised he must send his friend Hank an email. Tony had heard about the bus crash, everyone had.

******

Margaret and Ethan agreed to stay in Brisbane safe house. They arranged for Di to collect a few things from their house in Keeala Resort. As far as the other residents knew, they were still with friends in Adelaide, so no one wondered about the empty house.

The couple settled into their new, temporary home. They both took Tony at his word and sat down daily to write about their abduction. There was no thought that their story would make money. It was simply a means to exorcise the demons that roamed Margaret's dreams at night, and give Ethan an outlet for his anger and frustration. They did not compare narratives, but checked facts and confirmed dates from time to time.

For now, it was a waiting game. They relied upon Detective Inspector Frank Pekalski to keep them informed of events in the investigation. He had delayed telling the Doughertys the name of their abductors, as he had been concerned that another shock of that magnitude would be more than they could take. Ultimately, he had no choice. He visited them in their hideout and told them everything he knew so far.

"So, we think we know who is responsible for the crime," said Pekalski. "We have motive, opportunity, and some damming facts as far as identification by witnesses and forensic evidence is concerned. We now have to find them. I think they've been pretty careless as far as leaving a trail is concerned, but of course they never expected you to leave that mine, so they really overlooked a lot of details."

After a long silence, Margaret looked down at her hands.

"Thank you, Frank. It isn't the surprise it could have been to me. I had a feeling all along that one of the men was familiar to me, but I just couldn't place him. In hindsight, I feel so stupid. I still can't believe Patrick and Judy would do such a shocking thing to anyone, especially to us. I feel responsible for them, and I know that's unrealistic, but they spent years in my care and now they are murderers, as far as they know." Tears slipped down Margaret's cheeks and she pushed them away with the back of her hand.

Frank put his hand on Margaret's shoulder and said, "I believe the damage was done long before you ever met them.

If you researched the criminals locked up in gaol, you would find that most of them had a poor start in life. But Patrick and Judith are old enough to take responsibility for their own decisions now, and they will have to do just that."

Margaret knew the detective was right, but the sadness of the situation threatened to overwhelm her. There had been changes in Margaret since the abduction and she began to doubt whether she would ever get back to being the joyful, loving woman Ethan married.

******

Matthew sat in the office with Di and Jim. Neither manager had slept well, but they were anxious to come to grips with all the unfinished business in the resort.

"Sonja has not been in contact with the head office since she left. Of course, there may be more recriminations coming from the family of Elaine Steinberg, but we can only hope not," said Matthew.

"How's she going? I'll go and see her today." Di looked anxious.

Matthew said, "You can tell me when you get back. Last I heard she had improved, but that would be expected once she survived the stroke. Long term is the problem. How has all this affected her ability to live anything like a normal life again?"

Di thought for a moment, before she continued, "You know, even if she had instantaneous assistance there is a possibility her brain damage would be irreparable. There's no reason to believe it was all Sonja's fault. She would only have been able to ring the ambulance anyway, and I gather her neighbour Greta did that as soon as the alarm wasn't answered."

"This is true," Matthew replied, "and I guess it depends on the son and how far he wants to take it. In the meantime, I suspect Sonja has flown the coop anyway. She was hopeless, though.

"Now, what about Kevin?" Jim asked Matthew.

"Well, he hasn't been seen for a month or more, but he has left a few of his tools of trade behind, although well hidden. I want to catch the bugger and so does Pekalski. I have issues with him and the detective believes he was the one who nearly killed him on the path. I suspect he has something going on, something illegal. That guy couldn't lie straight in bed. I think now that you're back I'll take the opportunity to check out some of his old haunts. He most likely doesn't know I'm around and won't be expecting to see me, so I'll have the advantage."

"Hmmm," said Jim, "and what about this pair of murderers now."

"Well I don't know too much, but I'll tell you what I do. Pekalski will have to buy a house here soon if he spends any more time hanging around. He's the one with the whole story of course, and it's on going. They don't expect the murdering bastards, sorry Di, to come back here, but they don't know we're on to them, so who knows?"

The room was quiet while everyone mulled over the possibilities. The clatter of crockery came from the servery and there were a couple of men already playing pool at the end of the big room. "Well, Matt, you'd better bring us up to date on everybody else. Di is going to arrange a memorial service for the residents to honour Lorna McDonald and Ralph Johnston, as soon as she's contacted the relatives. We should take a look at the books now, and how are sales going? Did we have a response from council about that faulty drain?"

"Whoa, mate, give us a break, what was the first question?" They both laughed and Jim started over.

Chapter Twenty-Seven

When Patrick returned later that night, he threw himself down on the lounge and went to sleep. The fact that he had had too much to drink may have had something to do with it. He woke with a rotten taste in his mouth and a headache, sometime the next morning. He looked around for a clock and realised they did not have one. He squinted at his wristwatch. *Eleven fifteen. Shit, that time already. Jude, where are you?* He got up, made his way to the bedroom, and pushed the door open. Empty. He called her again. No reply. He went from room to room and realised he was completely alone in the house. Patrick went to the front door and looked out. Their car stood the driveway. *So, she hasn't driven somewhere this morning. Must have gone for a walk. She had been talking about starting to get fit, do exercise, must have started today.* Patrick went to the kitchen.

He made coffee and toast, brought it back to the lounge room, and turned the television on.

He woke with a start. He realised he must have fallen back to sleep on the lounge. The glow of the television set lit the room and Patrick could see evening had fallen. Patrick clicked the TV off with the remote. He could not see any lights in the house. He jumped up and ran to the bedroom again, but still no Judy. He called her name as he once again searched the house. There was no response. He knew there was something very wrong. She always let him know where she was, and she had never gone off before.

He turned on the lights and looked around for a note. He could see none. He went into the bathroom to see if there was anything missing. Her toiletries were not there. He ran into the bedroom and checked the wardrobe. All her clothes and shoes were gone. He was furious. He clenched his fists and gritted his teeth. He kicked the wall and hurt his toe. "Bloody hell, what are you doing to me now, girl?" he shouted.

Think, think. He rapped himself on the head with his fist and tried to imagine where his sister could have gone. Patrick walked up and down the hallway, racking his brains, but he had no idea where to start.

Over the last five years, the two had done everything together. They knew each other's mates and they met the same people; most of their jobs had been together. They spent harvest seasons picking fruit; they worked at gardening together and waiting on tables at conventions and functions. They did pet minding and even house sitting. There were times when one got a job and the other stayed at home, but they were always so close, so close.

Patrick sat on the lounge with his head in his hands. *Oh don't do this to me baby, please don't do this to me. I've done everything for you; I've even murdered two people for you. Don't leave me now. Please.* He felt as though his heart was bleeding. He had a pain in the chest as he sobbed and sobbed.

Silence hung in the room. Half an hour had passed. The feeling of loneliness was complete; all reason to go on living had evaporated. Patrick lay spreadeagled on the lounge and depression descended on him like a cloak. He began to see that his behaviour toward the old couple in the mine was abhorrent. He knew there was no way for him to change anything he had done. This was the first time he had really thought about Margaret and her husband since he had left Coober Pedy, and for just a moment, he put himself in their place.

No, he shook his head. *How did I come to this? I should just go and confess, get it over with. But then what? Would it bring the old people back? No, and would it help anyone? No!*

Patrick sat as night descended. He knew there was nothing he could do to atone for his actions. His mind went numb, he had no sense of self-awareness, not even to see himself thinking or crying or feeling. His depression was total. He sank into it, and in the process he annihilated the pain.

******

247

Judy sat in a coffee shop in the city of Parramatta, west of Sydney, trying to pull herself together. When she had argued with her brother the previous day, she sensed that everything in their relationship was suddenly changing. She also knew that this day had been coming for some time. That realisation gave her the impetus to act. She was grateful to her brother for keeping her out of the physical abduction and murder of her stepmother and stepfather, but was distressed that she had not had the opportunity to prevent Patrick carrying out such a shocking crime. So much of their behaviour had been a joke before. They had made fun of other people's misery, and conned or stolen whenever the chance came their way. They had cared about nothing, no one; their responsibility was to one another only, and other people or their property meant nothing to them. The end always justified the means. Not anymore.

Why has it taken me so long to grow up? Judy wondered, as she watched the passing parade out on the footpath. She wondered what her brother was thinking and doing right now.

Judy had never made any plans for a situation like the one she was in now. She had never thought she would leave Patrick. Now it was done and she wanted to do it well. She would never think about going back to him or even make contact with him. She knew she would not be able to resist his pleas or face his anger. She knew she had to be decisive and act quickly.

The first thing was more money. She didn't want 'blood money', but she knew she could withdraw about another thousand before dipping into the money Patrick and Russell had so recently stolen from her stepmother's bank account. Next, she would have to get a job, a place to live and she would eventually need a vehicle.

Judy found a bank and withdrew exactly one thousand dollars. She hoped Patrick would not be tracking her withdrawals yet; she needed time to build a base for herself. She knew it was very expensive to live in some parts of Sydney, so she had to stay away from those. She could not afford to spend her little reserve on travel so she would be staying put.

A suitcase, a backpack, and a shoulder bag would be too much to drag around all day and Judy, dressed in jeans, a long sleeve tee shirt and a jacket, realised it was much colder here than where she had been in the past few months. Winter in Western Sydney can be very cold. Accommodation was her first priority. *A backpacker's hostel would be good,* she thought. She and her brother had spent enough time on the road to not be intimidated by homelessness, but Judy did not want the insecurity of that for herself anymore; this time she wanted to do things right.

"Excuse me, can you please tell me where I can find a backpacker's hostel?" she queried a cab driver at a cabstand. When he said there was a place seven or eight minutes away, she asked him to take her there. On the way, she had him stop so she could buy a paper with the classifieds.

"You looking for a job love?" the cabbie questioned

"Yes, you want me to relief drive for you?"

He laughed, "If only it was that simple. I'm serious, what're you looking for?"

"Anything really; I've just moved down from Queensland. My mum died and I have to get a job. I'm hoping to go to university when I get some money behind me, but in the meantime, I've got to make a living and pay off my mum's funeral expenses."

"Well, that's the saddest story I've heard all day. Good on you, love, there ain't many young ones around these days that take their responsibility so seriously. Maybe I can help you."

"Really, do you know someone looking for a person with few qualifications but lots of motivation?" Judy had been part of many a con with Patrick, and lying came as naturally to her as breathing.

"I might. Tell me what you know about gardening."

"Oh, I did my family garden. It was quite large, nearly three quarters of an acre, and I often helped a neighbour with his. I love gardening and being outdoors, and I'm very fit."

"Well if you want to, come with me tomorrow I can take you to meet someone who is looking for some help. He does a very prestigious garden in the area and I happen to know he is looking for an energetic assistant, someone reliable, who's not lazy, and will turn up on time. I also know he's not against women because his best offsider ever, was a girl."

"That sounds very promising and I certainly don't have any better offers. By the way, how far is it to Blacktown from here?"

"I could take you there in half an hour from here. Why's that?"

"No reason, just have a friend there and wondered how long it would take me to get there. Is there backpacker accommodation there?"

"Sure is. There's a place I pick up and drop off at quite often. Never heard a bad word said about it – in fact, just the opposite – only ever heard good things about it."

"Sounds good. Could you take me there then, please?"

Thirty-five minutes later, the cab pulled up in front of the backpacker's hostel. "Here we are love; you'll be okay here tonight. I'll pick you up at eight in the morning. I'd like to see you settled, know what I mean?"

"Yes, thank you very much. How much do I owe you?"

"Nothing love. It's on the house – and tomorrow as well. This is my own cab, so I make my own rules, okay? And don't worry, I'm not a dirty old man. You remind me of my daughter, that's all – you're about the same age. I'd like to think someone would help her if she found herself in your position."

"I really do appreciate all this. Perhaps I can return the favour sometime."

"Don't worry about it, love, I'm happy to do it. I'll ring my mate tonight and tell him to expect you tomorrow. By the way, my name is Eddie."

"Judy. Bye, and thanks again, Eddie." Judy waved to the cabbie as he drove off, leaving her on the steps of the hostel. *So,* she thought to herself *I must be doing something right because so far it's all been so easy.*

That night, Judy shared a room with two other girls who talked for hours. While she listened, she became more aware of how different her life had been. They talked about their travels and adventures and so many interactions with other people. They had been all over Europe and the United States and Judy went to sleep listening to the easy conversation. She wondered if it might ever be her turn to travel and see the world.

Chapter Twenty-Eight

Harold kissed his partner on the forehead. "It's good to have you back in the land of the living, my dear. It's been very lonely without you. I've been missing your bad jokes and constant nagging."

Robert smiled up at his dearest friend. "Where am I, Harold?" Robert lifted his head and took at his surroundings. "There was a crash in the bus, wasn't there? I feel as if I've been away for a very long time. So many dreams, so confusing, so lonely. I thought I was awake several times, but now I see I wasn't, or maybe I'm still not – awake, I mean. Maybe this is more of my dream." Robert took hold of Harold's hand with both of his, not wanting to drift off again.

"No, don't go there again, stay with me." Harold lifted Robert's hand and squeezed it; "From now on I think we will stay at home and just exercise and eat healthy."

"Hah, you really have missed me, haven't you?" Robert looked around again and then directly at his partner and said, "Am I hurt?"

Harold smiled and shook his head. "No, you're fine. It's time you stopped malingering and we both went home. I can't wait to tell you all about it

They both shared a laugh and enjoyed the comfort of each other's company.

"They want to keep you here for a few more days," said Harold. "You've had a bad knock on the head and they just want to make absolutely sure there is no permanent damage. It will be nice to get home though, back amongst friends. Hey, we could even write a novel when we get settled."

Harold kept in touch with the Resort, and spoke to Jim and Di. He assured them that all was going well. He heard their news and said he was looking forward to hearing about their cruise when they all caught up at home.

Jim had been busy and let Di organise the memorial service for Lorna and Ralph. It was set for the following day in the Community Centre. The ashes of Ralph Johnston would be there; to be sprinkled in the garden at the end of the ceremony, according to his wishes.

Lorna McDonald had already been buried but her friends and relatives would need for closure for many of the people attending the ceremony, and this hopefully would provide that.

Di and Jim had seen little of their family since their return; they had been busy and wanted to make sure everything was handled properly. They had a need to give the support they were not available to give at the time of the crash. At these times, they all felt like an extended family.

******

"I've just seen him. Call Pekalski, quick." Matthew raced into the manager's office late on Thursday afternoon. He shot back out, then turned quickly and came back and looked at Jim and Di, who were still stared after him in amazement. "I mean Kevin, and I've just seen him hanging around Unit 27. I'm going to sneak up behind him, keep hidden, I mean. Don't anyone scare him off." Matthew was gone.

Di looked at Jim as he picked up the phone. "This must be our lucky day," she said.

Matthew flattened himself against the wall of the unit next door. He was in deep shade, and he remained very still while he watched his old friend, Kevin, casually but quietly walk up to the side gate of 27, open it with a key, and slip inside. Matthew moved to the fence and looked over. He spotted Kevin as he moved toward the shed. Matthew saw him open the shed door and duck his head as he disappeared into the dark interior. He pulled the door closed behind him.

Matthew stationed himself outside the gate. He was not going to let Kevin get away again. He did not hear a sound. He knew Rachael was home from the trip, but she had gone to see her family today and the unit was empty.

He waited. The minutes ticked by and Kevin did not reappear. Matthew chanced another look over the fence. No sign of Kevin. The shed door was still closed. Matthew knew Kevin had now had plenty of time to discover that his box was empty. He waited. Then it hit him, Kevin had already left. Matthew pulled the gate open and dashed to the shed.

Empty.

Matthew flew around the front of the house just in time to see his old friend disappear down the path toward the car park.

"Kevin!" Matthew shouted, and kept running.

Kevin did not look back. He ran toward a ute parked near the gate. He jumped in, started the motor, and slammed the gear lever into reverse.

Then, everything happened at once. The gates slammed shut and automatically locked. Jim ran to the scene and waved his arms. Kevin sat behind the wheel and revved the engine, not knowing where to go.

Outside the gate, a police car pulled up, its siren still going. Pekalski jumped out, followed by two men of his department. The driver switched off the siren. Kevin was surrounded. He sat completely still, and watched while Jim opened the gate for the police car. The policemen converged on the ute.

A crowd had gathered at the gate as Kevin was arrested and placed in the police car. No one could resist a bit of excitement of this kind. Everyone was talking at once. Suddenly, Detective Pekalski stopped as he was about to enter the car. He turned and looked toward the sound of Lil Gossett's voice.

"So," she was saying, "I told them both where their parents had gone, and I even gave them a morning tea.

Strange is the only way I could describe them. He was a bit overbearing, if you know what I mean."

Lil looked at Di for confirmation, and then she turned to see the wider audience were paying attention. Lil noticed that the Detective was listening now, and she began to address him directly as she took a step toward him.

"She, the sister, Judy was her name, was a pretty bad mannered sort, not like I would have imagined Margaret's daughter to be. Well, I've been wondering if they caught up with their parents and maybe all gone on another holiday together. I noticed that Ethan and Margaret weren't home with the others on the train. You know, I just had a strange feeling about them. Sort of."

Di looked at Pekalski and he shrugged, not prepared to add any fuel to Lillian's fire.

"Interesting," was his only comment as he changed direction and walked back to the office with Jim and Di. The police car cruised along beside, then stopped out front.

"What did you make of that?" was Di's comment inside the privacy of four walls. Pekalski frowned as he sifted through the conversation again.

"Must have been the famous relief manager, Sonja, who gave them the details of the trip." said Jim.

"Yeah." Pekalski was still thoughtful "It does explain a few things. A picture is emerging, and it's possible now to see where they got their initial information from. They joined up with someone and travelled to South Australia when they had the bus's itinerary. They were in Coober Pedy before the bus and they had the whole deal set up ready. They were well prepared. But not that careful, however. They had no idea the couple would ever leave that mine and didn't expect the crime to ever be uncovered."

Jim tried to expand the picture a little. "So now we know the brother and sister team left Coober Pedy with the other guy. Do we know who he is yet?"

"Yes. His name is Russell Mills, a bit of a computer hacker. We've tracked them all to Mildura where he was treated in the hospital emergency ward for a broken nose."

"Really?"

"Yes, he used his Medicare card and was told to see a surgeon as soon as he got home. So now, we know they headed back east and probably not to Victoria, judging by the route they took. We haven't picked up their trail since they crossed the Blue Mountains. That was the last sighting when they refuelled there. So, our next lead could come from one of the surgeons we've put on notice. It's been a big job searching out all the possibilities Mills may choose from, if he does decide to get his nose fixed. Sounded as though it was pretty bad so we're hopeful."

******

Detective Inspector Frank Pekalski stayed for the memorial service. There was music, speeches and then food and drinks. Lillian Gossett was not satisfied with the 'brush off' she had from the detective that morning, so she approached him at the end of the food table just as he filled his plate with Pavlova.

"I see you have a sweet tooth detective. Like me, you can't resist a bit of cream."

Pekalski inwardly groaned, then smiled, and nodded. He looked around desperately for someone to rescue him. He quickly gave up when he could see Lillian had him cornered.

"I've been wondering where Margaret and Ethan are now."

"I believe they went to see a sick friend in Adelaide," Pekalski said.

"I don't think so. I know how much they'd been looking forward to this trip, they wouldn't just abandon it like that."

"Sometimes friendship overrides everything else, doesn't it."

"Well, how come you know so much about them anyway?"

"I listen to gossip. It's amazing what you can pick up hanging around here. Just this afternoon I've heard all about Harold and Robert, who haven't come home yet, and how Hank and Peter passed out in the vineyard in South Australia." He looked, smiled and nodded as he said, "Excuse me, Lil, its time I went back to work. That's about the limit of my public relations for today." He stepped around the woman.

"Is that what you call it?" she said to his departing back.

Chapter Twenty-Nine

Russell was, by any standard, good looking, however his girlfriend, Megan, screamed when he turned up on her doorstep in Bryon Bay. His nose was beginning to heal in a very bad position. He was no longer handsome.

"God, Russell, what happened to you?" she asked, without moving from the front door.

"Walked into a door."

"Pig's arse! Whatever you did, can't you get it fixed?"

"Yes, I can, but first I 'ave to find a quack that can do the job. It 'as to be a particular kind of surgeon, one that only does facial stuff, and I'm just gettin' 'ome today, so give me a break will you. All in good time. Shit, what sorta welcome is this, anyway? "Ow about givin' us a kiss, eh, and lettin' me in?"

"Bloody hell, you scared the bejesus out of me. Aw, come on in."

"The guy that gave me this is a total lunatic, and I sure as shit ain't ever workin' with 'im again," he told Megan later, as he lay back allowing her to give him a massage. "E's lucky I can control my temper or I would've cleaned 'im up completely."

"I bet."

******

"I still don't understand why you want me to come with you," Russell said to mate, Justin.

"Told ya, a couple of yer old mates wanted to catch up with ya – thought we'd 'ave a couple a beers – catch up on old times, like."

"Yeah, okay, but I don't want to stay long. I've got a lot of people I need to see."

"Sure, mate."

Russell hung on to the passenger grab handle, as Justin drove on both sides of the road in his usual haphazard way. *No wonder 'e's lost his licence twice*, Russell thought.

"I didn't know you got your licence back," he said. "When did that 'appen?"

"It didn't. I probably won't get it back. Got nothin' to lose now."

"Well I 'ave – plenty. You could've told me."

"It ain't the world's best kept secret, mate."

"S'pose not."

"Anyway, tell me again. Where we goin'? 'oo we gonna meet?"

"To Ollie's. His mum's gone overseas and they've got a nice big 'ouse with a pool and 'eated spa. Perfect spot to 'ave a beer with Greg and Mikey, eh. And it's nice and private – you can 'ave a skinny dip."

"Yeah, maybe. I don't feel like 'angin' out in some of the 'oles you patronise. No offence mate, but you've lived in some really crappy dives over the years. "'Ow many times you been evicted?"

"Lost count, mate!"

Russell shut up and Justin drove in silence. Justin had a secret, and he wasn't about to tell Russell.

They could not get close to the house. Cars lined the narrow cul-de-sac; all parked more on the grass verge than on the road. Justin parked seventy metres away on the main road. He and Russell walked to the side gate into Ollie's yard and pushed their way through the palm fronds and ferns that spilled over the paved path, down the side of the house.

They reached a pool gate at the end of the path. The backyard was in darkness.

"So where's Ollie? And the others? There's no one 'ome, mate," said Russell.

"Don't worry, they'll be 'ere soon."

Justin slid the safety catch up, stepped inside and held the gate open for Russell. He followed.

The backyard flooded with light, as forty-odd people shouted, "Surprise!"

"Bloody hell. What's this in aid of?" Russell looked at the sea of faces. His girlfriend, Megan, walked toward him with a glass and a smoke in her hand.

"Good to see you made it, lover," she said, as she kissed him passionately on the lips.

A huge cheer, interspersed with wolf-whistles, erupted from the guests.

Russell put his arm around Megan. She lingered in the embrace, then gave Russell the   full glass of wine which she had managed not to spill.

"That's more like the 'omecomin' I'd expected," he said. They mingled with the crowd. Much back slapping and hand shaking ensued. The guest of honour spoke to lots of people he knew, and he met a few new faces.

Everyone he saw commented on his nose, and Russell resolved to see his GP next week.

Russell had spent most of his adult life in Byron Bay, or at least, used it as his permanent base. He went away to what he called 'work', almost on a regular basis. Depending on the degree of legality, this income could tide him over from a couple of weeks, to a few months. As these nice little earners were all cash jobs, he still looked forward to a regular deposit into his account each fortnight, courtesy of the friendly Australian taxpayers. On this occasion, he would have enough to last years, provided he invested his ill-gotten gains wisely in some worthwhile project. His biggest concern was to figure out how to launder the money first. He, of all people, knew how easily Big Brother could trace financial transactions anywhere in the world. Trouble was, he could not trust anyone to help him. He was on his own.

Russell had gone to the party with one of his oldest friends. He thought Justin, although a mate of many years' standing, was not the brightest star in the sky, and it did his reputation no good at all to be seen hanging around with him so much. However, Justin hero-worshipped Russell and tried to monopolise his time. Russell found his constant presence hard to shake off without offending him. He could not afford to alienate Justin; he had proved to be very useful from time to time in some of Russell's, more questionable ventures.

Russell often had a quiet chuckle when he thought of Justin's bad choices in women. Justin invariably dated women who were a lot smarter than he was, although, given his capabilities, that was hard for him to avoid. His average relationship lasted one night. Typically, the women ditched him quickly. His physical prowess in bed could not surmount his less appealing failings. He was an alcoholic and addicted to any mind-altering substance he could get his hands on, and Russell sometimes wondered if he bordered on schizophrenic. Justin was not the most sought-after prize in the lucky dip of life. Russell believed his lap dog was an unhappy soul, going nowhere fast; certainly not up the ladder of success. He felt Justin didn't have the potential for a long-term future unless he changed his way of life, soon.

******

Megan woke the next morning wondering why she could not remember getting home. They had both smoked only one joint, and they didn't drink any more than usual. Russell was careful about all forms of drugs; he had a good brain and had no intention of flushing it down the toilet like some of his friends.

"I don't know what you 'ad girl, but you passed out and I brought you 'ome just after midnight."

"Well maybe someone gave me something. You know I never get that drunk. Did anyone give me a drink, besides Justin?"

"I've no idea. You may 'ave y' answer there, anyway. I've enough trouble watchin' me own. How ya feelin' now?"

"Not real good. That's the last time I'm going to anything at Ollie's. I've heard he's into some heavy stuff. Bugger him."

"So what was all that about anyway? I didn't even know half the people there, and you said you'd tell me, later."

"Yeah well I wish I hadn't bothered now. I shouted all the grog and Ollie paid for the food. Easy to see who got the best end of that deal. It was for you, but I had no idea he was going to ask so many or maybe they were just gate crashers that he didn't bother to unask."

"So 'ow could you afford all that? Last I 'eard, you was broke."

"Well, of course I drew some of my share from your account. I couldn't tell you or it wouldn't have been a surprise."

Russell was stunned. "You what?"

"You know our partnership. We agreed to share before you went away. I shared all I had with you."

"You only bloody 'ad three 'undred bucks."

"Well I see you got plenty now. Don't worry, you can afford it."

"Ow'd you get your 'ands on my money?"

"Your card. I borrowed it and drew out a thousand. You know I have your number."

"I must 'ave bloody well forgotten. I wasn't supposed to use that account for at least a month. Now I can be tracked down. Thanks very bloody much!" Russell paced around the room and Megan cringed in the corner, beside the bed.

"I'm sorry. I really am. I had no idea. You should have told me."

"Where's my friggin' card now?" He put his hand out.

"It's back in your wallet."

He dashed over, grabbed his wallet from his pants pocket, and checked it. He threw it down on the bed.

Megan stood with hands on hips and said, "You know you should be grateful. Anyone else having access to your account would have cleaned you out, especially that best friend of yours. You know I'm honest. Anyway, that's still much less than you owe me."

Russell flopped on to the bed, grabbed Megan by the hand, and dragged her over. "You're right. It's just that the money in that account was supposed to sit there for another month, so as not to attract any attention to it. No activity at all."

"I really am sorry, Russ."

He accepted her apology and then some.

Later, they sat in bed drinking orange juice and eating leftover pizza. "I'm wonderin' now if we shouldn't piss off for a while," Russell said. "If we empty that account and move, we can stay out of sight and sort of lie low, you know."

"Sure. I don't mind."

"I'll think about it, but we got to have a plan and stick to it. It's a lot of money and it was too 'ard to get, to lose it now. Maybe I can 'ave a complete face change when I get my nose done. You know, fingerprints filed back, the works."

"I don't want to know what the job was. Don't tell me."

"I wasn't gonna."

Chapter Thirty

Patrick was distraught. He could not have felt worse if he had been told Judy had died. However, not knowing where his sister was may have been worse than knowing she was buried in some spot where he could at least go and visit her, and even talk to her. This was a betrayal and Patrick had no idea what to do next. Normally in charge – the decision maker – he was bereft of any idea about what the meaning of his life was, without Judy. He also had no idea it would be this way. He had often thought she played a bit part in his life; he had no idea until now that she was his life.

She had been gone almost a week, yet still he wallowed in his own self-pity. His nerves were on edge and jumped anytime he heard a sound. He would listen, but it was never Judy. The food in the fridge went rotten, uneaten, and he had not showered since he had found her gone. Patrick had paced around the little house and spent hours sitting, staring at the wall, hardly aware of thoughts other than those involving his sister.

On a Friday morning, as he sat curled up on a lounge chair, he heard a loud knock on the front door.

"Jude!"

He sprang to his feet, ran to the door and threw it open. He was disappointed – again. A young man stood on the doorstep. The visitor offered his hand and introduced himself. Patrick registered, after a few seconds that the man was a 'Bible basher', as he referred to those who evangelised from door to door. He stared at the man and had no idea what he was saying, until the young man said, "Sir, are you alright? Is there anything I can do to help you?"

Patrick looked at the man's eyes. He began to cry. Soft sobs turned quickly into a loud, convulsing wail. His shoulders shook and tears wet his cheeks. He held on to the young man and buried his head on his shoulder.

The man looked around and signalled, with a jerk of his head, to his friend who stood behind him. The two men took Patrick inside and sat him in the middle of a three-seater divan. They sat either side of Patrick and physically supported him while he blubbered.

A couple of minutes passed, before Patrick raised his head and focused on the men. Both had such a benign countenance that he had the feeling he was in the presence of God himself.

Patrick's shaky, husky voice whispered, "I'm so sorry, I'm sorry about everything. I don't expect anyone to forgive me. After what I've done, there can be no forgiveness and I don't deserve to have Judy here. I would poison her life. I may have already done that, it's too late for me, but it's not too late for her, she had nothing to do with it. I 'm sorry, I'm honestly sorry." He cried again, this time more quietly.

The two young men looked at one another in astonishment, held a hand each and rocked Patrick into some kind of peace. They all sat there like that for nearly half an hour, before Patrick sniffed, and looked at the young men.

"Who are you?" he asked.

"We're the ones God sent to help you through your hour of need," said the first young man.

The second young man took his partner's lead and said, "God has guided us to help you in your sadness and to show you His light. He is all-forgiving and no sinner needs to struggle without His help."

"We can show you the hand of God; you only have to take hold," the other followed.

Patrick took some deep breaths and sat back. He listened while the men explained their presence in his house. They offered to help, and said he would be welcome in the church anytime. They said they could pick him up if he wanted; he only had to call. They gave him reading material and pointed out the numbers for him to ring, if he needed help. Finally, they said they had to go. The first one suggested Patrick have a shower and then eat something, then go to bed and pray for a peaceful sleep. They told him they would return the next day, if he wanted them too.

"I'll call if I have need of you again," he said as politely as he could manage. He thanked them sincerely and saw them out. As he closed the door, he knew something had changed; he felt different – as though an almighty weight had been lifted from his chest. He began to see where he had been the past week, and for a moment, he was terrified he would return to that state. *Was it a place, or was it a state of mind*? he wondered. He knew he had hovered on the edge of madness, and he knew why. Now, he felt his strength returning.

A shower, that's what I want. They were right, I need to pull myself together and for the next five minutes he did not think of Judy once. Then, her face flashed across his mind. He knew he had to be on his guard.

He decided to go out and eat, and he made his way to the local RSL Club. Patrick talked to a couple of men at the bar, people who seemed as alone as he was, and he realised how deprived he had been of any kind of empathetic human company. He resolved to contact his Good Samaritan friends again. *They literally were a Godsend*, thought Patrick, as he left the club.

That night, he slept without dreaming. He woke with the sun.

******

As promised, Eddie the benevolent cabbie, picked Judy up from the hostel and drove her to an estate outside town, where he introduced her to the gardener.

"This is the young person I rang you about, Al. Judy says she can pull her weight in the garden and so it's over to you now, she's all yours."

Al immediately smiled and shook hands with Judy. "So you like a bit of hard work do you, love?" he said.

"I don't mind," answered Judy. "I enjoy being in the garden, and I definitely know the difference between a plant and a weed."

"Well, you just passed the first test. Come in, please."

Judy smiled at Eddie and followed it with a kiss on his cheek.

"Thank you so much, Eddie, I really appreciate your help," she said.

"It's an absolute pleasure, love, an absolute pleasure. You find you need any help, you have my number, okay? Bye."

"See you Eddie. I'll look after her, don't you worry," Al said, as the cabbie walked to his cab.

Al stood back and allowed Judy to walk in front of him, as he showed her around the small estate. There were beautiful cottage gardens, a small vegetable garden, and little pocket-handkerchief size lawns, dotted here and there. There were hedges, tall palms, and bordered paths – all immaculate.

Judy's head swung left and right trying to take it all in.

"It's all absolutely beautiful. What a lot of work, but it must be such a labour of love." Her mouth hung open and Al watched with a pleased look that said he approved of her appreciation.

"I normally do almost everything myself, but now Mrs. Jamieson, the owner, wants me to start driving her around, because she isn't as confident to drive as she used to be. Getting a bit long in the tooth, and, had a little motor vehicle accident recently. Anyway, now I'll be a bit preoccupied with being a chauffeur and won't have as much time to spend in the garden – which of course I'd rather do, naturally. However, I've been with Mrs J for nearly twenty years and she trusts me, so I'm going to need a little help. I'll try you out for a week, and at the end we can talk again. In the meantime, don't do a thing without checking with your's truly, first. Okay?"

"Sure." Judy nodded and looked around. "What do you want me to do first?"

"Can't wait to get started, huh? I like that. Come over here and I'll show you the tool shed and the equipment. You'll find it all top quality stuff and the right tool for just about every job, but if you find there's anything you need, just ask. Mrs. J is a generous lady – no expense spared and she provides you with lunch, but of course, you can bring your own if you prefer."

"Wow, sounds great." Judy looked into the tool shed and was very impressed. What time do you want me to start work?"

"Well, in winter it's 8am am to 4pm, and in summer, it's 6am to 2pm. Sound alright?"

"Yep."

"I hear you may be looking for a place to live for a while."

Judy looked straight at Al and nodded.

"I live here, in that granny flat," he said as he pointed to what was obviously an add-on to the original dwelling. "I know where you can rent a garage near a friend's house for a hundred bucks a week. Well, call it a garage, but it's really quite comfortable – has its own toilet, shower, bench top stove and stuff. If you want to negotiate a deal she may be interested in offering you free rent for gardening. I'll give you her address if you like."

"Thank you, I'd love that. Is it far from here?"

"No you can walk there from here."

Judy was truly overwhelmed, almost too good to be true, her heart was fluttering and she realised she was smiling.

"Anything else?"

"No, you seem to have covered everything, Al. I'll try to do a good job and I'm punctual and reliable, you'll see."

"Not quite everything. You haven't asked me about wages."

"Oh yes. I feel like I should pay you, letting me work in this beautiful garden."

"Oh, I think you'll need a bit of cash to go along with, as well," he laughed. "Cash in hand, since you're only a learner and the country owes you an education, so to speak." One hundred and twenty bucks a day, six hundred for five days. Sound agreeable?"

"It does. I'm very grateful, thanks again."

"Okay, let's get to work."

I've never known such kindness, Judy thought, *and from complete strangers.*

As soon as that thought had passed, Judy felt a pang of conscience stab her heart. *My God,* she thought, *what am I saying? Margaret and Ethan were so good to me, I realise that now, and yet I've totally abused their trust in the worst possible way.* A tear fell down her cheek, as she followed Al under a rose bower, and down a cobbled path lined with all shades of beautiful camellias.

Chapter Thirty-One

Keeala Resort looked 'great', according to Robert when they drove in from the airport. He and Harold had flown home that morning and within an hour they were sitting on their front veranda, drinking tea and holding court to Robert's sister, Meredith, who returned their King Charles spaniel, Gypsy.

"It's just as well you came home when you did, or you were in danger of losing Gypsy. I feel I've had her long enough now to call her mine."

Robert hugged the little dog on his lap and ran his hands over her head. "I've missed you so much my pet, don't even think of staying with that silly old girl."

"I expect to hear all about your trip, especially the accident and the poor people who died," Meredith said.

"So, does that mean you only want the morbid parts, and none of the fun or educational parts?"

"You silly man, I want to hear everything, and I plan to sit here until I've heard it all."

"Robert will not be sitting here that long," interrupted Harold. "He needs his rest and I intend to see he gets it. We nearly lost him you know."

"Yes, of course. Well, I'll hear it all in instalments then."

"In that case, why don't you wait until the book comes out?"

"Good idea," agreed Harold. He liked Meredith but found prolonged exposure to her was very wearing.

The phone rang. "Yes Di, we can hardly wait to see you as well, but Harold here has just ordered me to rest, so we will have to make it tomorrow. Goodbye."

The phone rang again; it seemed word was out. Harold picked up this time and explained Robert would have to hold court again tomorrow.

"At this rate, I'll have to post an announcement. I had no idea you were so popular, Rob."

******

Elaine Steinberg improved, and according to her son, she may actually soon return to her independent living home after more rehabilitation. This pleased everyone and Helga, for some reason, had made a special effort to visit Elaine in hospital.

"We'll see, people can change, look at Helga – positively unselfish and out of character. I do believe this trip had a big impact on everyone, in many different ways," Di announced to Jim while they discussed current resort affairs.

"Time will tell if the change is permanent or temporary," Jim responded, unconvinced.

******

Patrick woke to the morning breeze fluttering the thin curtain against his window. A shaft of sunlight filtered through the leaves of the overhanging tree outside. His eyes traced the movement and he blinked, then again, as he adjusted to the morning. His mind shifted into gear, thoughts began to wander aimlessly, and images played across his screen of consciousness. He pulled some back into focus while others wandered off to the side, waiting in the wings for a chance to return.

In his imagination, he saw the two young men who had rescued him the previous day. He saw the faces of the lonely souls at the club, with whom he had shared a drink. Front and centre, he saw Judy again. She took up the whole screen and he felt his heart rate begin to pick up speed, then his breathing and he started to move around the bed as the tension built in his mind and transmitted the thoughts to his body.

His remorse was gone. His self-pity was gone, and so was his understanding. Suddenly he had a moment of enlightenment and knew where she was. *She's gone to meet him, they had it all planned out, they must think I'm really bloody stupid.* Patrick could see Judy getting into the car he had helped Russell buy. In his mind, he saw them laughing together as they drove along the highway to Byron Bay, laughing at him. They had all the money they needed, a good car and one another. They had dumped him; he was such a joke. He clenched his fists and ground his teeth as jealousy filled his heart. He imagined them driving out of the picture and off the screen.

NO! I made it all possible. I risked my freedom, my life.

Patrick threw his legs over the side of the bed and strode to the bathroom. He tried to think but all he could do was feel anger, as he washed away every trace of regret or concern. The men who had comforted him yesterday would not recognise this person. They would probably be afraid of him now.

Patrick did not really need to think or plan; he knew what he would do. Byron Bay was not such a big town. He could track them down easily, and he had all the time in the world and plenty of money.

By 9am, he was on the road leading to the Great Western Highway, thence the Pacific Highway and on, nonstop, in a push to that beautiful, idyllic town at the most easterly point of Australia. White sandy beaches and rolling turquoise, white capped waves welcomed travellers, especially those from the south when the weather was cold and the cities claustrophobic.

The drive was a blur to Patrick, his head filled with images and constantly changing impressions of Judy and Russell. He only stopped for fuel and coffee, and then almost passed the motorway exit to Byron, late in the evening, after eleven hours driving. He pulled into a rest area and slept in the car. The sounds of highway traffic woke him, as dawn spread its light through his windscreen.

It was not so hard to run Russell down, once he began his enquiries. On his second day in Byron, Patrick stood outside an old house, divided into three flats. Russell's name was on a letterbox, but Patrick would find that was the only vestige of Russell that remained in Byron Bay. Patrick knocked on the door of Flat 2. Russell was gone.

"Yeah, mate," said a blond-headed teenager. "He and his girl took off yesterday, dunno where he went, but he'll be back. Always comes back after a while."

"You say he had a girl with him?"

"Yep, good lookin' bird too. He's always got some chick chasin' him, dunno why, especially now his face is all smashed in. He ain't the prettiest flower in the bunch, not anymore."

"So you have no idea where I might find them?" Patrick had caught the young surfer with his board under his arm as he stepped out of the door of the neighbouring flat.

"No, mate, but someone you might ask is that useless excuse for a human being, ah ... Justin. Yeah, try him. At this time of day you'll prob'ley find him sleepin' it off in one of the bus shelters, if he's homeless. Otherwise, just hang around the pub down near the roundabout, you know, back that way," he said as he pointed. "He'll turn up sooner or later. He keeps tabs on Russell and a few others."

"So what does this Justin look like?"

"Like a pitiful excuse for a grown man that doesn't work for a livin' and never showers or cuts his hair."

"I see."

Patrick nodded and thanked the font of information. He got back into his car and headed to the pub down the road.

Before he got there, he saw a few men near a bus shelter. One stood apart from the others, leaning against the sidewall of the shelter and concentrating on rolling a cigarette dexterously between thumbs and forefingers.

Patrick rolled to a stop and wound the passenger window down. He leaned across. "Your name Justin?" he asked the cigarette roller. The man shook his head.

Russell rolled the car forward. "Any of you guys know a bloke named Justin?" he asked, as he stopped level with the group.

They all turned their attention to Patrick, checked him out, and shook their heads. Patrick started to move away, but one put his hand up and shouted, "Yeah, mate, I just saw 'im down by the public toilets. Back that way." He pointed in the direction of the beach.

"Thanks." Patrick started to move off, but stopped. "Hey, mate, what's he look like. What's he wearing?"

The youth gave Patrick a description. *The red hair should make it easy,* thought Patrick, and it did. He sighted his quarry within a minute, walking toward the pub. He pulled alongside him and shouted, "Hey, mate, are you Justin?"

"Who's askin'?" said the redhead.

Patrick parked his car and jumped out. He walked over to where Justin stood staring at him. He was tying his knotty hair back in a bandanna.

"My name's Tom. I'm looking for an old friend - his name's Russell Mills. I was told by his neighbour you might know where he is."

"I might, and I might not. 'Aven't 'ad me breakfast yet though. You shoutin'?"

"Sure, jump in."

They drove back to the pub and walked in past the group Patrick had seen a few minutes previously.

"Found 'im, eh?" said one of them.

Patrick nodded, and walked into the bar with Justin. They ordered burgers and beer and took it outside to eat under the shade of an old, spreading Jacaranda, where the seats were benches and the tables made from rough-hewn logs. They filled their mouths and ate in silence for a couple of minutes, each one sizing up the other.

"So whaddaya lookin' for 'im for then, hey?"

"Well as a matter of fact, I owe him some money, and since I was on my way home, passing Byron, I thought I'd look him up."

"Yeah, bullshit, mate, pull the other one. No one looks someone up to give 'em money. But if you really wanna, you can give it to me, and I'll see he gets it when 'e comes home."

Patrick laughed, "You're a real comedian, aren't you. Where is he? I need to know."

"So do I, mate. Like I said, give me the dough and I'll see he gets it after I take out what he owes me."

Patrick leaned over the table and grabbed Justin by the front of his shirt.

"Where the fuck is he?"

Patrick's face was getting redder by the second. He glared, inches away from Justin's face. Justin could now see this was no amateur.

"Yeah, yeah, alright, I dunno. 'e left yesterday, never even told me where 'e was going, nothin'. Just packed 'is car up and took 'is sleazy bird and pissed off."

"In which direction?"

"Like everyone else, mate, the Pacific bloody Highway."

Patrick let Justin drop to the seat and stood up himself. He walked around in circles, and pumped his fist into his palm. He looked back several times at Justin, and his indecision threw him into a fit of frustration and anger. He kicked an empty beer can into the trunk of a Norfolk Pine. Finally, he walked away from the pub, pushing his wallet down in his back pocket and ramming his sunglasses into place on his face. He pulled his car door open, got in, and slammed it shut. He left his audience in no doubt he was in one shit of a mood.

Chapter Thirty-Two

Margaret and Ethan had become used to wearing a disguise when they went out, which was kept to a minimum. However, it was not much fun being 'dead' to the rest of the world.

They dearly wished to be back in their own home, where they could mix with friends and play Bridge with one group on Thursdays, and golf with several close friends on Friday. Then there was the Book Club on Tuesday afternoon and relaxation classes, Tuesday and Thursday mornings. They shopped on Wednesdays, and Monday was either swimming or walking, depending on the weather. The weekends were filled with entertaining or eating out with friends, or going to the theatre. To say they had a full and happy life would be no exaggeration. They both acknowledged how much they loved their life and how hard they had worked to arrive at this point where gratifying their own needs was their fulltime occupation. They even had time to volunteer for Lifeline, two days a month.

Staying out of sight and not participating in anything social was becoming more tiresome every day. It was beginning to stress their health as well as their marriage. Margaret complained of headaches nearly every day, and spent many nights wandering around the little house they now occupied, and for all intents, in which they were held captive.

"Can't you sleep either?" she asked Ethan as she bumped into her husband leaving the bedroom at three o'clock one Sunday morning. They had stayed up late watching television, trying to fill in some of the endless night.

"No, I've caught it too; just too much sitting around doing nothing. I think it's time we considered how we can do more with our time beside just writing and television, eating and sleeping."

"I agree. How much longer can we go on like this? It's been a month now and I'm sure we're no closer to an end."

They both sat on the lounge, thinking and restlessly fidgeting. "What about moving home," asked Margaret. "Don't you think we might as well get on with our lives now?"

Ethan nodded, "I'm beginning to think so. There's not much to gain in hiding out from someone who's not looking for us, since to them we are dead. I really don't think they'll come looking for us in the Resort, and draw attention to the fact that we aren't there. You know?"

This time Margaret nodded, and said, "What say we ring Pekalski tomorrow, and suggest we reincarnate ourselves and maybe that in itself may stir up a little action?"

"I agree. Good idea. Let's go to bed."

They made their way back to the rumpled sheets with a smile and a commitment to a much better tomorrow.

******

They did not need to ring Pekalski. He rang them as they were having breakfast, and suggested he come to see them for an update and a discussion.

Two hours later, they all sat down together with coffee and immediately the detective could see the Doughertys were apprehensive.

"How're things going?" he asked.

"We planned to ring you today, but you beat us to it. In fact, we've both 'had it' with hanging out hiding and putting our lives on hold. We've given it a lot of thought. Margy is having lots of headaches, and we're both suffering from insomnia. We keep asking ourselves – all for what?"

"That's what I wanted to discuss with you today. We've lost the trail. It ended in Sydney and no one has put their head up since they got there, no sightings. They're smarter than we gave them credit for, or, maybe they've split up and they may have even left the country."

"How could they do that?"

"Plenty of ways. Private charter plane or boat, false papers, changed identity. I must admit I'm disappointed. I had the feeling we were very close when we got to the Western

Sydney area. But they just disappeared and the fact that they have not re-emerged in the past three weeks is pretty telling."

"So what now?" asked Ethan.

"What did you have in mind? Moving back home?"

"Yes, we did."

"I see."

"Not a good idea?"

"I'm not sure. I realise you can't hang around here forever, but we do want to get them."

"So?"

"I was thinking about advertising."

"What!" said Margaret.

"What if we put a notice in the classifieds, looking for relatives of a missing couple? Maybe with a view to an inheritance. You know, 'Couple missing, believed dead, solicitors trying to find eligible family to pick up inheritance'. That sort of thing."

"Wouldn't they know that when they come forward, and the solicitors check the bank account and find it empty, they may be under suspicion?"

"Not necessarily, but it would be a big temptation for them, don't you think?"

Margaret and Ethan looked at one another.

"That would mean us staying under cover, and all our friends would think we were dead. At the moment, they think we are on a visit with family in Adelaide. This is getting pretty complicated."

"True. But what if it flushes them out? They are greedy, we know that, and stupid in some ways. Greed will cloud judgement, and if you go back now all this sacrifice may be wasted."

"Oh ... I don't know. How would we do it again?"

"I think we could let the media have a story about a couple who have been missing for more than a month. If that were the case, we would want to be in touch with anyone in the family who might lead us to them or stand in line for an inheritance, if the couple never turned up. I think we may even put up a reward for information leading to relatives. Uncle Rod could help us out there."

"Gee, I don't know, Frank. It seems a bit of a long shot," said Ethan.

"Well, I guess it is, but let's face it, at the moment our enquiries have met a brick wall. We need to be pro-active on this, wouldn't you agree? You can't live like this forever. We have to force their hand. Remember they believe you are dead. They think you will never turn up and therefore they will eventually have to inherit whatever you have left behind anyway. However, they have to put their hands up first. They have no idea we are on to them, and that's our ace. They could come back, looking completely innocent, and seeming to be just as distressed as the rest of us that you have disappeared. They may even offer to help us with our investigation. If they were innocent, that's how they would be expected to behave. They could also think they might lead us away from the trail to Coober Pedy. The game would be one of cat and mouse."

"Can we think about this, Frank?" asked Margaret.

"Certainly. Get back to me as soon as you decide, and if you don't want to go ahead, then we will make arrangements to get you both settled in at home again."

"Great," said Ethan.

He and Pekalski stood up together and shook hands. Margaret smiled and nodded, as she thought about the plan Pekalski had suggested. The men walked to the door.

Pekalski reassured Ethan once again, that they would get their culprits in the end.

"Don't worry, we won't give up. One way or another, we will bring them in. I promise."

Ethan closed the door, deep in thought. It sounded like a complicated plan. Still, what else could they try, he thought. They had already invested so much of their energy, their health, and their money. He walked back and sat down. Ethan knew that the longer this dragged on, the more it would take its toll on his wife's health, especially emotional. He looked at his wife. Neither spoke for a couple of minutes.

Ethan broke the silence. "What are you thinking?"

"I really don't know, love. I had made up my mind to leave here and go home – get on with our lives. Maybe they'll never catch them, but I can see how determined Frank is. The police won't give up anyway, so maybe we could give it one more shot. What about you, do you think it's worth a go?"

"Maybe, maybe, but I'm really worried about how this is affecting you. I'm going to think about it today."

Margaret started to think about the effect her so-called 'death' would have on her friends and Ethan's family. It seemed such a lot of distress to put so many people through and it may not even work. And how would she feel if it did. How would she feel when she came face to face again with her adopted son and daughter, knowing what they tried to do to her and Ethan. Tears filled her eyes and splashed on to her chin; so much unhappiness, and all caused by the two natural parents who neglected and abused their children and allowed them to grow in the darkness, not in the sun.

"Oh, the waste," she whispered.

Chapter Thirty-Three

"Hey this is pretty good." Megan jumped on the bed in the hotel room they had just checked into, in Brisbane.

"It'll do for the time bein'. I like to look after my girl. Just remember, I'm puttin' all my trust in you, now all that dough's in your name."

"You already know you can trust me, lover. When did I ever not tell you what I spent our money on?"

"Sure. Come on, I 'ave my appointment in 'alf an hour. Let's go."

Megan grabbed her handbag, and Russell put the key card in his pocket as they swept out of the room and down in the elevator to the lobby. Their next stop was a consultation with the surgeon who would be reconstructing Russell's nose.

******

"Make it a good one, mate; I can't go round scarin' the girls no more."

The surgeon nodded. "This has already been left too long. Why have you waited so long to come and see me?"

"No choice, mate. We were away and just been gettin' 'ome all this time. Do you think you can fix it?"

"I think you will be happy with the finished effect, but I am going to have to break it again, because of the length of time you've left it, so it's going to take quite some time to heal and there will be considerable bruising. Don't expect to look like Brad Pitt on the first day."

"Jesus, Joyce," was all Russell could say. He immediately regretted having ignored the advice of the doctor in Mildura.

"Be here at 0800 hours tomorrow. Lucky for you, we have a cancellation and you will be first cab off the rank. You can expect to stay in overnight. We'll need to monitor you until the next day, before you'll be able to go home. Oh, don't eat anything after nine o'clock tonight and only a sip of water tomorrow morning, if you have to. Okay?"

"Sure, thanks Doc."

They shook hands, and the couple left the surgeon's rooms and went to see a movie. That night they ate in style and both were relaxed and happy when they finally got to bed.

Megan did consider taking the money out of her account and leaving. Just for a moment. When Russell was in hospital the next day, she wandered around the shops and knew she could really buy anything she wanted, but then she would have to explain it to Russell. She was very fond of Russell, and had never had a boyfriend who treated her as well as he did. If she did take off, she wondered, where would she go that would be better than where she was now, and who would she rather be with?

So, she stayed, and was genuinely worried when she first saw how bad Russell looked after the operation.

"Shit, you look bloody awful"

"Thanks."

Russell's tardiness in seeking the specialist's help meant that what should have been a relatively straight forward operation, had become quite a complex challenge for the surgeon. Consequently, Russell's stay in hospital extended to three days. He still managed to look like a train wreck when he came out and they went back to their hotel room.

"What now?" said Megan.

"Hows about a little holiday, a little fun?" Russell said. His attempted smile was masked by the swathe of bandages around his head.

"What do you mean?"

"I think we could take a break, time out – while my face 'eals, before we start our next adventure."

"Yeah! What do you have in mind? Tell me."

"I want to buy a business. Somewhere. I can do graphic art, paint a bit, and one thing I've always wanted was my own shop. You know those pictures you see on the side of trucks and vans and buses?"

Megan nodded.

"Well, I can do that. I used to work with my dad, until 'e kicked me out. After that, I never wanted to do it again. But now, I feel differently, and I thought about nothing else while I was in 'ospital. It cost a lot for me to get that surgery done, and I feel like I've 'ad it with scams and 'acking. I'd like to start my own business and settle down. With you." A smile started. "Shit, don't make me smile or laugh!" Russell sucked in his breath from the pain.

"Settle down with me? Are you serious? You don't mean like getting married or anything?"

"Yes, I do."

"Wow. What can I say? So this is like a proposal or something, isn't it?"

"Yeah, it is. What do you say?"

Megan put her arms out and spun around like a ballerina. She jumped up on to the bed and did a little dance.

She smiled and said, "I say yes. I say yes, yes, yes." She jumped down into his arms and they held each other. They knew this was a very special, life changing moment for both of them.

"I do 'ave a few regrets, especially about this last job this bloke and I did. It was pretty messy, and to be honest, even though the money was good, I still wish we 'adn't done it. However, we can't change it now, so we 'ave to go on. He was such a bastard, treated everyone like shit, you know, even his sister. He slept with his sister, you know, acted as if she was 'is possession, wouldn't even let 'er speak to me. That's how I got this nose. I was just talking to 'er, an' 'e came in an' started world war three. He exploded all over the place and could do that anytime, the minute 'e got pissed off about somethin', you know, 'e'd just explode."

"Are you serious about him sleeping with his sister?"

"Yeah, wouldn't let 'er do anythin' alone. No wonder she was such a mess. I feel sorry for 'er bein' stuck with 'im; I reckon he'd kill 'er if she tried to leave."

"You're joking?"

"Nah, I mean it; I wouldn't wanna meet that bastard in a dark alley. 'e's capable of anythin'. I 'ad no idea 'ow bad 'e was until this last job."

"Please don't tell me about it. I can't worry about what I don't know."

"Right."

"So what's our first step?"

"Well, I think I'd like to close down things at Byron, let my flat go and move to some place where I can make a livin' doin' what I like for a change. And you need to do the same, pack up and tidy things up at 'ome."

"Mrs Mills."

"What?"

"I said, Mrs Mills. That'll be me."

"Yeah, and I'll be able to say, 'meet the wife'." They both laughed. Everything was working out great, really great.

******

It was a shock to find Patrick waiting for them when they drove into Russell's driveway in Byron Bay, much later that day. He was sitting on the old veranda, rocking in a chair, as though he had expected them to drive in any minute.

"Fuck! What the bloody 'ell is he doin' here?

Megan looked at Russell and saw he was very upset.

"Don't move," he said. "Don't get outa this car, y'ear me?"

"Yeah, yeah, sure." she shook her head. "Who is he?"

"The bastard I told you about. What the bloody 'ell's he doin' 'ere, now?" He got out of the car and walked to meet Patrick.

"So, the lovers have returned."

Patrick stood. He brushed past Russell to the car, and pulled the passenger door open. He stared at Megan.

"Where's Judy?"

"Who's Judy?" asked Megan quietly, as she stared back into dark, bloodshot eyes that she knew she would never forget.

"Where the fuck is Judy?"

Patrick swung round and launched himself toward Russell. He almost lifted him off his feet as he grabbed the shirt of the other man.

"What've you done with her?"

Russell knew immediately that Judy must have left Patrick, and he was after her.

"I ain't seen 'er, and that's a fact, Jack – not since the day I left you in Sydney."

Russell put his hand up to protect his nose, and was ready to kick Patrick in the groin if he made any move to hit him.

Patrick let him drop.

"So where is she?"

"How would I know, I got my own business to worry about. And my own girlfriend."

Patrick suddenly felt the air go out of him. He slumped down on the steps of Russell's place and put his head in his hands.

Russell walked back to the car and told Megan to drive off to her house and he would come and see her later. She reversed out of the driveway and was gone.

"I've been waiting here for days for you," said Patrick, as he stood up and sat on the chair.

"So?"

"I thought she was with you."

"Yeah, I gathered that," said Russell, as he tried to figure out what to do next. "Why don't you let 'er go, mate? She won't turn you in. Even I know that."

"What do you mean?"

"Well, if she's taken off, she must want out. So let 'er go, eh? I know you're 'er brother an' all, but she needs a life of 'er own. Find yourself someone else to sleep with, and move on, mate."

Patrick rose up and made a grab for Russell, but Russell moved too quickly and ducked out of reach.

"Be 'onest with yourself, mate. It aint 'ealthy. I know you 'ave your reasons, but it's time you guys grew up and started to act like normal people."

Patrick sat on the step and looked around as if for an escape. He did not want to hear this, especially not from this 'fuckwit', as he referred to Russell in his own mind..

"Shut your mouth, Russell."

Russell turned to walk inside. Patrick got up to follow him.

"Where are you goin'?" asked Russell.

"I've been staying here this last week, and I'm getting my gear."

"How the 'ell did you get in?"

"Oh, mate, give me some credit. Your piddly little locks are a joke."

Russell said nothing. He watched Patrick move about his home collecting his stuff, and piling it into his car, parked around back of the old house.

Patrick got into his car and drove off. He said nothing.

"Yeah, and kiss my arse too, you prick," said Russell, as the car disappeared.

Russell knew he should get away as quickly as possible, before this arsehole came back. Russell sat down and thought about what had just happened. *I'll change my name as well,* he thought, *maybe to Megan's. I've heard of that.*

Chapter Thirty-Four

"They're all treating him like a movie star," said Harold to Di, when he walked into the manager's office, looking for Jim. "He's lapping it up, a born actor. And he's putting on weight – all that sitting around, resting and writing his memoir. It's beginning to take its toll on me, the carer."

Di laughed. She knew Robert had extracted all the attention he could get from being a 'famous casualty' of the luckless bus trip.

"He is much improved I'm happy to say," said Harold. "I'll be getting him back on the running track sooner than he thinks. What about tonight, coming to our musical soiree?"

Di nodded and said, "Wouldn't miss it for quids."

******

The atmosphere in the resort had been electric after everyone came home, and all the travellers had a story to tell.

Jim and Di were coming to grips with their end of things, and barely did a day pass that Jim did not mention the fact that he was never, ever, ever going to take another holiday. Matthew Weatherlee had left everything in good order, maybe just not how Jim would have had it.

"My next day off will be the day I retire," he said to Di. "I never want to go through all this hassle again."

The book was closed on Elaine Steinberg. She was home now, and recovering well. Her son was content when Jim told him that Sonja Steele would not be back. Keeala Resort was humming along nicely, again. Ethan and Margaret had not returned, and no one seemed worried about them, that was, until the announcement Jim made at the resident's meeting.

Before he got up to address the gathering, Jim thought about the meeting he had had with Frank Pekalski the previous day. Pekalski had laid out the scheme to trap the kidnappers.

"Margaret and Ethan have agreed to stay undercover for a little longer," Pekalski had told him. "We are going to try to bring the suspects out into the open. They went to ground after they reached Sydney, and since then, the trail has gone cold. We plan to bring the search for the couple and their companion into the spotlight, and also offer a reward for anyone coming up with a good lead to their whereabouts."

"But the suspects won't respond to that. Surely, they don't want Margaret and Ethan found, ever," Jim had said.

"Sure, but if they weren't the murderers, wouldn't they come forward as though they cared about mum and stepdad. They have the incentive that they will be the beneficiaries of the Will, or were, until a few days ago. We're hoping this might flush them out of their hiding place. If not, we will have to play a waiting game. The Dougherty's want to return to their old lives. They just hope that in time, the trio are caught."

"Hmm, all a bit exciting really, but can we expect to see the suspects around here maybe?"

"It's possible, but if they to take the bait, we expect they will contact the police. They assume we know nothing about their involvement, and we want to hold the door open and let them walk in. There is enough evidence to hold them as soon as they're sighted. I really want to slam the gate on this lot," Pekalski had said as his final comment to Jim.

Jim brought himself back to the present as the chairperson called on him to address the meeting.

"I'm afraid we have had no word from Mr. and Mrs. Dougherty and there is to be a police investigation launched tomorrow into the whereabouts of the couple," he said.

"Not again! Just what we need another police investigation. We haven't got over the last one. What about that lout Kevin – what's he up to now?" someone said. These questions and many more were thrown at Jim from around in the room.

Jim explained that Detective Inspector Pekalski was once again in charge of the investigation, and he was anxious to hear any information leading to the whereabouts of the missing residents. Jim stressed that he was telling Margaret and Ethan's Keeala Resort friends first, before they saw it in the media, and in case anyone had information they thought useful.

The room immediately broke into animated discussion and speculation. Jim wanted everyone to have a chance to speak, so he called for order, through the chair.

Jim went on.

"So you see, we are hoping to find them and would appreciate any help we can get. You can see me or contact Detective Pekalski direct, that's his number on the whiteboard. We have no reason to think they've left the country, and they really aren't the type of people who would just drop out of sight without telling anyone."

"Has anyone contacted their kids?" It was Lillian Gossett.

"We would like to, but do not have a contact number, however, if anyone sees the son or daughter around, please contact Di or myself immediately."

"What about a car registration number, would that help?"

"Of course." Jim looked at Lillian questioningly.

"I might still have it, I think."

Everyone now turned to look at the resident with the smile growing on her face.

"Yes, I wrote it down when I saw the brother and sister parked out front of Margaret's old unit, just after the Doughertys went away. I told the detective that I had spoken to them and given them a cup of tea. Before I spoke to them, I had written down their rego number. It's a habit of mine. I just have to find it, I have quite a collection."

Jim's mind was racing, but he needed the meeting to stay under control. He continued the meeting to its natural conclusion, and then walked with Lillian to the door.

"I'll come to your house with you Lil, if you don't mind. That registration number may be just what we're looking for." Jim knew the police would have already crosschecked their name with their vehicle, but maybe something would come from Lillian's information.

******

Patrick looked in his rear vision mirror and saw him.

"Shit, shit, shit."

It was a motorcycle policeman in pursuit. The siren wailed and the red and blue lights flashed. Patrick put his foot to the floor. It was instinct – flight, and then fight. They hit the road in tandem, taking the bends left, right, left, right, and on it went. The patrolman was sitting right on Patrick's tail, but Patrick had absolutely no intention of pulling over. He put his foot down and ate up the highway.

The patrolman stayed with him. He could have backed off and radioed Patrick's description in, but he was challenged and could not let go. They both overtook on double lines, passed a caravan and car, then a truck. This was madness. Neither of them backed off for a second. The road wound along the hills behind the coastline. Patrick saw a semi-trailer ahead of him and he pulled out to overtake. He came face to face with an enormous truck heading straight for him, not fifty metres ahead. His heart beat rapidly and adrenaline surged through his body. Patrick slammed on the brakes and dived back into his lane behind the trailer.

It was too late for the motorcycle policeman. When Patrick had braked, the policeman's bike clipped the rear of his vehicle. Out of control, the bike veered onto the wrong side of the road and hit the truck head on. A body flew into the air, over the top of the handlebars. The patrolman soared over the guard rail at the side of the road and landed down the side of the escarpment on the right hand side of the road.

Patrick saw it all in his rear vision mirror. He kept going. His mind was completely numb, but somewhere he registered that the semi he had been following had pulled off into a heavy vehicle rest area. The road ahead was clear.

******

Jim sat in Lillian's lounge while she sifted through her diary. She talked nonstop and Jim made minimal replies, so as not to encourage her. He looked around the room, and saw soft furnishings and the floral lounge, highly polished coffee tables, and artificial flowers in pots and vases on every flat surface.

"Here it is. I think. Let me just check this. You know, I've been meaning to get all this sorted out, in some kind of order, with dates and so on. But it comes down to these three."

Lillian copied the numbers on to a piece of paper.

"Maybe that, not so busy detective can check the numbers on his police computer. Do you think it will help?

Maybe I'll get a reward if it does; you never know what it could lead to, do you?"

"Thanks Lillian, I'd better be going – not finished my paperwork in the office." Jim grabbed the note and slipped away while Lillian watched him open-mouthed.

No manners today. I would have thought he could have stayed a while; he's just like all the rest. Lillian closed her door and picked up her diary. *I knew it would come in handy, sooner or later.* She closed it and put it back on her desk, next to her computer, the one she was going to learn soon.

****

Margaret and Ethan sat huddled together. They looked at one of the five newspapers stacked on the coffee table. Ethan read aloud to his wife, as she held him around the waist and listened to him reading about their disappearance.

"Missing, believed dead ... not seen since going to bed in a motel in Coober Pedy, S.A ... looking for relatives ... wanting information leading to ..."

Wounds, not yet healed, began to weep again. The story brought back every scene, frame after frame. Margaret sprang up from the lounge.

"Please don't read anymore, it's all so vivid and all so painful."

Ethan dropped the paper on the floor and strode over to his wife's side. He put his arm around her and pulled her close. She sobbed into his chest. Quiet little tears rolled down her cheeks.

"I so wish this was over," she said. "It just goes on and on; more suffering, and I'm not sure I even want the men caught now. If I think them being caught, and if Judy is with them, what can I say? To go through a court case – watching more suffering – this time, my own children."

"Not your children, remember. I know you doted on them and treated them as if they were your own flesh and blood, but they rejected you more than once."

"I know, I know, but to think of them in gaol and how terrible that will be for them."

"But there are others involved here as well, Margy. They can't just be let off. What if they try to murder someone else?"

"Oh, yes, I can't bear to think of that. I know they must be brought to justice, but I wish there was some humane way. Isn't there something we can say that will alter the sentence?"

"Maybe you can make a plea on their behalf, but I don't want the likes of them out in society, when I think of how cold blooded they were about just leaving us to die in that mine. They had no idea if we suffered, or died of thirst, or blown to pieces. They have no conscience, so how can we let anyone like that back onto the unsuspecting public?"

"I do understand, and I agree," Margaret said, as she walked around the lounge room, wringing her hands. "I feel we should do something more though, some sort of rehabilitation, not just make them worse by punishment."

Ethan sat down and picked up the next newspaper. "I'm sure if you want to introduce some kind of diversion, or self-improvement activity after they go to gaol, anything's possible, but the system is the system." He read the rest of the notices in silence.

"Well, if anything's going to bring them out, this stuff in the papers should."

A week of almost sleepless nights for the couple followed that day.

The following Friday, they had a call from Detective Pekalski. "Not a word, I'm afraid. All is quiet. We wait. How are you two holding up?"

"Fine, yeah fine. Not sleeping too much, but I guess we'll get used to it, the waiting I mean."

"I was hoping I would have some good news for you but it looks like we have to hang in here a little longer." They made small talk and then Pekalski rang off. Margaret and Ethan sat, disillusioned. They wondered how long it would all take.

Chapter Thirty-Five

Judy was really enjoying her new job. She and Patrick had worked at all sorts of jobs in the past, but mostly on a casual basis, and with no sense of loyalty or commitment to their employer. It was different this time for Judy, and she began to identify a sense of belonging and responsibility. She was doing a good job and feeling proud of herself.

Al had introduced her to the friend with the garage to let. Judy had scored the garage in exchange for her attending to the lawns and gardens. The garage was set among natives in the large garden, quiet, hidden and very private.

When Judy first saw it, she was speechless.

"I'm a trifle overwhelmed," she said to Al the next day. "Have you seen it?"

"No, not inside, what's wrong with it?"

"Not a thing. It's perfect – has three rooms, shower/laundry, then a bedroom with a television, and a kitchen/lounge with everything I could want."

"So you like it?"

"No, I love it."

They both laughed. "Well I'm happy for you, and by the way, I was real pleased with what you did with that new garden I left for you to develop."

"Thanks. I think it will be pretty good, given a bit of time and a little more attention."

"I agree. Now, something I wanted to ask you. How do you feel about driving Mrs. J. around today?"

Judy looked at Al questioningly. "Why me?"

"I have several other commitments, and I thought that if you were as good a driver as you are a gardener, then I should give you a go."

Hesitantly, Judy nodded. "Okay, tell me what I have to do."

Al sent Judy home to change into her best jeans and collared t-shirt, then took her to meet her employer. Mrs. Jamieson met them in the little vegetable garden where she was picking parsley. She looked up at their approach.

"Oh good, you're here." Mrs. J. put her hand out to greet the young woman. "I hope you're a good driver Judy, and don't mind a change today. Al would be better employed at other chores this afternoon, and I am loathe to drive myself."

"That's fine with me," Judy said. "I've been driving for about six years now; no accidents, no speeding tickets or anything. What sort of car do you have?"

"A Honda Legend, lovely to drive and so comfortable," answered Mrs J.

"Wow, I can't wait." Judy smiled as she said it.

Al looked at Mrs. J., and they both grinned.

"Al has told me how pleased he is with you, Judy, doing a great job in the garden, he says."

"Thank you."

Judy really did not know what to say, so unaccustomed was she to any sort of compliment or praise.

"We'll have a nice day out today, and you could probably do with a change of scenery as well. How does that sound?"

"Good," nodded Judy.

"So, I'll see you back here in about half an hour, my dear."

"Sure." Judy nodded, and she and Al walked over to the tool shed.

At 11am, Judy drove the car up the driveway to the front door, as Al had instructed her. She watched Mrs J open the back car door and wondered if she should have jumped out and held it open for her, like a proper chauffeur.

"Where to Mrs. Jamieson?" Judy smiled into the rear vision mirror.

"Into the city, Sydney, that is. I'll show you where when we get closer."

"I'm a Brisbane girl, not a clue about getting to Sydney, so you're going to have to tell me which direction to go in to begin."

"Oh, I see. Turn around here and then go left when you drive out the driveway. I'll direct you."

Half an hour later Mrs. Jamieson acknowledged they were lost. "It's so easy to take a wrong turn; I can't believe I brought you all the way over here. Perhaps it is time we used the ah ... ah, sat. nav. Is that what you call it?"

Judy smiled to herself and looked around for the satellite navigation.

"Look at that! We're off," she said a few minutes later, as she made a U-turn and headed in the direction the navigation system was directing her.

"You young people, you're so good with computers. I'm very impressed." Mrs. Jamieson put her hand on the back of the front seat and leaned close to Judy's ear. "Do you have one in your car dear?"

"I used to, but I don't have any wheels now, I'm getting around on shanks pony, and cabs."

Mrs. Jamieson had heard a brief version of what Al knew about Judy, and it had made her curious to hear more.

"May I ask what happened to your car then?"

Judy sighed and wondered which story to tell to this woman. The truth? A modified version of the truth, or should she stick with the story she had given the cab driver?

"I've had some problems and left my home. I can't really talk about it right now. Maybe some other time. I took very

311

little with me. I really need to start my life over. I am indebted to Al for giving me that opportunity."

Once again, Mrs. Jamieson leaned forward and put her hand on Judy's shoulder.

"I understand dear, not when you're driving; we'll talk some other time. Please feel free to come to me if you have a problem, and call me Mrs. J., like Al does. What do you like to be called?"

Judy thought for a minute, maybe it's time for a whole new image.

"My mum used to call me Judith and no one else ever has, perhaps that would be nice for a change."

"Judith it is then. Are we nearly there, Judith?" They laughed together as she turned the car.

Mrs. Jamieson was very clear with her directions to the building in Pitt Street, where she went every second week for her meetings.

"You can drop me off and either wait in the parking station, or go off for a little sightseeing. I'll be about two hours, so if you line up here at the drop off area, I'll come out that main door there." She pointed to the large glass entrance door, set back from the drive-through area where there was already a line of vehicles moving slowly. "See you at three. Don't be late," Mrs. J. called to Judy, as she stepped out and moved toward the door. She waved to several other ladies of similar vintage, as they too emerged from their own vehicles.

Judy looked left and right, and then drew slowly into the line of traffic. She had no idea where she was going so she drifted along with the flow and decided to see where it took her. She ended up going round in circles and she decided to reset the sat. nav. to take her to the botanical gardens, where she was lucky to find an empty parking spot.

She turned off the engine, and leaned forward with her elbows resting on the steering wheel. She allowed her focus to relax and she stared into the middle distance. She became aware of how far she had come, and how much she had already changed since leaving Patrick.

She had metamorphosed into the person who had always been waiting just below the surface. She recognised the young girl, crying for her mother and ultimately attaching herself to Patrick in loneliness and fear. Judy knew this was her new beginning, and it was a rare gift, from someone. Maybe God. She could not let it go; she would not let it go.

Judy thought about what she really wanted. She asked herself the question. *Love, companionship, and a home,* she thought, *but not right now. Now I want freedom, freedom to develop, travel, and become educated and to know what I'm capable of. I want to make my own decisions, find out what I believe in and what my opinions are. Do I have any?* She smiled. The possibilities were endless, and she had no idea why it had taken her so long to get to where she was right now.

Judy looked at the clock and decided to make her way back. She turned on the ignition and set the sat. nav. again. She shifted into drive and joined the traffic. *Like joining the human race again,* she thought.

She got on the slowly moving line winding through the pickup area and made her way to the entrance to Mrs. J.'s club. She saw her employer and put the brake on. She jumped out of the car and opened the door as Mrs. J. smiled and walked toward her.

"That's very kind of you dear. Have you been waiting long?"

"No I timed it well. I went to the botanical gardens, but got so engrossed in my own thoughts I forgot to get out of the car. So here I am again, having done nothing at all."

Judy had the experience of feeling completely open, with no need to tell lies or make up stories. Maybe it was Mrs. J.'s easy manner, or maybe it was all part of the new person who was emerging. She had a sense of being empty inside, but a good emptiness, her mind no longer clouded with dubious schemes and sad feelings and worries.

"Well I'm sure the time wasn't wasted if you got lost in thought. It's a healthy occupation and we all find it necessary at times," said Mrs. Jamieson. It was late afternoon when Judy drove into the garage. She grabbed her bag and the old newspaper off the back seat, and took the keys back to the house. Mrs. J. took the keys and handed her an envelope.

"It's a Myers shopping card. You'll need some more clothes if we go out in future. Take tomorrow morning off and do some clothes shopping for yourself. Al will let you take the ute. Just get something smart and comfortable to go out in – a couple of outfits, suitable to your age and personality."

Judy looked quizzical. "Do you want me to drive in the future then?"

"I do. It was pleasant having you with me today, and I believe Al would much prefer the garden. It is heavier work and he more suited to it. Don't you think?"

"Thank you, Mrs. J. for everything. I would love to drive for you anytime. I'll get some new gear in the morning and bring it back to see what you think."

"Absolutely, Judy. Go home and get a good sleep and we'll talk more tomorrow."

Judy walked home in a pleasant state of confusion; things were opening up for her. She threw her bag and the newspaper on to the table when she walked into her little home. She pulled off her boots and turned on the TV She wondered what to cook for dinner; it was nice to only please herself and she discovered she had a taste for all kinds of things she had never even tried before.

Chapter Thirty-Six

Russell and Megan had moved fast. They did not want Patrick to catch them again, and they made sure there were no traces for anyone to follow. Not even mail, they would redirect any mail after they were settled.

Russell applied for an Easy Name Change Kit. Megan knew Russell had been involved in illegal deals, and she did not want that to influence their future. She agreed they should take her name when they were married.

They moved to a suburb just north of Brisbane.

Russell found an advertisement for a business for sale. Similar to the one he wanted, it was graphic design and sign writing. He made an application to the bank for a loan.

He was turned down. Not enough history of employment and nothing to mortgage.

"Back to square one," Russell said to Megan, when he got the call from the bank the day following his application.

"Why don't you just work for a while, for a boss," Megan said. "At least you can find out if you really want to do this." Megan tried to placate Russell; he was so obviously disappointed.

Russell turned from Megan and went outside to light up a smoke. They were renting a small unit at Woody Point. It was modern, close to the water and shops, and they both liked it. Now they needed to get some money coming in.

"I want my own business. I 'ate the idea of workin' for someone else. I dunno know what to do now. I was so sure we could borrow a piddly little amount like $100,000. With $200,000 of my own, I'd no idea it was so 'ard to borrow money." Russell stamped around, puffing on his smoke.

"I'm applying for a job tomorrow."

"Doin' what?" Russell looked at Megan.

"Bar work, at that little pub on the corner."

"I don't want you workin' there."

"Why not, I've got experience and the money's fine. It's better than nothing right now. We don't want to dip into your savings, do we?"

Russell looked at his new partner and knew she was talking sense.

"Yeah, you're right, good luck then and I'll think about applyin' for a job too."

One thing Megan really liked about Russell was his flexibility. When it came to making decisions, he was never stubborn; he always heard both sides and he was sensible. They were really well suited that way. She had a feeling they were going to have a good life together. Bugger her parents, she thought, they would never approve of anyone she chose to marry. So to marry without their approval was her only course of action.

The next day Megan applied for the bar job and was employed on the spot. She gave Russell the news.

"To you," Russell said, as they clinked glasses and gulped down a beer.

"Isn't it funny," said Russell, "I never thought I would be the type of person to get married, or use someone else's name, or apply for a job from some stranger, or 'ave more than $200,000 in the bank. I'm changing, I really am. I must be gettin' old."

"Here's to getting old." Megan raised her glass again.

They both knew they were in grave danger of becoming like everyone else. Ordinary. The scary part was, neither of them cared.

The next day, Russell bought the paper to look up the classifieds. On the second page, he was confronted with a half page photo of the Doughertys. He almost fell over and only just made it to the chair.

"Missing. Believed Dead." The headline was stark and simple.

He looked at the photo of the couple, taken on their wedding day. He sat and stared at it. *They both look so happy, just like me and Megan will on our wedding day. Anyway, what do I care about them. They're dead, and that's that.* He knew this day would come eventually and there would be an investigation, but he had become complacent and pushed the whole episode into the back of his mind. He knew he would have to lie low. He could not attract any attention. Suddenly, he realised that either Judy or Patrick could expose him, if they were caught. He had always known one of them could talk, but it seemed unlikely when they were together. Now they were separated, there was no telling what either of them might do.

They are both such loose cannons, capable of anything; especially Patrick, and especially now he is obsessed with finding his sister. Russell sat and brooded for some time. He knew he had done everything in his power to slip under the police radar, except leave the country, and then he may be caught using his passport. All he could do was carry on with his current situation, and hope they eventually would stop looking for the Doughertys.

******

Twenty minutes after he saw the police bike crash, Patrick arrived in Ballina, a beachside town, where he pulled over at a park. He got out of the car and walked around, looking at the ground. He was shaking, his whole body, shaking so badly he almost fell over. Eventually he went and sat on a park seat and clasped his hands together on his thighs and tried to make himself settle. He reminded himself to breath slowly and then he noticed spots before his eyes A red cloud passed across his vision. Suddenly he gasped.

Blackness descended on him. He fell off the seat and landed unconscious on the grass.

Several people saw him fall and they ran to his aid.

"Call an ambulance," shouted one young woman, as she leaned over Patrick.

Another girl pulled out her mobile phone and dialled triple zero. The first young girl knelt down and checked his pulse, then his breathing. She sat back on her heels and spoke to her friend.

"I really can't tell if he's alive or dead, can you see if he's breathing?"

The second girl shook her head as she leaned over him. Several kids, a man and a woman quickly surrounded them.

Both girls shrugged and the man pushed his way to Patrick's side, turned him over, and tried to clear his airway. He shouted and slapped his back but got no response. Next, he turned Patrick on his back again and commenced mouth-to-mouth resuscitation.

"What do you want me to do?" asked the first girl.

"Try and find a pulse, both of you."

They both picked up a wrist each and moved their fingers to find the slightest movement.

"I have one," the second girl said excitedly.

"Me too," said the other.

They smiled briefly. They heard the ambulance siren coming toward them.

"Go and direct the ambos over here," said the man to his wife. She ran off, with two kids following.

Patrick began to stir and the three people near him sat back. They watched as he put his hand to his head and rolled his head around. Two paramedics arrived with a bag and a trolley, and everyone made way, as they set about assessing the situation.

"No, I don't know what happened," was Patrick's very weak reply to their questioning.

They continued to check his vital signs and put an intravenous drip in place. A few minutes later, they had him in the ambulance and were about to take off when he said, "My car?"

"It's alright mate, we'll take care of it. You just relax and breathe in this oxygen I'm putting over your nose."

One medic sat next to Patrick. He continued to monitor his vital signs as the other closed the doors, and walked around to the cab. One of the girls ran over to the second medic and handed him Patrick's car keys.

"No, please just leave them in the ignition. I'll call the road service and they will organise someone to drive it to the garage for safety. They should be here any minute. Thanks for your help, you all did great."

The ambulance drove away more slowly than it arrived. It went directly to the hospital and passed the tow truck on the way.

The tow truck driver's offsider was about to step into the driver's seat of Patrick's car when a police vehicle drew up behind him.

"Hey mate, where are you taking that vehicle?"

"To our holding yard. The owner's just gone off to the hospital in an ambulance. Had a turn right here and we were called in by the Paramedic to put it in the yard for the night, until the owner collects it."

"Right. Just leave it be for a minute."

The police officer got on his radio. A couple of minutes passed. He walked over to the tow truck driver and said he believed the car was one sought in relation to an accident on the highway about an hour ago.

"Uh huh. So what do you want me to do?"

"We'll impound it. Take it to our yard, fellers."

"Fine."

The towies winched Patrick's vehicle on board and headed for the police compound. That afternoon, Patrick's vehicle was positively identified as the one involved in the death of the highway patrol officer.

* * * * *

Meanwhile, Jim had given the registration number Lil Gossett had provided, to Detective Inspector Pekalski. He had it put into the computer. It belonged to Patrick Robilliard. The vehicle's description circulated immediately throughout Australia as wanted in connection with the investigation of the missing couple in Coober Pedy. The information flashed up on a computer screen at the Ballina Police Station minutes after Patrick's car was seized. The Ballina police were anxious to interview Patrick.

Chapter Thirty-Seven

"So I gave the number to Frank, and he says that connects a few more dots. Everyone will be on the lookout for that car now. We had checked the Robilliard registration before, but now we know it was the car sighted in Coober Pedy, and here, just after we left on the bus trip. There is also a bulletin out for a car recently registered to Russell Mills, purchased in Sydney a few weeks ago. I do believe we are getting closer to our culprits, and it may not be long now before Margaret and Ethan can come home." Jim pulled a chair out for Di, and they both sat down to dinner.

"But what if they don't drive their cars or if they've already left the country?"

"Frank says they're still around and he bet me they are still driving. Remember, they have no idea the cops are after them."

"Well, I sure hope for everyone's sake it's all over soon."

They finished their meal and later were relaxing in the lounge when the phone rang.

Jim answered.

"Really? Well, the long arm of the law finally caught its man, hey? I appreciate the call, Frank, and hopefully the rest will fall into place very soon now." He hung up and turned to his wife.

"Guess what?"

"Tell me"

"Patrick Robilliard has been caught in Ballina, in New South Wales. Apparently, he was part of a high-speed chase on the Pacific Highway, between Byron Bay and Ballina. A motorcycle policeman died while in pursuit and they tracked Robilliard to the hospital in Ballina, where he was admitted by ambulance after some sort of a turn in a park. His car was spotted and now they have him."

"Wow, that's great. Do the Doughertys know yet?"

"Frank has just spoken to them, and he's on his way down to Ballina right now. They will only have to get Mills now, and hopefully he's living locally also. I wonder what it must be like to be caught and arrested, knowing there's a life of imprisonment ahead."

******

Judy picked up the newspaper to check out the television programme. She flicked it open and saw the faces of Margaret and Ethan. 'Missing feared dead ...' she read on, her heart beat faster as she did. *So now, the police are looking for them, how far will they go in their search?* She sat and stared at the face of the woman who had tried so hard to be a loving mother to her and her brother. Knowing she had no direct part in the murder of the couple gave her no sense of satisfaction. She began to wonder what she should do. To turn Patrick in was unthinkable. What would it achieve? It would not bring back the two wasted lives. It would mean gaol for all of them, probably for the rest of their lives. No, there was not a thing she could do, except hope Patrick stayed out of trouble and that they did not find her.

She stood and walked back and forth, pulled at her hair and punched her head with her fist. *Think, think, what to do?* She had absolutely no idea what she should do next. *Pack up? Move? Call Patrick, or the police. No, no, none of that.* Ultimately, she sat and agreed with herself to leave well enough alone. Lie low and wait; maybe they won't be looking for her.

******

"Patrick Robilliard?"

Patrick sat upright in the hospital bed and slowly nodded. He realised the man standing in front of him was a cop, and not a doctor.

"My name is Detective Inspector Frank Pekalski and I'm here to arrest you on a charge of two counts of attempted murder..."

Pekalski told Patrick his rights and said he had been given the go ahead by his doctor to take him into custody immediately. Another medical practitioner would see him in gaol. Pekalski opened the door and admitted two uniformed police officers to escort him to the wagon, waiting downstairs.

"Get dressed. You're going for a ride, son."

With a great sigh, Patrick simply looked at the three men and shook his head. He threw the bed covers back and put both feet on the floor. He reached into his locker and pulled down his clothes. A couple of minutes later, he was dressed and walked over to the young police officer with the handcuffs extended.

Together, they walked out of the hospital and down to the waiting wagon. As Patrick stepped up into the back of the vehicle, he turned to Pekalski who was moving away toward his own.

He shouted, "Attempted murder, did you say?"

Frank walked back to where Patrick stood poised in the doorway, with the two police officers standing either side.

"Yes, they escaped the mine blast. Walked away. Both looking forward to seeing you in court." Frank slammed the paddy wagon door and nodded to the waiting men.

******

The following day Margaret and Ethan drove over to their home at Keeala Resort. They parked their car outside the community centre and quietly walked in, hand in hand. Suddenly, a shout came from the lounge where a meeting of the social committee was in progress. Lil Gossett flew up from her seat and ran over to the smiling couple. She threw her arms around Margaret, and was quickly surrounded by a group of residents, all wearing grins and cheering.

Ethan attempted to shake hands, but was bear hugged by all the men and kissed by the women. Another group walked in from the bowls green and headed over to the activity, to find the Doughertys were the centre of the celebrating. Jim came out of his office and the window cleaner was standing on his toes trying to see what was causing the commotion.

Someone pressed the community centre alarm and a few minutes later the place was swarming with anxious faces and running feet, only to be delighted to find no emergency but a homecoming in full swing.

Within the next half hour, a proper celebration commenced with beer, wine, lemonade and cups of tea all being handed around and everyone clamouring to hear the story of the Dougherty's return. Margaret and Ethan had no idea what a lot of great friends they had, and were almost overwhelmed by their own celebrity.

******

Megan wiped the bar down and turned to stack the last of the glasses from the dishwasher onto the glass shelf.

"How do you like it love?" asked her boss, as he walked into the bar and looked around. He always checked before anyone finished his or her shift. He was very particular and Megan liked that.

She smiled and turned to pick up her bag from under the counter, just as Russell walked in the side door and sat at a table.

"That's my fiancée over there," she said to her boss, and pointed to Russell who waved back.

She skirted the small tables and bent to kiss Russell as he stood up. They walked outside and down the path together. Megan's boss looked at the television fixed above the counter and was about to turn it off when an image caught his attention. He stared at the face of the man who had just walked out with Megan. He hesitated for a second, then reached for the phone and dialled the number of the local police station. He gave Megan's address to the local constables over the phone, and five minutes later he saw a police car drive past his pub in the same direction as Megan and her man had walked.

Russell answered the loud knock on the door a few minutes later. Megan stood horrified in the background as she listened while they read Russell the charges against him and his rights. They handcuffed him and walked him out to the car.

Megan stood in the open doorway, tears streaming down her cheeks, her knuckles white as she gripped the doorknob.

Russell looked back from the police car window.

He mouthed, "I love you."

They drove him away.

******

Life slowly returned to normal at Keeala Resort. Just about everyone agreed that Keeala Resort had surely seen more action and excitement than all the Over 50's resorts in Australia, put together. They also agreed that it was the friendliest resort around; they had been through so much, and the bonds of friendship would grow and endure into the future.

******

The following spring, Detective Pekalski called in at Keeala Resort. He found Di and Jim coming out of their office.

"Hi," Frank said, "just the people I was hoping to see. I was going past, so thought I'd drop in and say hello."

"Oh, it's so nice to see you, Frank," Di said, with a beaming smile.

"Yeah, long time no see," said Jim, as he offered his hand. "What have you been up to, mate?"

"Oh, still catching crims for a living. What's new, eh? Sold my house a few days ago: been on the market for nearly a year. I had to get out – never felt comfortable since my wife died a couple of years ago. It just wasn't the same without her – you know, too many memories – all that stuff."

"So, a new life awaits, Frank. Where are you going to go?" Di asked.

"Well, I don't need a big house any more. Been there and done that, as they say. Thought I might get myself a nice little bachelor pad."

The sound of someone clearing his throat turned Frank's head.

"I think we may have just the thing you're looking for, Detective."

"Oh, hi, Matt."

"Sorry, but I couldn't help overhearing as I came out, but yeah, I reckon I've got just the place for you."

"What, here?" Frank asked.

"Sure, it would be perfect for you. May I borrow him for a few minutes, Jim?"

"Be my guest."

"Follow me," said Matthew.

After a few seconds, Frank fell in beside Matthew on the paved path.

"Take your time, Frank. Have a good look. We'd *love* to have you here!" yelled Di, with another wide-eyed smile.

Jim sighed. He did *not* smile.

"What?" asked Di.

The End

Author Kumari and husband John live in an Over 50's resort in Queensland.

In their past careers, John was a business manager and Kumari, a registered nurse.

After their marriage in 1992, they combined their skills to manage retirement resorts in N.S.W. and Queensland. They used to joke that the many interesting characters and unusual situations they encountered would one day provide a wealth of material for a book.

When Kumari became wheelchair bound following foot surgery in 2010, she realised the period of physical inactivity presented her with a golden opportunity. She decided to weave her memories of those management years into a fictionalised story. The result was not one novel, but a series.

The series follow the trials and tribulations of the residents, employees and diverse characters of Keeala Resort. Kumari also introduces social comment about ageing issues and some of her characters draw her readers into a dialogue about the social and practical questions encountered in people's mature years.

Sixteen grandchildren fill in the spaces when she is not writing.